C

"Escapist, chemistry-fueled, and with the perfect amount of Christmas magic, *Christmas at the Ranch* is the perfect book to whisk you away this holiday season."

—Emily Stone, author of *Always, in December*

"If you're looking for a second chance holiday romance filled with heart, soul, and a sexy cowboy hero, look no further! You'll want to bust this baby out every year."

—Codi Hall, author of *There's Something About Merry*

"*Christmas at the Ranch* is an emotional and romantic, snow-kissed love story about rediscovering your first love when it matters the most."

—Heidi McLaughlin, *New York Times* bestselling author of *Forever My Girl*

"Tender, transporting, and impossible to put down. *Christmas at the Ranch* is a heartwarming holiday escape filled with snow-dusted second chances, soulful romance, and the kind of magic that only comes when you return to the place that once held your heart. Julia McKay writes with so much charm—and this book is a winter dream."

—Chantel Guertin, bestselling author of *It Happened One Christmas*

Praise for
The Holiday Honeymoon Switch

"Mayhem and romance!"

—Entertainment Weekly

"Not just one, but two gorgeously romantic and heart-warming love stories set in two of the most idyllic locations you could imagine. The perfect book to snuggle up to this winter."

—Paige Toon, international bestselling author of
Only Love Can Hurt Like This

"Unexpected adventures, personal growth, and the potential for love."

—New York Post

"Full of sugar and spice, and comfort and joy, *The Holiday Honeymoon Switch* is everything I love about holiday movies in book form. Savor this one in front of a cozy fire with a warm drink. Delightful."

—Laura Taylor Namey, *New York Times* bestselling author of
A Cuban Girl's Guide to Tea and Tomorrow

"McKay delivers a sweet holiday romance focused on two best friends and how their support of each other leads each to new romance. . . . This charms."

—Publishers Weekly

"A story of enduring love—of the BFF variety. Holly and Ivy were meant to be! How fun to then watch them stumble their way into romantic love, too."

"Dual love stories as well as a tribute to ride-or-die friendships . . . A delightful addition to the holiday romance subgenre."

"A bighearted story filled with ride-or-die friendship and swoony romance, times two . . . best enjoyed with a cup of cocoa!"

"This book sucked me in immediately and never let go of my heart. Twice the swoon! Twice the romance! Prepare to be swept away on holiday by this funny and charming gem of a novel!"

Also by Julia McKay

❊ ❊ ❊ ❊ ❊

The Holiday Honeymoon Switch

Writing as Marissa Stapley

Three Holidays and a Wedding
(with Uzma Jalaluddin)
The Lightning Bottles
Lucky
The Last Resort
Things to Do When It's Raining
Mating for Life

Writing as Maggie Knox

All I Want for Christmas
The Holiday Swap

Christmas at the Ranch

Julia McKay

G. P. Putnam's Sons
New York

PUTNAM
— EST. 1838 —

G. P. Putnam's Sons
Publishers Since 1838
An imprint of Penguin Random House LLC
1745 Broadway, New York, NY 10019
penguinrandomhouse.com

Book design by Shannon Nicole Plunkett

Library of Congress Cataloging-in-Publication Data

Names: McKay, Julia, author.
Title: Christmas at the ranch / Julia McKay.
Description: New York: G. P. Putnam's Sons, 2025.
Identifiers: LCCN 2025008742 (print) | LCCN 2025008743 (ebook) |
ISBN 9780593716304 (trade paperback) |
ISBN 9780593716311 (ebook)
Subjects: LCGFT: Romance fiction. | Novels.
Classification: LCC PR9199.4.S7327 C47 2025 (print) |
LCC PR9199.4.S7327 (ebook) | DDC 813/.6—dc23/eng/20250227
LC record available at https://lccn.loc.gov/2025008742
LC ebook record available at https://lccn.loc.gov/2025008743

Target Exclusive Edition: 9798217178933

Printed in the United States of America
1st Printing

The authorized representative in the EU for product safety
and compliance is Penguin Random House Ireland, Morrison
Chambers, 32 Nassau Street, Dublin D02 YH68, Ireland,
https://eu-contact.penguin.ie.

For Maia,
because this one was her idea

Christmas at the Ranch

※ ※ ※ ※ ※

Dear Diary,

I met a guy.

I kissed a guy.

Twice, actually. Three times. Four?

Possibly forty.

I kissed him so many times I lost count.

His name is Tate Wilder. He has amber-brown eyes and a voice like hot maple syrup poured on snow. I know you had to wait eighteen years for the story of my first real kiss, but trust me, dear Diary, it was worth the wait . . .

It all started last night. Another one of my parents' parties with the crowd of friends and family they invited to this huge "cottage" we've rented for the holidays. Screeches of laughter drifted up through the floorboards, waking me at, according to the clock in my cavern of a bedroom, just past one in the morning. It's not really a cottage we're staying in, it's a mansion—but at least the monstrosity is perched at the edge of a frozen lake in the Algonquin Highlands, surrounded by snow-topped pines and ice-glazed granite cliffs. So pretty. So serene. So obvious no one in my family got the memo about peace and quiet.

As I tried to go back to sleep the music started again: Cousin Reuben, playing his <u>New Wave Xmas: Just Can't Get Enough</u> record for the tenth time. He and my dad had some kind of falling-out in their thirties and didn't speak for over a decade. But apparently, that's all water under the bridge now because they're starting some new business venture together.

Earlier in the night I was down in the kitchen, pouring glasses of water and gently suggesting my family members eat some real food instead of nibbling on or ignoring the canapés my mother served before she and Aunt Bitsy got into the martinis. As I reheated the platters of beef tenderloin and potatoes dauphinoise the hired chef had prepared and no one had touched, I overheard Aunt Bitsy and my mother talking about me.

"She's <u>so</u> responsible, Cass," Bitsy said. Then, in a sotto voice that wasn't sotto at all, she leaned toward my mother and added, "And a bit boring, honestly." At this, my mother laughed lightly and looked over at me, her smile apologetic. But then Bitsy raised her voice and said, "Shouldn't you be out somewhere, causing trouble with the local boys, Emory? That's what I would have been doing at eighteen. And why didn't you invite any friends here? Aren't you bored?"

My parents had suggested I invite a friend or two, and I had to pretend they were all busy over the holidays. When the truth, as you know, is that I don't fit in at Blackford Academy, the private school I go to. Just as I don't fit in with my family. I even did a science fair project on DNA, asked my parents to provide samples, secretly hoping the findings would reveal I had been switched at birth. Maybe my real family lived in a cozy house in the suburbs . . . Maybe I had brothers or sisters or both . . .

But no. I'm one hundred percent the only daughter of

Cassandra and Stephen Oakes. My great-great-grandfather opened a distillery in Gananoque during Prohibition and turned it into a booze empire. My father then added a financial arm of the company, and hoped I would work there with him one day, allowing his ne'er-do-well cousins and other relatives to run the distillery portion of things. He didn't take it well this summer when I finally worked up the nerve to tell him I was planning to study journalism instead of business in college. We've been distant with each other ever since. I guess he thought I was someone else entirely—and, for my part, I'm hurt that when I tried to let him in on my true dreams, he acted like they were nothing.

My mother, meanwhile, used to be a charity fundraising executive but she stopped working outside of the house after I was born and is now known for throwing great parties and overseeing at least one home décor refresh per year. She still fundraises for charities, but sometimes I wonder if she thinks about why she's doing it—or if it's turned into a social thing for her, rather than any sort of philanthropy.

I somehow turned out quiet, studious, introverted—and, up until tonight, someone who had never even had a proper first kiss.

I'm getting to that part.

"Our Emory is eighteen going on forty," my mother said to Aunt Bitsy—and she may have meant it as a compliment, but I abandoned the platters of food to go back upstairs, feeling stung by her words, laden with even more disappointment than before.

Back in Toronto last month, when my parents told me

we were renting a lake house for the December holiday break, I imagined quiet nights in, just the three of us. Reading by the fire, playing board games. Exactly the kind of holiday an overly mature eighteen-year-old would want. Finally, I thought. For my last Christmas officially at home before university next year, they've decided to do something they know I'll love. My dad has forgiven me for disappointing him. For wanting to chase my own dream instead of his.

Instead, my parents planned an elaborate three-week party beginning the moment school break started. And they ignored me when I suggested that sharing a house with the relatives they spend the rest of the year—and portions of their lives—avoiding was probably a bad idea. Now my dad and Reuben are in business together, and I can't put my finger on why that feels like trouble, but it does.

Anyway. This is not about them.

Because—the guy. I'm getting there, I promise. I just need to make sure I have all the details straight, so I never forget any of this. I'm like a reporter, and this is my own life—and I finally have an exciting dispatch!

Annoyed by the noise coming up through the floor, I got out of bed to open my window for some fresh air, but was greeted instead by cigar smoke and the loud voice of another one of my father's cousins—Richard? Hank?—telling my father what a genius idea all this was. Who wouldn't want to stay in a luxury "cottage" on my parents' dime, eating and drinking for free? I thought, as the densely bitter-smelling cigar smoke billowed through the window.

I felt so lonely.

But just before I closed the window, I heard a sound. Like a ghost, wailing from the direction of the lake. I think my father and his cousin heard it, too, because they stopped talking abruptly. Then, the howl started up again. It was mysterious, otherworldly, the strangest noise.

My first thought was that maybe someone was hurt, and I had to get outside and help. I pulled a sweatshirt over my flannel pajamas, found a parka and winter boots by the back stairs, and crept outside. No one noticed me leave. My father and his cousin had gone back inside through the patio doors. I stood still, listening, until I heard it once more: the groaning sound bubbling up from underneath the still-thin ice of the lake. I headed for the shore to check it out.

"Hello?" I called. "Is anyone out there? Are you hurt?"

The light of the full moon was fading the stars, but still, I'd never seen so many of them. I stopped walking when I reached the edge of the lake. I looked up and took the cosmos in. I wonder now if I made a wish on all those stars, perhaps for a cure for my loneliness.

I heard the crackling of sparks and embers. I looked to my left and saw a bonfire down the snowy beach, some-one sitting in a Muskoka chair, staring into the flames. He was wearing a plaid jacket and a Stetson hat.

"What's that noise coming from the lake?" I asked. He waved me over. As I got closer, I realized he was about my age. He had a strong jaw and full lips—the bottom one fuller than the top. Eyes that flashed like sparks from his fire. The words "Wilder Ranch" were stitched in white across the pocket of his flannel jacket.

"It's the sound the lake makes when it freezes every year," he explained when I was close, and the way he spoke to me made me feel like we were continuing a conversation we had already started—like I hadn't just appeared in front of him out of nowhere.

I'll admit, I forget most of what he said next. Something about how it was sunny today, so the ice melted a little, and now it was dark, and the ice was refreezing. Expanding and contracting, science, et cetera. As he spoke, all I could think about was how his smile flashed at me like a shooting star I wanted to chase, to coax out again and again, to keep for my own. He stood up from his chair and I realized he was very tall. I'm tall, too, so it's nice when I'm not looking down at a person. Especially a guy. He was slim, kind of gangly, but his shoulders were broad under his flannel. And his hair, peeking out from beneath that Stetson, was sandy brown with sun-kissed ends, as if he hadn't had it cut since summer.

He continued with his explanation about why the water made that noise under the ice, but all I could think was how unexpected it was to be standing on the shore of a lake in winter, talking to a handsome guy in front of a bonfire—when moments before I had been stuck in my bedroom, staring down three weeks of misery.

Was I dreaming?

I must have shivered then, and he mistook it for my being cold. He invited me to come sit by his fire and pulled over another Muskoka chair. I explained who I was and apologized for all the noise my family was making, disturbing the peaceful setting. He just shrugged and said it was fine, he hadn't heard anything, really. Then he looked over at me and smiled again. I was mesmerized.

"I mean, hey, who doesn't love hearing 'Last Christmas' by Wham! on repeat something like . . . eleven times?" he said.

In that moment, I knew I liked him. Already. And I decided I wanted him to like me back so badly. I needed to try to be someone else. Not the shy awkward girl I'm known as at school. The one who had worn bottle-thick glasses until she recently got contacts and would rather stay home with a book than go out on weekends.

"I'm Emory," I said, hoping the smile on my face was as casual and appealing as his. I nodded at his beer bottle. "You don't happen to have a drink for me, do you?"

There it was, that smile again—now wider. He was looking at me with the interest I had been seeking, the same delighted surprise I felt the second I saw him. I tossed my hair over my shoulder, glad I'd allowed my mother's stylist to have her way, pre-family reunion. My normally flat chestnut-brown hair was layered into a long bob that flipped up at the ends.

"So, a city girl just walks onto my beach, asking for a drink?" he said, his eyes dancing in the firelight. "What do you think this is, a bar? Maybe I should be asking for ID."

I tilted my head, doing my absolute best at insouciance. I pretended I did this sort of thing all the time. "What makes you think I'm a city girl?"

At this, he laughed—and if his voice was maple syrup on snow, his laugh was butterscotch in a double boiler. "The haircut, the outfit . . ." he began.

I looked down at myself. "I'm wearing flannel pants with snowflakes on them."

"Hmm, that's true. And yet there's just something city-ish about you."

Now it was my turn to smile. "You're right. I'm from Toronto."

"I'll try to overlook that," he said as he pulled a half-empty six-pack from under his Muskoka chair. "Here you go, City Girl."

Crooked smile. (Him.) Heart palpitations. (Me.)

"Help yourself," he said.

I don't usually drink beer, or anything at all, but I pretended I did, taking a bottle and twisting off the cap like I had done it tons of times before, then casually sipping while trying not to grimace. He saw it anyway and raised an eyebrow.

"I guess Labatt 50 isn't exactly your flavor," he said, and my heart fluttered again because, dear Diary, we were flirting. I've never flirted with anyone—unless you count Maxwell Corbett at school, who told his friends last year I'd be "pretty without glasses" and "maybe if she weren't so tall." Then, the next time I saw him, I said "hi," started to blush furiously, and ran away. But you know all that already.

"It's my favorite," I replied, taking a longer sip—and then, embarrassingly, gagging and nearly spitting it out. Beer is gross.

"I can get you something else," he offered.

"Maybe this really _is_ a local bar?" I countered.

"Yeah, it's a real dive," he said with a laugh. "But actually, there are some nice parts."

He gestured behind him and I realized that just beyond us, down a snowy hill, were fenced paddocks and stables. The wooden boards of the buildings were hung with red and white Christmas lights. I peered into the moonlit darkness at the magical setting spread out before me, feeling as if I had wished it into existence.

"Wilder Ranch," he said, and I could hear the pride in his voice. "It's mine. Well, mine and my dad's."

"I <u>love</u> horses," I breathed, because this is true. It was a relief to drop the pretenses. "Why is it called Wilder?"

"That's my last name. I'm Tate. Tate Wilder."

"Nice to meet you, Tate." I tried one more sip of the beer and sighed. After just five minutes of pretending to be a cool girl from the city, I was tired of it. "I don't actually drink," I said, handing him back his beer bottle. "But I would love to see your horses."

He tilted his head then. "You ride?" he said.

I told him about the stables I used to take lessons at, just outside the city limits. "I joined the show team and practically lived there until I was sixteen. But then I stopped," I told him.

"Let me guess, because you got a boyfriend?"

I could have said yes, kept up the charade—but I shook my head. I didn't want to lie to him. I liked him too much, already.

"Actually, I discovered the honor roll. And my desire to get into a good university."

He looked away from me then, seemed thoughtful. "Well, sure," he finally said. "I'll take you on a tour of the ranch if you want. Just let me finish this." He shook the beer bottle I had just returned to him and tipped it back.

"Meantime, do you know how to skip rocks? They make a cool sound at this stage in the lake's freezing process."

Since I wasn't pretending to be someone else anymore, I was able to tell him I was the kind of person who avoided throwing or catching things at all. This got me a rumble of a laugh that made me feel like the bonfire had transferred itself to my chest.

"I'll teach you," he said, moving down the shore, gathering stones as he went. When he returned, he set a pile of them at my feet.

"It's all in the flick of the wrist," he said—or something to that effect. I was distracted by how close he was to me then. And how good he smelled. Like leather soap and hay, pine needles and woodsmoke, and something else I suspected was just <u>him</u>. I watched as he demonstrated, keeping the stone in his hand instead of releasing it. When he finally let the stone fly, the deep pinging sound it made as it ricocheted across frozen water reminded me of a video game or a spaceship's controls.

"That can't be real." Much like the otherworldly groaning from beneath the lake ice I had listened to earlier, the noise the stone made as it skipped didn't sound like it should be coming from a lake at all.

"Lakes in winter are full of surprises."

Honestly? I was feeling the same way about him.

"Now you try," he said, handing me a smooth, flat stone. My first attempt was a fail: I threw too hard and the stone landed several feet out with a single resonant clunk. He stepped even closer and said, "May I?" His hand hovered just above my wrist.

I wonder if that was the moment everything changed—

or if everything had changed already by then. As I was standing on that shore with him, under the starriest winter sky I had ever seen, Tate Wilder touched me and a shower of sparks flooded my system. My stomach swooped, my knees weakened, I truly understood the meaning of the word "swoon." This could not possibly be what it's always like when one person puts their hand on another person's wrist. Could it? Is this what I've been missing?

With the utmost effort, I dragged my thoughts away from how his touch made me feel and back to what he was trying to show me. I perfected the snapping motion and my stone did exactly what it was supposed to: ricocheted across the ice four times, then five, pinged and ponged while I cheered and laughed. So did he.

"Okay, so, that ranch tour," he said. "Still interested?" He thought for a moment. "There's also a party in town I was invited to, if that's more your speed."

"I want to see your ranch."

I helped him put handfuls of snow on the fire to extinguish it. Then he led me down the snowy embankment into the valley.

Soon, we were standing at the edge of a paddock, watching a herd of about a dozen horses gallop in the moonlight. He whistled. One of them, her gray-white coat shining palely, trotted over. When she reached the fence, she nuzzled Tate's shoulder while he laughed and patted her, then reached into the pocket of his plaid flannel jacket to pull out a bag of mints, those round white ones.

"I have to keep these on me at all times," he said with

a sweet laugh I was <u>almost</u> getting used to. He popped a mint in his mouth, offered me one, then held a mint out to the horse while she stamped her hooves, appearing to protest the order in which the mints had been distributed. But then she picked the mint delicately from his palm.

"She's beautiful," I said.

"Isn't she? Her name is Mistletoe. Because of the marking on her face, see?" He ran his finger along the pure white blaze running from between her eyes to just above her soft muzzle. Indeed, there was an unusual shape at the top, just like a little sprig of festive leaves.

I was wishing he would touch me that softly. I was wishing a lot of things.

"She was born on Christmas Eve, five years ago. Mistletoe was the perfect name for her."

"She really seems to like you." The horse was nuzzling him again, rubbing her face against his broad shoulders—and I have to admit, I was still envious.

"It's the mints," he said with another laugh, stroking her muscular neck while she nickered in his ear. "But yeah, she's pretty much mine. I helped train her. We get along well." Now his voice became even softer and the horse pricked her ears forward. "You're a good girl, aren't you?" he murmured.

Diary, I cannot stress this enough: Listening to Tate Wilder croon sweet nothings into a horse's ear was probably the most charming thing I have ever experienced. I had the sudden urge to say something stupid like, "Well, since we're standing near Mistletoe, maybe we should . . ."

But that's not how the kissing happened.

He told me Mistletoe was expecting a foal in the new year and that he and his dad were so excited about this. He then pointed out the other horses in the small herd that were his favorites: a compact chestnut Thoroughbred gelding named Jax, a beautiful bay Dutch warmblood mare named Dolly, a sturdy quarter horse named Walt.

"But Mistletoe is the prettiest," I found myself saying, earning a nod of approval and agreement from him.

He showed me the stables next. Inside, they were cozy, dimly lit. The air smelled of the bodies and warm breath of the horses in their stalls. Of sweet grain and hay, leather soap and dust. He explained that they boarded some of the horses, owned some of them, currently operated a small breeding facility—but that he wanted to start a riding school someday so they could keep all their horses, rather than have to sell any of them.

He asked me questions about the show team I had been on, and my time on the Trillium circuit. He asked if I missed it, and I told him that until tonight, I hadn't realized just how much. Not the competition element, but being around horses.

"Maybe I shouldn't have given it up so easily," I said.

"It's never too late to start again," he replied.

The last stall at the end of the final row contained a donkey named Kevin. "He's a rescue," said Tate.

A rescue donkey, dear Diary. He's a stout little character with a spiky gray mane who, apparently, prefers carrots to mints—so we gave him a few of those from a bucket near his stall while Kevin hee-hawed happily.

Eventually, we climbed up into the hayloft to sit side

by side on a tall stack of bales, talking some more as the moonlight flowed in through a hole in the roof covered in waterproof clear plastic, which Tate said was on his and his dad's endless list of things to fix at the ranch.

We passed one of his beers back and forth and I got used to the taste. He asked me about my school, where I lived in Toronto, how I had ended up at the huge rental house next to his property for the holidays, how long I was staying. I asked him more questions about life at the ranch, who else besides his dad was around to help with that long to-do list. He said it was just the two of them; he didn't have any siblings. And his mom was gone, she had died. In the silence after he said that, the words "I'm so sorry" faded on my lips. I wasn't sure what to say at all. But then, he turned and stared into my eyes so intently I couldn't speak or move. He took a deep breath, then held it—as if weighing whether to speak again or not.

"It was one year ago tonight, actually," he finally said. "That my mom died. I never talk about her, but . . ." He let that sentence wander off, unfinished, then began again. "I was feeling pretty bad tonight, just wanted to be on my own, to light a fire and look at the stars, hoping that might"—he paused again, swallowed, looked away from me for a moment—"make me feel better, I guess. And then . . ." Our gazes connected once more. Those eyes, like the embers from his bonfire. I couldn't get enough of his gaze. His smile was slow, transforming his face from sad to sweet to everything I had ever dreamed of in a person. His voice was husky when he said, "And then, City Girl, you walked onto my beach, and I forgot my problems altogether."

Kissing him was, all at once, the only thing I could think about. I had to take this chance or I'd regret it forever. I leaned toward him, tilted my head, and his lips met mine.

So, what exactly was my first kiss like? Maybe the first few seconds were awkward, sort of like riding a bike until you figure it out. Scary, a little wobbly—and then, all at once, you're balanced, you're rolling, you feel like you're flying, wind in your hair, beautiful confidence filling you up. That's how it felt to kiss Tate Wilder. Like I could fly away, go anywhere, be anyone. Like being too smart or too tall or too weird didn't matter anymore.

His hands were in my hair, and then he was pulling back and stroking my cheek, telling me softly that he thought I was so beautiful, so unexpected. "Where did you come from?" he said. "Did I dream you?"

"I've been wondering the same," I replied.

His hair and skin smelled like woodsmoke combined with the clean, cool tang of winter air. I remember my hand on the back of his neck, the warmth of his skin under my fingers, the softness of his hair with its leftover sun-kisses at the ends. His Stetson had fallen onto one of the hay bales.

He tasted a little bit like beer, and those scotch mints he kept in his pocket for his horse, and something else spicy, like cloves or cinnamon. He tasted like the best parts of Christmas.

I will remember my first kiss until the end of time, I swear.

Hours must have passed, because when we finally stopped kissing, I pulled away from him and opened my eyes to see the first streaks of dawn in the slip of sky vis-ible through the barn roof.

"I'd better get you back to that big old house before anyone in your family notices you're gone," he said.

I didn't want to go, but I suppose all kisses must end—even absolutely epic ones that last for hours. I felt sad about it being over, but then he looked at me like I was a treasure he'd just found and didn't want to lose. It made the fact that we weren't kissing anymore a little easier to bear.

We held hands as we picked our way along the snowy shore. When we got to the back door of the rental house, he said, "Can I see you again?" Which was precisely what I'd been wishing on the very last star flickering out in the sky that he'd say.

Before I could even think about it, the words "I'm yours for the next three weeks" flew out of my mouth.

Instead of making him appalled at my forwardness, they caused him to pull me close and kiss me again. "Don't tease me, City Girl," he murmured. Then, "Come by the ranch later today, mid-afternoon? I'll be done with all my chores by then, and we can go for a trail ride if you want. Get you back on a horse, since you said you miss it so much."

I told him that sounded perfect, because it did. Then, I opened the back door and stepped inside, already filled with longing for him. I watched him through the little window at the top of the door as he made his way down the snowy forest path, back toward the magical place where he lived.

When he looked back, I didn't duck away in embarrassment: I waved, and he waved back—and then, dear Diary, I melted. I drizzled down the door, landed on the welcome mat, and lay there, an Emory-shaped puddle, daydreaming about him until who knows how long later, when I heard my mother in the kitchen and had to reassemble my atoms and sneak upstairs to bed.

It was the most perfect night of my life—one that feels like it could be the beginning of everything.

One

Ten Years Later . . .

*G*ood morning! Can I interest you in an orna-ment from our Fit-mas Tree?"

The woman at my gym's reception desk has been asking me this for weeks. The tree is one of those fake glittery ones, heavily decorated with multicolored Christmas balls—all of which, according to a chart on the wall beside it, have a corresponding exercise to go with their color. A two-minute plank, twenty push-ups, something called a reverse sit-up, which I'm un-clear on the mechanics of.

My gym routine these days consists of running slowly on the treadmill while watching news headlines scroll past on the televisions above the machines. Then I tick "went to gym" off my mental list of "Ways Not to Turn into a Complete Sloth While Working from Home." This is a list I started six months ago, when I was laid off from my news reporter job at *The Globe and Mail* and went freelance.

"No, thanks," I tell the receptionist as I scuttle past on my way toward the stairs that lead to the basement changeroom. But today, she gives chase, waving a white T-shirt in her hand like a race flag.

"Maybe this will provide some incentive," she says, handing me the shirt. It's emblazoned with the words "Do you have the balls to try the Fit-mas Tree?" I cringe but still take the shirt; I don't want to cause a scene. I shove it into my gym bag and flee, resolving to find a different gym in the new year.

Soon, I'm taking my place in the line of treadmills beneath the row of televisions. I increase my speed to a light jog as I gaze at the revolving ticker tape of headlines, weather squares, and local event listings. I usually leave my phone in my locker when I'm at the gym, because I recently wrote an article for *Chatelaine* magazine about the fact that our smartphones are turning our brains into dopamine-addicted mush. Taking a little time without my phone attached to me is just like meditation, I tell myself—which checks off another item on my daily wellness list. Even if watching news channels is probably just as brain-addling as staring at a phone.

I read the subtitles as a red-haired woman, her eyes shining bright blue from the talk-show square, does a segment called "Meal Prep Monday." She somehow manages to make four complete meals out of one store-bought rotisserie chicken. "Now, *that* is going to help us get through the busy holiday season," the host says. Next, a dermatologist talks about how preventative Botox and fillers are the key to never getting wrinkles.

"Ever," she says, staring wide-eyed into the screen, her forehead alabaster smooth.

I reach up and touch the light furrow between my eyebrows, which I've been jade-rolling nightly in an attempt to un-crease. I can tell it's not working. But I still always say no when my mother looks at the wrinkle and shakes her head sadly, then offers me her next coveted appointment at the dermatologist she and my father both use.

I think maybe it's because I'm thinking of my parents that I believe I'm seeing them on the television screen—but then I realize it's really them. It's a photo that was taken in the fall, at a fundraiser gala for the Art Gallery of Ontario, otherwise known as the AGO. I know because I was there: The long skirt of the shimmering forest-green gown I wore is visible in the corner of the screen before the image flips to one of my father alone, gazing sternly at the camera. It's his corporate headshot. I remember when it was taken. It felt like he was frowning at me in particular, his only child who refused to take her place at his side.

At first, I assume this is just some holiday society item, until I squint at the chyron running across the bottom of the screen—deepening my furrow, I know—and realize it's not that at all.

PROMINENT TORONTO BUSINESSMAN
ARRESTED FOR FRAUD

My heart rate surges and the treadmill beeps frantically. I think I'm hitting the down arrow to slow myself but have actually pressed the emergency stop button. I yelp and scramble, just managing to avoid skidding off the treadmill onto the floor. It seems like everyone in the gym is staring at me. The receptionist is rushing over to see if I'm okay.

"I'm fine," I mumble, now feeling as conspicuous as an out-of-place fluorescent pink ornament on the Fit-mas Tree. I step to the floor, where I stand still and stare up at the televisions, horror slowly dawning as the news item flows past.

> The North York corporate headquarters of TurbOakes Money Management were raided by police early this morning. CEO Stephen Oakes was arrested, along with Reuben Oakes, his cousin and TurbOakes's CFO. Both men have been charged with wire fraud, mail fraud, securities fraud, money laundering . . .

Now, there's a picture of Cousin Reuben, his smarmy grin causing my stomach to churn the way it always has. Meanwhile, my mouth has gone as dry as an over-cooked Christmas turkey.

Then the story disappears and it's on to the next catastrophes: a staph outbreak at a local nursing home making holiday visits to aging family members a challenge. A shortage of the year's hottest toy causing a skirmish at a local big box store. I'm still frozen in place. I want to go back to being the person I was five minutes ago, someone whose biggest concern was not wanting to participate in the Fit-mas Tree promotion. Instead, the thoughts careening around in my head are moving faster than Santa's sleigh. Still, I dutifully wipe down the treadmill I just used because, I remind myself, *I* am not a criminal.

But you knew.

I hate my inner voice sometimes. Because in this case, she's not wrong. I'm shocked that I just saw my father on the news being arrested for fraud. I'm upset. But somehow I'm not surprised.

"Excuse me, are you done with this treadmill?"

A man holding a shiny red Fit-mas Tree ball is waiting politely behind me. I rush past him toward the stairs to the changerooms. Downstairs, I stand in front of my locker and stare at the cool metal. I can hear my phone buzzing inside the locker like an angry bee.

So far, there are ten missed calls from my mother. Then two from my best friend, Lani, and a string of texts from her, too.

I saw your dad on my Apple news alert.

Are you okay???

Call me. I'm here for you.

Various other texts from friends and acquaintances stream in, but I can't bring myself to open any more of them. I'm getting email notifications, too. When I see the names of a few of my newspaper and magazine editors pop up, my heart sinks even further. I don't have to open any of the emails to know what they say. My editors are looking for the scoop. Or maybe—and this thought makes me feel worse than I already do—they're writing to tell me my byline is no longer suitable for their publications.

I open Safari and type my father's name into a news search. CBC has the story of his arrest, and so does the *Toronto Star, The Globe and Mail*, the *National Post*. All of them detail a monthslong investigation, a dossier of evidence. And as I watch, a CNN hit appears. Then *Forbes*. The story has crossed the border. I click and read. Some reports discuss the victim impact. Retirement funds, nest eggs. All gone.

A tsunami of guilt engulfs me. And shame. I'm a member of the Oakes family, despite fantasies harbored as a teen about having been switched at birth. Yes, I have a trust fund, but I don't touch it unless it's an emergency. I donate the interest dividends to charities, work to pay my own rent and bills. My independence, paying my own way, has always meant so much to me.

And it was never enough.

One of the articles is showing the AGO gala photo I saw on the news. There's my leg again, and the glittering hem of my green dress. I'm in the picture, no matter how much I want to deny it.

Another text from my mother arrives: Emory. This is urgent. CALL ME!

And she's right, of course. I really should be calling her back, but I just can't. Not yet. I throw my phone into my gym bag and zip it shut. Then I walk upstairs and nod at the receptionist as she trills out a friendly "Goodbye and season's greetings."

Outside, I pull my parka hood up against the win-

try blast of air that greets me on Liberty Street. I battle
the wind blowing in from the desolate middle of Lake
Ontario in December as I walk to my nearby condo-
loft.

Suddenly, all my senses go on high alert. And I see
it: My mother's navy Jaguar is pulling around a corner. I duck into an alley, press myself against the wall
of a building, and pull my hood tight against my face.
I feel like a horrible person for avoiding my mother
when my family is completely falling apart. But I stay
where I am. I wait, then peer through the faux fur ruff
as her car slides past like a shark patrolling the road.
Which isn't fair—she's not a shark. She's my mother.
But I can't face her yet, can't deal with any of this.

My phone vibrates in my bag. I pull it out and read:

I'm at your condo. But I think I see a news truck.
I'm being followed. Are you there? Can you let me
into your parking garage?

I'm not at home right now, I text with numbing fingers. I'm at a work interview in the north end of the city. I
won't be home for a while, I'm sorry.

It's true, I am sorry. My eyes are filled with tears. I
close them, and I can picture my mother. Her eyes are
green, like mine, and her mouth matches mine, too:
cupid's bow. But that's where the similarities end. She's
glamorous; I'm minimalist. She's sophisticated; I'm
awkward. She has, all my life, been focused on keeping
up appearances—and so I know how much this is
hurting her, to see our family's dirty laundry aired on

the news. But she'll want me to empathize with her, and I know I can't do that. Not now, and maybe not ever. This is starting to feel like it has to be happening to someone else. Because while I love my parents, I have always felt like an outsider in my family.

I watch as my mother's car pulls around, then away. Her face, completely smooth and free of lines, a slight downturn of her mouth and a darkening of her eyes the only way to tell she's upset, flashes past. She doesn't see me. Still, I count to thirty before stepping out from the alley. I keep my hood up and my head down. I let myself in the side door of my building's parking garage and walk quickly to my car. Once I'm inside it, I put my gym bag in the back seat and turn on the heat, full blast. My heart is racing. I take deep breaths to try to calm myself down, but it doesn't work. My inner voice is no longer all-knowing and calm.

Now there are only three words in my head, on a repetitive loop: *fight or flight.*

Two

I choose flight. With a modicum of fight, since navigating Toronto's perpetual gridlock is always a battle. I inch toward the Gardiner Expressway and persevere until I'm sailing down the Don Valley Parkway in my Prius. Past the icy river and the valley filled with the leaf-bare, snow-dressed trees. Past happy kids sledding down the hill beside Riverdale Farm, which gives me a twinge to see. I don't have any core memories like that and couldn't imagine either of my parents pushing a child version of me down a toboggan hill, ever. Back when my dad and I used to be close—which now feels like a different lifetime—his idea of bonding was taking me to the Toronto Stock Exchange to hear them ring the opening bell, then out for what he called a power breakfast. I asked him once if we could go to the library instead and he told me we were the sort of people to donate money to the library, not actually use it. But I loved the library and went on my own whenever I could, taking the subway two stops from our neighborhood in

Rosedale to roam the stacks of the reference library, to drink coffee in the café and dream of one day writing for the newspapers my father spread on his desk every morning, keeping the business sections and leaving the rest for me.

I'm on the 404 now. I keep driving north because it feels good to do this. Because my brain is telling me that as long as I keep moving in this direction, I'll be okay. Which is not true, of course, but it's working in the moment. When the news comes on the radio station and they start talking about my family, I spin the dial away and onto 96.3. Soon, I'm being lulled into complacency by Michael Bublé's vanilla-sundae-with-a-cherry-on-top voice, singing about having myself a merry little Christmas. I only realize how far I've traveled when I speed past the sign for Webers, an iconic BBQ institution at the gateway to Ontario's cottage country.

My phone rings. It's Lani.

"Emory! I've been so worried!"

"Lani, I have to tell you something . . ." My voice wobbles and I grip the steering wheel tight. But I can tell my best friend anything. Ever since Lani and I met in our first year at Concordia in Montreal, at a Halloween party where we were both dressed up as Encyclopaedia Britannica volumes in protest of them going out of print that year, we've been soulmates. I was still heartbroken over Tate, my first boyfriend, when I met her, and she helped me through it. But this is worse. This isn't a teenage heartbreak I should have gotten over well before I did. It's my family. My culpability.

"I always knew something was going on with my

dad's company," I say. "Right from the first moments he and Reuben went into business together. If I had told someone—"

"Oh, Em. Don't do this to yourself."

"He wanted me to work with him at the company, and I refused. I never would have let this happen."

"No. Just because your parents have never made it feel safe to be who you are doesn't mean who you are isn't great. You were supposed to abandon your dreams just to make your dad happy? Now, where are you? Do you want to come here?" A baby's wail in the background punctuates her words. "Hang on, let me just get this one on the boob and"—the cries reach a desperate pitch, then stop suddenly, making me realize my best friend has way too much on her plate with twin newborns to be dealing with my stuff.

"Which one is that?" I ask with a smile.

"Cece."

"And Matt is on shift?" Her husband is a pediatric cardiologist who works long, often erratic hours.

"Yes, but my mom and her sisters are getting here tomorrow—at which point I'll be lucky if I even get to hold the twins for the foreseeable future. It's you I'm worried about. Come here. Stay with me. Let us take care of you, too."

I can't help but feel a tug of longing at the idea of Lani's mom, Isa, and her many aunties fussing over me during the holidays, feeding me Filipino food until I want to burst.

"It's you and the twins they should be doting on," I say. "And besides, I need to keep driving north."

When I say these words, they make perfect sense.

"Driving *north*? Where are you?"

I look at the next highway sign. "In Orillia."

"*Why?*"

"I needed to get out of the city."

"You should probably stop soon, Em," she says gently. "There's a blizzard coming." I hear a second baby wailing in the background. "Hang on, just let me get these two settled and you'll have my full attention again."

"You go take care of them. I'll turn around soon. I'll call you in the morning."

"And text me later so I know you're okay?"

"Promise."

I hang up and keep going. Soon, the winter scenery I'm passing makes me feel like I'm driving through Narnia. Thick white snow covers the tall coniferous trees lining the highway, so they all appear to be wearing regal white robes. The walls of blasted granite that signal the official entrance to Ontario's northern cottage country are frosted with snow so thick it could be mistaken for layers of marzipan. Crevices in those rocks are festooned with waterfalls stilled by ice. Creeks line the shoulder of the road, their frozen surfaces shimmering in the light of the descending sun. Through the trees, I see a snowy river ribboning away along snowy banks. It's so beautiful, so perfectly wintry. Like the Christmas cards I used to tuck away and save, making me feel nostalgic for the sorts of holiday seasons I had never had.

Except once.

Is that what I'm driving toward? That single, magical Christmas that broke my heart, yet still remains one of my most cherished memories? I push the thought away and just keep going, chasing this impulse I don't fully understand.

One more corner, and the rivers become lakes. Everyone in Ontario raves about cottage country in summer, but lakes in winter are their own special thing. In the quiet still of the coldest season, when thick snow tucks in the world with snowy blankets, a vast frozen lake is truly a marvel. So calm, so still. The sight of each one of them soothes me a little, dulls the sharpest edges of my agitated state. Their names are comforting, too. Cranberry. Maple. Moose. Loon. I turn up the radio and hum along to Beyoncé's rendition of "Silent Night."

And then, all at once, it's as if ten years slide away like the miles between my car and Toronto. I've let my guard down, and I can hear his voice. That charmingly shy way he had of speaking, that crooked half smile.

I actually like it best here in winter, City Girl.

I crank up the music even louder, but it turns out you can't silence a memory.

Well, I've never been here in summer to be able to compare the two, I remember replying with a smile of my own. In that moment, in his arms, I was certain I'd get the opportunity to visit Evergreen as often as I liked.

But it wasn't meant to be.

My phone ringing again jerks me out of my nostalgic reverie. It's my mother, and I'm far enough away from Toronto that it feels safe to answer.

"Hello, Emory," she says, her tone measured and cautious.

"Mom," I say, and I don't know what else to add, because asking how she is feels like a powder keg question. But I have to. "How are you holding up? And . . ." I swallow hard. "And Dad? How is he?"

"So, you've heard."

"The news is everywhere, Mom. It's impossible to avoid."

I hear a strange sound on the line, like a repressed sob. "Where are you?" she asks me.

"I'm in Muskoka," I say.

"I thought you said you were doing an interview uptown."

"Yeah, it ended up being farther north," I improvise. "I'm hours away. I'm sorry. It can't be avoided." This feels true, as if I've had no choice but to drive and drive, away from this catastrophe. "Tell me how Dad is," I press. "Where is he?"

"It's a setup. Our lawyers are on it, and it will all be resolved soon."

As she speaks, I can tell she really believes this—or at least badly wants to. And she wants me to believe it, too. She's trying to protect me, in her way. Which still doesn't make any of this okay. And is one of the reasons I didn't want to talk to her yet.

"Mom, I saw it on the news. The police raided Turb-Oakes's headquarters after months of investigating. They found evidence, they must have—"

"Stop!" Her tone is one of horror. Then she continues in an urgent whisper. "The police might be listening, our phones might be tapped."

"Mom. If our phones are actually bugged—" I have to pause; this idea fills me with such deep dread. "Whispering isn't going to help," I conclude.

"I need you," my mother suddenly says.

This is new. My mother has never sounded this way with me before. She has always been so good at keeping up her perfect veneer. I'm not sure I've ever even seen her cry. But I can hear tears in her voice now, and I hate to hear her sounding this way.

"What can I do?" I ask her.

"Your trust fund," she says, her voice still low. "You still have most of it, right?"

"I do," I say.

Now her voice contains notes of musing. "You've been so good with it over the years, haven't you? So . . . frugal." The word sounds odd in her mouth, like she doesn't truly understand what it means. The way she talks about me often makes me wonder if she, too, has sometimes questioned our genetic relationship. How could Cassandra Oakes, who once asked me what I thought a reasonable price to pay for a pair of sneakers was and then told me she was surprised it was around a hundred instead of a thousand, ever have given birth to someone like me? A daughter who drives a used car on purpose, rents a condo, resolutely works to pay for these things when she doesn't have to. *You're like Lorelai Gilmore without the kid,* Lani always says.

"It's just for now," she says, her voice so quiet I almost

can't hear it over the rush of road beneath my tires. "We'll pay it back once this is all cleared up."

I drive in silence for a moment. It's so hard to think straight right now—until all at once, I feel clarity.

I know what I want.

To be free.

If I give her the money, and I never ask her to pay it back, ever, will this absolve me in some way? The idea feels the same as driving north does: unreasonably appealing. A solution I can't resist, even if it turns out to be a Band-Aid rather than a tourniquet.

"Okay," I tell her, pulling over to the side of the road and clicking on my hazard lights. "Do you have a pen?" I find the files in my phone, recite account numbers and passcodes.

"Thank you. I'm so relieved," my mother says when we're done.

"Me, too," I tell her as I pull back out onto the highway and press my foot on the gas again.

"You'll come back for the Christmas party—"

"Wait, really, Mom? You're still going to have your Christmas party this year?"

"I'm famous for that party, Emory!"

I pick up speed, trying to put even more miles between myself and my city, my family.

"But right now? Are you sure—"

"It's more important than ever! What would people say if I didn't have the party? It would practically be an admission of guilt for your father, and he is not guilty."

"Mom," I begin—but then, with a crackle, I lose

both the cell signal and the radio station I've been listening to.

Which is when I see the sign.

EVERGREEN, Population 1023. And then, the town slogan, still the same after all this time.

Feels like home.

I find myself blinking back sudden, confused, and lonely tears. "What am I doing?" I ask the empty car.

The only response is the hum of my engine. Then plump snowflakes begin to fall, fast and thick. I manage to slow down enough to keep my abruptly fishtailing car from veering into the ditch just as I realize I haven't gotten around to putting on my snow tires yet.

Lani was right. This is no weather to be driving in, especially without a properly outfitted car. I've been trying to outrun something that already has me beat. And yet, in a moment of weakness and fear, I drove as fast as I could to the last place in the world I should be.

Evergreen, Ontario—the only place that has ever felt like home.

Three

'll just drive past, I tell myself. I'll just have a quick look at the place where I stayed with my family ten years ago. Then I'll leave town and try to find a hotel somewhere before this blizzard gets too fierce.

Soon, I'm driving along Schafer's Road. What feels like an internal compass directs me to turn left where the lake appears beside the road. The snow is falling on the frozen, glass-like surface of the water, covering its smoothness with a white blanket. I pass rolling hills, snow-covered trees on the banks of a roadside creek. My breath catches in my throat. *It's so beautiful here.*

But the snowfall is getting thicker still. Near the bottom of a hill, my tires begin to slide—meaning I almost miss the driveway leading to the place my family rented that fateful Christmas. I regain control of my car just in time. There's a sign there now, the letters glowing soft white against a forest-green background. **EVERGREEN INN**. Then, in smaller letters, **Your home away from home**.

The emotions I'm experiencing are all jostling for a spot at the front of the line—and then, relief pulls ahead. An inn is exactly what I need right now. Even an inn set squarely atop some of my most complicated memories. And it makes such perfect sense that the enormous cabin my parents rented would become what it was likely always meant to be: an actual hotel.

The long driveway is lined with gas lanterns that flicker in the fading afternoon light and the falling snow. There are only two cars parked in the small lot in front of the redbrick Victorian. The windows are lit up, turning the house into a welcoming beacon, shining through thick-trunked spruce with their huge, gray-blue needled branches, some of them so laden with snow they bend to touch the ground. The house is as large as I remember, and so are the trees. The hardwoods surrounding it still dwarf the structure, enclose it, make it feel as though this place is in the middle of a forest all its own, completely isolated from anywhere and anyone else.

But it isn't, and I know it.

Do not look to your left, I tell myself as I pull into a parking spot. But the urge is too strong; I allow myself a glance. All I see are trees and more trees, snow and more snow.

Maybe Wilder Ranch isn't even there anymore. I wonder what it would be like, to know that for sure—and just the thought makes it feel as if my heart is being driven through with splinters.

A tap at my driver's side window startles me from

my thoughts. I release my grip on the steering wheel and hastily wipe at the tears that have pooled beneath my eyes. A girl of maybe nine or ten is standing outside in the snow-dappled late afternoon light. She's adorably elf-like, with dancing brown eyes and dark corkscrew curls poking out from beneath a holly-berry-red hat topped with a forest-green pom-pom. Even though my mood is bleak, there's something about her sweet, welcoming grin that makes me feel, for just a second, like everything will be okay.

"Please tell me you didn't just take a wrong turn down this driveway," she says when I open the window. "You're an actual guest, right?" She clasps her woolen-mittened hands together in front of her heart, and I think that even if I had taken a wrong turn I would probably ask for a room at the inn just to make her happy.

"I'm definitely in need of a place to stay," I say, and her eyes light up like Rudolph's nose. "Just for one night, but—"

"Yessss. We only have two other guests staying here right now, so you get your pick of the best rooms!" She pulls my door open and yanks me out of the car by both hands while I laugh in surprise.

"I'm Samantha," she says when we're both standing in the snow. "But everyone calls me Sam."

"I'm Emory," I say.

"Nice to meet you, Emory. I assume you came from"—she looks me up and down—"Toronto? You look city-ish."

My already wounded-feeling heart seizes. *Hey, City Girl . . .* It's as if I can hear his voice on the wind through the trees. I shake my head to make it stop.

Sam looks perplexed by my expression, my head-shaking. "You're *not* from Toronto?"

"Oh, no, sorry, you got it right. I am."

"Knew it!" She grins again. "And your luggage?" She's peering into my back seat, then at me. "Is it in the trunk?"

"Oh. I don't really have any," I say. "Just that gym bag . . ." I nod my head toward it.

"That's all you brought?" Sam asks. I just shrug, not sure how to explain.

Now she's enthusiastically wrenching open the back door of my car and lifting my gym bag. When I insist on carrying it, she says, "Suit yourself. Follow me!"

I follow her little boot prints toward the house. The front door is different now: It was dark-stained wood when I stayed here; now it's painted a festive green. A large cedar wreath, festooned with red ribbon and studded with berries and dried flowers, hangs from the door knocker—which, I notice with yet another twinge, is in the shape of a horse's head.

Sam pops open the door and we step inside. Back then, the entrance transitioned into a large main living area, but now that's hidden behind a wall and the front of the house is a cozy little lobby. There's a knotty pine desk. Overstuffed chairs covered in red-and-black-checked upholstery. Through an open door, I hear logs crackling, see a welcoming fire, couches and love seats that match the chairs facing the fireplace or turned toward a picture window that looks out at the woods.

"So. What brings you here? Business or pleasure?" Sam asks as she steps behind the desk, clearly trying to sound as grown-up as possible. It's adorable. But I don't know how to answer this question and so, guiltily, I lie.

"Business," I say. "I'm a journalist."

At my words, her eyes become fully-decorated-Christmas-tree level bright. Then, she squeezes them shut, as if she has just gotten exactly what she wished for under that tree. What have I done?

"Are you a reviewer?" she asks in a reverent whisper. Then she opens her eyes, takes a step back, and says, "Never mind! Forget I said that! You don't have to tell me. Pretend I didn't ask." But under her breath I hear her whisper, *"Now Mom is definitely going to be able to afford horseback-riding lessons for me!"*

"Sam—"

"Really, it's *fine,* say no more!"

"It's just, I'm not exactly—"

We're interrupted by a woman with Sam's same lively dark eyes stepping into the room, a flour-dusted apron covering her jeans and red-and-white-striped button-up top. "Sam, what are you up to in here— Oh." She spots me. "Hello!"

"Mama, we have a guest," Sam says with a flourish. Then she gives her mother a meaningful look and I feel my cheeks flush as red as the ribbon on the wreath at the door. "We need to give her our best room. It is *very, very* important."

"I'm Reesa," the woman says, shooting a bemused glance at her daughter as I open my mouth to try to explain that I'm not really here on assignment. But then I pause. I could be, couldn't I? After I got laid off from the *Globe*, in order to pay my bills, and while waiting to find a new job in journalism that has yet to materialize, I started to freelance. News reporting is almost never done by freelancers and I miss the newsroom, but I also enjoy the lifestyle pieces I'm assigned at various newspapers and magazines. I throw myself into the research; I'm always trying and learning new things. Maybe I could pitch a review of Reesa and Sam's hotel. If any of my editors still want to hear from me, that is.

"How long will you be staying?" Reesa asks.

"Just one night. I need to leave first thing in the morning."

"You won't leave until you've had your breakfast, though, right?" says Sam. "You have to try our award-winning scones."

"Sam," Reesa murmurs. "My scones haven't won any awards . . ."

"They're the best scones in the world as declared by me," Sam says, and I can't help but laugh again at her infectious enthusiasm.

Reesa smiles. "Okay, they *are* pretty good," she says.

"I promise," I tell Sam. "I will not leave until I've tried them."

"Let's get you checked in, then!" She painstakingly writes up an invoice, but I have nowhere to be so wait patiently, staring out the window above her head as I do, the rhythm of the snow falling outside becoming mesmeric.

After Sam checks me in, we walk through the main room, with its fireplace and comfy seating, to get to the staircase. As we do, I clock the changes that have taken place in the past decade. The stairs I once used, off to the side of the kitchen—mostly to sneak out and see Tate—are blocked off now, and so is the kitchen. Both doors have signs that read **Staff Only**.

"There are bedrooms downstairs," Sam says over her shoulder as we climb. "But the best ones are up here." We've reached the top of the staircase. "There's the Loon's Nest, which in my personal opinion is the best one. See, it looks out at the lake from one window, and at the forest, and this *beautiful, magical* horse ranch next door from the other—"

"No!" I can tell both Sam and Reesa are surprised by my abrupt tone. "I don't . . . like horses," I improvise. "I'd have nightmares."

I can't bring myself to look out that window, but the knowledge that Wilder Ranch is still there flows through me. It's not gone. The truth of this beats in my heart, in my soul. I want to run outside and see it. But I can't do that, and I know it.

"Okay, then," Sam says, now looking at me like I'm the strangest person she has ever met. "Right this way, I guess. We also have the Great Heron Hideaway—"

But that was the room my parents had slept in, a high-ceilinged corner suite overlooking the lake on one side and the woods on the other. It's a beautiful room, but I know it will just remind me of them—and I don't want to think about my parents right now. "Do you have anything maybe a little smaller?"

She looks disappointed. "We have the Loonet's Lair, but that's just a kid's room. It has a bunk bed and only one tiny window, and it looks out into the front yard, which doesn't really—"

"Perfect," I say. And it is, I can tell as soon as she opens the door. Small, dim, doesn't remind me of anything. I can crawl into the bottom bunk later and hopefully fall asleep without also descending into the pit of nostalgia that is threatening to engulf me.

"Weird," I hear Sam say under her breath as her mother shakes her head at her.

"She's our guest, let her stay in the room she wants," Reesa whispers back.

Reesa explains that the Loonet's Lair has a shared bathroom, but since no one else is on this floor it will be my own private en suite. Then Sam begins to list activities.

"There's the guided snowshoe tour—"

"Sam," Reesa whispers, "we don't have that."

"*I* can be the guide," Sam shoots back, returning her gaze to me. "And the guided cross-country ski tour. Also, skating on the lake! Bonfire at dusk! We could even go next door and see if the Wilders would let us groom the—"

"I'm okay," I say quickly. "Really, no need."

"You don't want to do *anything*?"

Except wallow in my own shame, misery, and confusion? Not really, kid. But of course I can't say such a thing to this sweet, idealistic little girl—so I tell her I'm just going to go for a walk by myself, and look away from her crestfallen expression.

"Will you eat some dinner when you get back?" Reesa asks me. "I'm baking fresh bread and there's soup on the stove. Not much open in town on a Sunday, in the way of food."

My stomach is still in knots and I can't imagine eating much, but I tell her yes, mostly for Sam's benefit. She looks relieved that I've agreed to do something.

"After you eat, we could play a board game—" Sam begins, but Reesa puts her hand on her daughter's back, rubs it once, a silent signal that causes Sam to stop her excited stream-of-consciousness babble as she tries to suggest more activities for me to try. *Let her be,* Reesa is telling her daughter. I feel more grateful than ever, both for Sam's heartwarming zest—even if I'm not fully up to participating in it—and for her mother's quiet compassion.

"It gets dark fast this time of year, so I'll leave a lantern at the door for you to take on your walk," Reesa says.

Sam clearly wants to stay and keep offering me an itinerary of made-up activities, but Reesa suggests she come to the kitchen and help her with the scones for the next morning, so she follows her mother. Alone now, I send Lani a quick text to let her know I'm safe, then root around in my gym bag for the sweatshirt I know is in there. I don't have a hat, but I do have the hood of my parka and some thin gloves. This will do.

I pick up the lantern Reesa left for me, step outside,

and stand still, listening. The silence feels like a living thing, quiet but not. The snow is softening the sharp edges of the world. It already seems like a lifetime ago that I was on the treadmill, watching my family's transgressions written across the bottom of a television screen. I breathe in the cold winter air and step down from the stairs to begin my walk, careful to avoid turning toward or looking for any path in the woods leading to Wilder Ranch—intent on avoiding my past, even though I've just run blindly toward it.

Four

A sound I remember well pulls me toward the lake. My boots slip and slide on the granite steps that lead from the cottage down to the water, but I don't fall. The dock is out, pulled ashore to protect it from the ice, so I stand on the rock wall at the edge of the water and listen. There it is again: the noise that woke me in the middle of the night ten years ago and led me to Tate Wilder.

I lean down and pry a rock from the icy ground, practicing the motion of flicking my wrist to see if I still remember how. I do. Like so much about this place, it has left its imprint. I let the rock fly, and the noise it makes as it bounces across the new ice is a lilting, whistling pop that is so deeply satisfying, I do it again.

Eventually, my hands grow too numb to skip rocks anymore, so I turn away from the lake and walk down the lantern-lit driveway. I turn right instead of left, determined to walk away from Wilder Ranch instead of toward it. I have a view through the trees of the lake, silent, cold, and moody in the early evening light. It's the perfect visual match for my somber emotions.

I hear a car coming up the hill behind me and my heart seizes momentarily—*What if it's him?* But it isn't. It's a man and woman in a pearl-white SUV, and they wave at me as they pass—which I remember is the rule here in cottage country. I wave back and continue on my way, down the hill and around another corner. Most of the cottages are closed up for winter, and I'm completely alone—until a little red fox trots out of the trees, keeping to the opposite side of the road, glancing at me with cautious disinterest as he hurries on his way.

Next, I see two deer leaping up the snowbanks on the road's shoulder, then stepping gingerly onto the icy gravel. One glance at me and they're off, bounding into the woods. I stand still, feeling a sense of wonder that I let wash over me: a deep sensation of luck at spotting the fox and the deer. My heart has been racing on and off since I left the city, but now I feel it slowing. I've read and written articles about the health benefits of "forest-bathing." It's amazing that even in my agitated state, being so close to the woods makes me feel like I can really breathe, finally.

I walk again, my pace more relaxed, the lake at my side, until I realize the sun is about to set and I should get back to the inn. My stomach grumbles. It has unknotted itself, and I'm grateful that Reesa will have left me bread and soup. I think of all the elaborate food my mother had the chef cook that Christmas, when what I really wanted was a simple, comforting meal. I wanted a life that didn't consist of constant striving for the next level of status, to unlock a level of wealth that seemed pointless, like pouring more water into an already overflowing bucket.

I turn and walk back the way I came. Near the deer tracks at the side of the road, I spot other animal tracks. I lean down to take a look: They're large, paw-shaped, and there are no human footprints beside them to indicate these are from a dog. I feel a prickle at the back of my neck. Is there a wolf nearby? I remember listening to a pack of them howl one night with Tate, feeling thrilled at the sound—slightly scared, too, but sure I was safe in his arms. Now I think of the two deer I saw earlier and feel a sinking sense of doom for them.

The world's not a fair place, Emory. My father's voice is so real I look over my shoulder to see if he's there—and then remember where he is. In a jail cell, in the city. I wonder how he is, if he's feeling as adrift as I am, as my mother must be, too. If he's scared. I've never seen him scared. I look up at the darkening sky and keep remembering him, the father from my childhood. The idea that the world isn't fair is one of the bits of wisdom he sought to dispense as I was growing up, during our early morning bonding breakfasts on Bay Street, before our driver would arrive to take me to school. That was back when he believed that one day I would work alongside him. I'm seized with the urge to try to reach him, somehow. I want to hear his voice, hear him say to me, like he did when I was younger, *One foot in front of the other, Emory. It will all be fine.*

Now I'm swamped with more sadness. *One foot in front of the other.* He just kept doing that, but I think he started to forget why. And it hardened him. As his business grew, he never stopped pressing forward, didn't take a moment to look around and see what we already had. If he had done that, he might have, in the pause, seen who he was and who I really was, too. As opposed to who he had hoped I was going to become: someone just like him.

During one of our last conversations, he snapped at me that maybe the world didn't deserve his benevolence—and in his voice, I heard his father, my grandfather. I didn't know my grandfather well; he died when I was ten, but I remember him as stingy and mean, abrupt and judgmental. When did my father turn into him?

I've become lost in the wolf tracks, staring down at them and imagining different paths. I'm upset with my father for not really seeing me—but I let my thoughts of him get lost in the woods, too.

It's cold. My feet in my boots are growing numb. I walk again, until I can see the glowing lanterns on the inn's driveway. Once inside, I smell Reesa's fresh bread. It's comforting and welcoming. In the living room, I see that she's left the fire on for me, a note on the coffee table. *The soup is on the stove. It's called Saturday Soup; we make it every week. A little spicy, lots of vegetables. Bread on the counter beside it.*

I step into the kitchen, where I see the large pot of soup simmering on the stove. I ladle some into a blue pottery bowl, cut a slice of bread, spread it thick with the soft butter, then take my meal back out to the living room.

The soup is just as delicious as it smells, the peppery flavor heating me all the way down to my cold toes. The butter melts across the still-warm surface of the bread like the setting sun's reflection on a lake. I grow thoughtful as I eat this wonderful food in this cozy setting, more intent than ever on the idea of pitching an article or review of this place. Something about finding comfort and winter joy in the most unexpected hidden gem towns. I find myself smiling as I imagine how delighted Sam would be. Looking around at this silent, empty room, I also think they could really use the business an article could bring in. It would be doing a good deed—and I'll need to focus on good deeds going forward to make up for the havoc my father has wreaked in the world with his dishonest ways.

Once I'm finished with my dinner, I clean up, then find myself staring back out the window into the night. I feel a tug of curiosity, and of longing, too. My head tells me to go upstairs to bed—but my heart is getting away from me, and perhaps it was just a matter of time before it completely loosened itself from the ties I keep trying to bind it with. Fortified now by the soup and bread, I put my coat back on, pick up Reesa's lantern, and step outside, closing the door quietly behind me the way I used to when I was a teenager in love. I swing the light toward Wilder Ranch.

Slowly, I walk forward. I see a break in the trees, and what could be a path. I push aside snowy branches; the path gets wider. All at once, I can almost see the ghosts of us, two teenagers, kissing in the moonlight, our arms wrapped around each other, never wanting to let go.

They say the first cut is the deepest, but I've often wondered if there's something wrong with me. I've dated, but I've never allowed anyone else into my heart in the same way, not since Tate. Not for a decade. After getting hurt the way I did, I've been so afraid to let myself be seen the way Tate saw me back then.

I keep walking, keep shining my light around. It lands on tree trunks, snowy branches—and then, a log cabin I didn't expect. Startled, I pull back into the shadows. But I already know what this cabin is. I cast the light on it again.

Tate's house. I feel as certain of this as I am of my own name. It's just how he described it to me, plucking it out of his dream life and painting it with words. *I've been dragging granite rocks out of the lake for years, and someday, I'm going to use them to build a fireplace with two sides, one in the living room, one in the bedroom. It'll be a log A-frame, with a great big wall of windows facing the valley, looking down at the ranch. I think you'll love it, too, Emory.*

The trunk of the tree I'm pressing my body against feels solid and reassuring on my back. I focus on it rather than letting my thoughts spin even further into the past, snake my hands around behind me and touch the bark, richly textured beneath my thin gloves.

You have to walk away. What if he sees you out here?

I turn away from Tate's cabin, from the stables and horses I know are there in the dark. Once I'm a safe distance away, I click my lantern back on and shine it on the path ahead. Soon, I spot the lanterns on the inn's driveway. I just have to walk toward them, *one foot in front of the other,* and I'll be okay.

As I get closer to the inn, I feel a bone-deep tiredness settling over me. It's still silent when I get inside. I hear some voices in the downstairs bedrooms, but no one is about. Upstairs, I wash up, pull out the Fit-mas Tree shirt to wear to bed, change, and head for my cozy little room.

In the bottom bunk, I close my eyes. Behind my eyelids, lights glimmer as if strung across the eaves of stable buildings painted red, weathered to a shade as soft as a beloved old sweater. And I can see his cabin in the woods. I open my eyes again and stare into the darkness, but the vision of his home is still there. It's with me in this room, and it's out there, too. Just beyond these walls, only a few hundred feet away from where I'm tossing and turning, trying to sleep.

I need to talk to him. How could I not if I came all this way? I need to finally get the closure I never had, and then I need to move on with this life.

As terrifying as I find this idea, there's also a strange sort of peace in it. I close my eyes, and a calm settles over me. And finally, I sleep.

❄ ❄ ❄ ❄ ❄

Dear Diary,

I'm sorry about the messy handwriting. I have to write fast because I'm on my way to the ranch soon to help Tate get the place prepared for the Starlight Ride. It's a week from today, sounds like the most festive (and frankly, romantic) thing in the world, and I can't believe I get to be a part of it. Everyone in the town comes. Some choose to ride horses, others to walk. They carry lanterns and sing carols and do a loop through the woods before ending up back at the Wilders' for hot chocolate, mulled wine, a bonfire, and more carol singing.

I'm telling my parents that I'm taking lessons over at the stable next door, and they're happy I'm having fun and keeping busy. I haven't mentioned Tate. Or the Starlight Ride. I just don't want them involved. I want this to be mine. So I'm keeping it to myself.

Anyway, my not being around leaves them free to stay up late smoking cigars, drinking martinis, and talking about politics (i.e., why late-stage capitalism should never end, ugh) and whatever business it is my dad and Cousin Reuben are cooking up. I don't know how I'd be surviving this holiday without Tate—and I don't know how, in a few weeks' time, I'm going to live without him. But I don't want to think about that right now. Not yet, dear Diary, not yet.

The day after we first met, I walked around like I was in a dream. I actually started to worry it really WAS a dream. Could the night before have actually been possible? I waited and waited, and finally at three (I had a hard time deciding what was "mid-afternoon"—two seemed too eager, four seemed too late, and at this time of year, it would almost be dark out), I told my mother the half-lie about riding lessons—and my mother ALMOST said she wanted to come with me. But then Aunt Bitsy started whining about how she had promised they'd go skiing, so off they went. Phew. I felt a little guilty; my mom likes riding, too. But Bitsy has zero filter and would just embarrass me. And my mom . . . well, she's a snob. There's no other way to put it. She likes upscale equestrian facilities, not cozy country ranch properties. Wilder Ranch would not be her thing.

I was so nervous about what it would be like to see Tate again. Would I feel the same? Would he? I was nervous, but as soon as I saw him outside one of the stable buildings, standing there in the snowfall as if he had been waiting for me, I could tell. What had happened between us was real. When our gazes locked, it felt like we were connected by a cord. He smiled that slow-burn smile of his, and I started to feel like I was melting again.

We went to see his horse, Mistletoe. She is so beautiful. I can only imagine how lovely her foal will be when she's born. We gave her some mints, and then walked farther out into the paddock to bring in the horses we would ride: Jax for him; Walt for me. Once we got them tacked up, we headed out. I've never been on a trail ride in winter—and wow, have I been missing out. The forest was blanketed in snow, the trees looked like they had been hung with lace. It was a sunny afternoon, so warm we both tied our jackets to our saddles, and our horses walked side by side as we talked.

The forest path we were on meandered up a few rolling hills and eventually we reached a clearing with a breathtaking view of the valley below. You could see everything from there: the forest, the lake, the stables, the town. It was perfect, and I told him that. He smiled and said this was the spot he wanted to build his house on one day. It felt like he was telling me a secret. He said he had been dragging granite rocks out of the lake for years—and someday, he was going to use them to build a fireplace that would have two sides, one in the living room, one in the bedroom. When he said the word "bedroom" I think I probably blushed, but if he noticed, he didn't let on. He talked about it being a log A-frame, with a big wall of windows facing the valley, looking down at the ranch. It sounded so perfect.

I asked him if that was what he did for fun: drag granite rocks out of the lake. Then I almost wished I hadn't. I think I was asking about friends, about girls. Maybe in that moment I was worried about there being someone else in his life. He just shrugged and said, "At my high school, you're either a football jock—and I'm not really a <u>Friday Night Lights</u> kind of guy—or a burnout—and I don't smoke weed. I have a few buddies and we hang out sometimes, but this"—and he looked out at the valley spread before us, the stables, the paddocks—"is where I'm happiest."

I almost said it was where I was happiest, too. But I stopped myself.

Instead, I asked him what he wanted to do after building that house—who he wanted to be. He told me he wanted to be here, running the ranch with his dad, that he hoped to eventually develop a riding school and train show teams. That maybe Wilder Ranch would one day be well-known for producing quality riders. Even Olympians. I told him I admired someone who had dreams like that—who knew exactly who they wanted to be. He asked me about what I wanted for my future, and I told him about my journalism school plans. He said, "Well, it sounds like you're sure about your future, too. You just won't be staying in one place, like I will."

We were side by side on our horses, looking down at the spot where he wanted to build his house—and I just felt so sad all of a sudden. Like despite all these intense feelings, I could see his future . . . and I wasn't in it.

Then he looked over at me and said, "What are you thinking?" I shook my head and told him it was nothing important. He said, "Well, I was just thinking that I hope we'll still know each other when I build that house. I hope you see it someday." Then he bit his lip (Diary, I can't express how it makes me feel when he does this) and his expression became searching. He wanted something, and I wanted to give it to him. To give him everything. But I settled for leaning over and giving him a kiss.

Have you ever kissed someone while sitting on a horse? It's not easy, but it's also magic.

I keep reminding myself I haven't known him long enough to be feeling this way. But my heart just won't listen to reason. I know he feels the same, and that makes it even more special, more intense. We're falling fast, and I'm not going to do anything to stop it . . .

Five

I wake up disoriented in a dark room. It feels like the middle of the night, but it's nearly nine. I slept in. I sit up, hitting my head on the bunk above—and it all comes rushing back. My dad. The arrest. My mother's phone call. Handing over my trust fund and just . . . driving. To Evergreen. Of all places. Whatever peace and certainty I experienced last night is gone. I only feel panic. *I have to get out of this town* is my first thought. I had an unsettling dream about dark woods and burned-out lanterns. Being utterly lost. Hearing a wolf's howl and feeling afraid.

What am I doing here? Why would I do this to myself?

I turn on the lamp on the little desk and pull on my gym clothes from the day before. Downstairs, I'm expecting the homemade scones Sam raved about, and for my mood to be brightened by her enthusiasm for absolutely everything—but all is just as silent as it was the night before. I don't even smell any coffee brewing; in fact, I don't hear any noise in the kitchen at all. That's strange. Sam made such a big deal out of the inn's early morning breakfast, but the kitchen door is closed tight. Am I late?

Out the window, I can see the snow falling in thick, white clumps, and when I step closer and peer out, I realize my car is half buried in snow. Sam and Reesa are outside, shoveling the walkway, silent and determined. I see a plow has already been in to clear the driveway, but my car has now been swamped. I pull on my snow boots and parka and open the front door.

"Good morning!" I call out. "Wow, what a blizzard! Do you have an extra shovel? Let me help."

Sam looks up at me, then away, back to her shoveling. Even from here, and through the snow, I can see the disappointment in her eyes. Did she already find out I'm not actually a hotel reviewer? I step gingerly down the front stairs and head toward them. But as I approach, instead of saying *good morning*, Reesa turns to her daughter and says, "Go inside, Sam," her voice tight. Sam scampers away without looking at me.

"Listen, I'm sorry if I gave her the idea I'm a hotel reviewer," I begin—but Reesa cuts me off.

"You need to leave, please," she says firmly. "I'll refund you for the portion that would have been for your breakfast. And then you can go."

I blink in surprise. This seems like an extreme reaction for giving her daughter the wrong impression about who I was. "I actually *am* a freelance journalist, I just don't write about hotels," I say. "But I was planning to pitch something to one of my editors."

"No, thank you," she says. "I don't think an article with your name on it would do us any good."

"I don't understand," I begin, but as I say the words, I realize I do. I'm a member of the Oakes family, and she somehow knows. But how? I realize I've said this out loud when she answers the question.

"It's all over the Evergreen Business Owners' group chat." Then she shakes her head and says, "Poor Gill."

It was one thing when I could think about the people my father hurt with his scheme as nameless, unknown to me. But my heart is aching already for whatever has been lost here.

"Gill—who is that?"

"He runs the fish and chips and bait and tackle place in town. Years ago, when apparently your family was staying right here over Christmas—an interesting fact you did not mention last night—your father and his cousin canvassed the town for investors. Luckily, most people didn't trust them, or didn't have enough money to get into TurbOakes at ground level. But Gill invested everything he had just received from his beloved late father's estate."

I feel like I'm on a fishing boat, lost in a storm, seasick. I can't believe my father and Reuben went after people in town. Did they even need the seed money? Was it just for sport?

"I'm so sorry," I say. "I had no idea."

"I saw the name Oakes on the article that was sent around in the chat. And then, there was a picture on the internet, at some gala."

Reesa takes her phone out of her pocket and turns it toward me. And there's the full image of me and my parents at the AGO gala last year. I'm no longer just cut off at the hem of my sparkling green skirt. I'm beside my parents, smiling, looking like one of them. Their darling daughter.

"I only went because my parents said I had to," I say, but this feels so disloyal. I love the AGO. I wanted to go. And I'm not a child. I don't have to do what my parents say.

"Then I realized it was you," Reesa continues, ignoring me. "I don't know what you're doing here in Evergreen, and frankly, I don't care. I just want you to leave."

Reesa turns away from me and calls out, "Sam? Please gather Ms. Oakes's things!" Moments later, my gym bag lands with a thud in the snow at the bottom of the stairs, and the front door of the inn slams shut again. I think I see a curtain twitch, and Sam's face peering out, her eyes filled with disillusion.

. . . .

By the time I'm done shoveling my car out of its snowy prison, I've taken off my parka and am covered in a cold, clammy sweat. I carefully lean the shovel against the porch and take one last look at the exterior of the inn. I'm exhausted, embarrassed. The only bright side is that I am not nostalgic for this place anymore. Once I get out of here, I swear I'll never think of Evergreen again. I get in my car and drive carefully down the inn's driveway and out onto the road—but I can already tell I won't make it back to the city without snow tires. The road is plowed, but the snow is still coming in thick.

I turn on the radio, scan until I find a local station called Kayak, just in time for the weather report. It's delivered by a man who sounds like he's eighty if he's a day. "Looks like we're in for a heck of a lot of snow to-day, folks. I can barely see my hand when I hold it outside the window of the station here, and there's a snowfall warning in effect. I think they're calling for"—long pause—"a couple more feet, at least, and in a short period of time. So, stay home if you can . . . and if you can't, best to put on some tire chains."

Tire chains? I don't even have snow tires on my car, let alone tire chains. As if to prove this, my car fishtails at the bottom of a hill. Reluctantly, I turn left, heading toward Evergreen instead of away from it.

Ten years, I tell myself. It's been ten years and this town is not going to look the same. This is not going to be another painful walk through my memories, like last night was.

And yet, somehow, it still is. There's the grocery store where Tate and I went together to replenish his stock of the mints the horses liked to eat. And then, on Christmas Eve, we went there to get the ingredients for his dad's fondue recipe: Emmenthal cheese, broth, apple juice, garlic, lemons, and cornstarch. There's the movie theater, now shut down and housing a closed-for-the-season beach toy shop instead. But the sign is still there, golden and red, the bulbs lining the words **Evergreen Theater** burned out or broken. We went to see the latest Minions movie there—which neither of us had any interest in. We used it as an excuse to kiss in a back corner until the credits rolled. There's Carrie's Café, and when I see the pink-and-white hand-painted sign, my heart skitters in my chest. I remember thick, dark hot chocolate and caramel chip cookies, the best I'd ever had. My stomach grumbles and my traitorous heart swoons, thinking of my teenage self sharing a cookie with Tate Wilder at a corner table.

I *really* have to get out of this town. My backward gaze is rose-colored, but there's only heartache waiting for me if I keep staring so intently into my rearview. I press my foot down on the gas pedal and keep going, looking for a garage. But first, I have to pass Gill's Fish n Chips n Bait n Tackle. I'm agonized over my father's crimes against this person. My family owes Gill—money, definitely, but also an apology. I don't feel brave enough for that yet.

As I continue past Gill's, another memory surfaces. Tate and I went there together, too. Gill kept polystyrene containers of worms and little buckets filled with minnows in a fridge in the corner, but the food was delicious. I can now recall Gill as a big man with bright blue eyes and a friendly manner—just like everyone in the town. Tate and I sat in a window booth with peeling vinyl, shared a huge plate of fries doused in malt vinegar and salt, fed each other pieces of crispy fried lake trout. I sucked on a lemon, then kissed him. I had to avoid lemon-flavored anything for a full year after.

"*Please* let me find a mechanic who can do my snow

tires fast," I mutter. And then, as if in answer to my wish, a sign comes into view out the windshield: **M&M's Autobody**.

I pull into the parking lot, breathing a sigh of relief as a young woman with wavy blond hair, wearing festive red coveralls, comes out to greet me. She gives my car a once-over as I get out. "Let me guess, you're here for the winter tire special?"

My relief increases as I tell her I am, then follow her inside. She slides a form across the counter at the front and I pass her my credit card. There's a long silence then, a sudden chill I know isn't simply from the blast of cold air caused by another customer opening the door and entering the shop. The woman—the name-tag stitched onto her coveralls reads MEREDITH—shoots a quick smile at the person who has just walked in, her glacier-blue eyes filled with warmth.

"Hey there. I'll be right with you." Then, to me, in a considerably less warm tone, she says "Just one second" before heading through a door behind the desk leading to the repair bay.

My credit card suddenly feels like it's an incriminating item, my toxic family name a glowing beacon. I cover my card with my hand as I wait. The person behind me clears his throat, but I don't turn.

After a few excruciating moments, Meredith is back. "I'm so sorry," she says, but doesn't sound sorry at all. "Unfortunately, we just ran out of the winter tires we have on special. All we have left are our custom European winter tires, which are quite expensive."

My heart sinks. "How expensive?"

The price she quotes seems absurd. I suspect she just made up the whole European-winter-tires thing, but what other choice do I have?

"It's fine," I say, perhaps to convince myself. "Please go ahead." I push my credit card toward her one more time and she looks down at it like it's a dead fish from Gill's.

"And it'll be a lot longer than an hour," she says. "These European winter tires are a specialty item. They won't be ready until just before we close today."

I'm even more dismayed than I already was. "But I need to get back to the city," I say. *I have to get out of this town.* "Please, is there anything you can do?"

Another throat-clear behind me, and then a deep voice says, "Of course there darn well is. Meredith, cut the nonsense, would you? We both know there's no such thing as European winter tires."

I know who it is immediately. And I can't decide if I want to turn and say hello or find a back door I can escape through so I don't have to face him.

It's Charlie Wilder, Tate's father.

Six

I close my eyes and wait, hoping maybe a sink-hole will open up in the floor of the mechanic's shop and swallow me before I have to turn around.

"Emory? That you?"

His voice cuts through my angst.

"Yes?" I say, my eyes still closed.

"Might as well turn around and find out what happens next."

I'm too miserable to *actually* laugh, but I'm smiling when I turn toward him. Charlie always did have the best sense of humor, and apparently this is still true.

"Hi, Charlie."

He's just as I remember him: tall, wearing a Stetson even in winter—just like his son—and with amber-brown eyes that match his son's, too, but on a more weathered face.

I can't speak. I find myself peering behind him, out the window, at the white pickup truck with the Wilder

Ranch logo—a red line drawing of a horse's head swooping into a curvaceous *W*—parked there. I can't help but look for him—but Tate's not in the passenger seat.

"It's been a while," he says, filling my silence.

"Sure has," I finally manage. "Ten years."

Then his smile fades as he seems to remember something. He leans around me, toward Meredith behind the counter.

"I don't care what the overactive rumor mill in this town is spewing out. Emory herself has done nothing wrong, and you can't be going and lying to her, overcharging her for something you know you and your brother can have done in an hour."

Meredith seems even more flustered than I am. Her cheeks turn as red as her coveralls as she apologizes. "I'll see what I can do," she says.

Charlie shakes his head. "Damn group chat. Now, I need a new winch. Mine's busted. Got any of those in stock for me?"

As she goes to fetch it, I turn toward the door, but Charlie calls out to me.

"You want to wait a minute there, Emory, so you and I can have a little catch-up?"

I nod and mumble that I'll see him outside. In the parking lot, the snow is still falling in feathery little bundles, and I let it land on me, in the hopes it'll cool me down after the emotional roller-coaster ride I've just been on.

Soon, Charlie is outside, too. He looks at me for a moment, then says, "You have an hour to kill while they get those tires on for you. I can't let you be standing out here in this snowstorm, waiting."

"I'll be okay," I try to insist. "I'll go to Carrie's Café or something."

He ignores this. "Why don't I take you back to the ranch for a nice warm mug of something, and by the time we're done getting caught up, Meredith should be done with your tires, too."

Now I'm as frozen as a snow sculpture. But not because of the cold. Is this really going to happen?

He shoots me a look, reading my hesitation. "He's not around," he answers my unvoiced question. "Went to a trade show in Barrie for a few days. Not back till Wednesday."

Something swirls around me along with the snow. I can't quite grasp it. Disappointment, I think. He's not here at all. So there's no chance of my running into him. But then a new emotion arrives: relief. I can relax now. Tate Wilder isn't in town. He's not going to see me, or know I was here.

Somewhat more at ease, I follow Charlie to his truck and climb up into the cab. Soon the heat is blasting, and he's driving down the familiar winding road toward Wilder Ranch. His radio is tuned to Kayak, the quirky local station I was listening to earlier; Céline Dion is singing "The Christmas Song," soulfully crooning about chestnuts roasting on an open fire and Jack Frost nipping at her nose. *This is nice,* I tell myself. *I'm going to have a pleasant visit with Charlie, and then, once the hour is over, I will be able to drive away and put this town behind me.*

. . . .

"Charlie, Wilder Ranch looks just the same!" And it does. Exactly like my dreams of the place—because I have dreamed of it, over and over as the years have passed. The paddocks are still fenced by sun-bleached wood, now iced with snow, hung with dangling icicles. Horses either stand still, covered in those same red-and-green-plaid Wilder Ranch blankets I remember, or prance and gallop, snorting plumes of frosty air.

"Well, now, you haven't been inside yet," Charlie says, turning off the truck. "We've made some modernizations—Tate's seen to that. But you're right. Wilder Ranch is still very much the same place you knew."

The snow slows enough that everything comes into focus. I can see the main house, which is made of logs like the one Tate built in the woods—except much larger, with a wraparound veranda in the same sun-bleached wood as the paddocks. I see a construction dumpster out front; Charlie must be doing some renovations. I look away from the gable I know used to be Tate's bedroom window and try not to think about the night I threw pebbles at it, trying to get him to come out and talk to me. He never did.

I turn instead toward the stable buildings. There's a covered arena, separate from the stables. Charlie explains that this is one of the modernizations he mentioned. And that the space that used to be a stall-lined riding ring is now a ranch office, with more stalls and a larger tack room. "For Tate's riding school," he says. Another one of his dreams come true.

I recognize the snow-covered outdoor sand ring, the paths leading to the fields and forest, the woods I know are filled with peaceful, snowy trails and Tate's house of dreams. I find myself wondering, *Does he live there with a wife? A family?* I want to ask Charlie questions about him, but I can't. I just stand still, taking it all in.

"Let's walk," Charlie says, and we do, heading toward the paddocks. "So," he says as we crunch through the snow. "Tell me what you've been up to all these years. What great things have you done?"

I feel embarrassed. What have I done that's great? "I worked as a local news reporter for *The Globe and Mail* after journalism school," I say, and he lets out a low whistle.

"Impressive! That's our national paper!"

"Not so fast. I got laid off last year, and now I'm a freelancer."

"Who do you freelance for?"

"The *Globe*, still. Sometimes the *Toronto Star* now, too. Just about any Canadian magazine you can think of. *Chatelaine. House & Home. Food & Drink.* Some websites."

He glances at me like he wants to ask me something. Instead he says, "Well, I've heard of all those publications, so I still find it impressive. You were always going places, Emory Oakes." I feel a twinge as he says this—because he sounds just like Tate.

I drag myself back into the present as Charlie says, "Okay, so let's address the elephant in the room." My heart seizes in my chest. "I'm sorry about the way you're being treated in town."

I blink a few times, catch my breath, slow my heart. He doesn't want to talk about Tate. And why would he? It was years ago. It was between me and Tate. And Tate's not here.

"I suppose I shouldn't be surprised that the Evergreen grapevine is still fully functional. It was always robust, from what I remember."

"Yes, well, now it's been streamlined. That Business Owners' group chat never shuts up." He shakes his head. "I keep meaning to ask Tate to tell me how to mute it but we always get busy with something else and I forget." Then he shoots me a sidelong smile. "Small towns, you know. Everyone's in everyone else's business. Sometimes literally. Now, let me guess what brought you here at this exact time."

Now my heart rate gallops completely out of control. How am I going to handle Charlie saying he can tell I obviously have never fully gotten over his son?

Except that's not what he says at all. Yet again, he doesn't mention Tate and me and what happened between us back then. "You came here to apologize to Gill on behalf of your family. To try to make things right."

"*Oh.*" I have no idea what to say to this. The fact that this isn't at all why I came jabs at the shame that is so close at hand, pulls it up into my consciousness again so it's all I can feel.

"And to offer him money, probably," Charlie continues, which just makes it all worse. "But I don't think you should do that," he concludes.

I open and close my mouth, but can't think of anything to say that will help. *Sorry, I didn't come here to apologize to Gill and I have no money to give him. I gave it all to my mother, who is still throwing her annual Christmas party while my father is in jail.*

"It's okay, kiddo. This is hard, I can tell. But I don't know that you talking to Gill will help. Emotions are running high, obviously. And while I think it's really quite admirable of you to have rushed here to try to make it right, I just don't know if you can accomplish that right now. Gill is a softie in some ways, but a proud man, too. It's going to take a while for him to accept help."

"Charlie, that's not why—"

"No, I must insist that it's just not a good time to go talk to Gill." He shakes his head, his voice still kind, but firm.

All I can do is nod and force a weak smile. Thankfully, we've reached the paddock fence, which is a distraction. Reflexively, I search my parka pockets for a mint. I place my empty hands on the wood of the fence and watch two horses in the paddock together, one a large bay—mahogany-brown coat, coal-black tail—running back and forth at the south end. She reminds me of Mistletoe until she turns her head toward me and I see the distinctive marking isn't there.

But there's another horse nearby, full of energy. Kicking up snow, dashing back and forth, almost as if she's showing off to the others. And then, she stops and looks over at us.

She has a coat the color of dappled sunlight. Spun gold. Fresh hay. She nickers and trots in our direction. That's when it comes into focus: the blaze up the center of her aristocratic forehead that ends in a star.

Charlie chuckles, his mood lifting. "Here she comes. Our Star."

He reaches into one of his pockets and hands me a scotch mint. I take it and hold my palm flat, filled with sudden reverence. *Star.* I was here the night she was born. Star dips her head to take the mint and her muzzle grazes my skin, a soft brush of velvet. Then she steps back, crunching and staring. Once she's finished the treat, she tosses her head and whinnies, while Charlie chuckles and tells her one is enough. She sidesteps one more time and paws the ground, as if waiting for a different answer, before shooting me what I'm sure is a haughty look, then turning and trotting back the way she came.

I turn to Charlie. "I haven't thought about her for years," I say, my voice filled with emotion.

"Really?" Charlie raises his eyebrows. "You've never thought of her?"

How can I tell him the truth? I haven't allowed myself to think of her is more accurate. I'll always remember my eighteen-year-old self breathlessly telling Tate and Charlie that the night Star was born was the most memorable night of my life. Helping during a foaling, especially one as complicated as hers, is an unforgettable experience. All at once, my eyes are filling with tears. I blink them away fast and turn back toward the paddock, hoping Charlie didn't see.

It almost seems as if Star did, though. She's stopped in her tracks, and her head is lifted, as if she's caught a scent. She turns to me, gives me a long look, then lets out a whinny before galloping in a circle. I think of something Tate told me once, years ago. *Did you know a horse can sense your heartbeat from four feet away?*

"That girl," Charlie says. "Even at ten years old, she still acts like a damn filly. And against all odds, too, since she was a preemie. You remember."

"I remember," I breathe, the words coming out in puffs of white air, lingering in front of my lips as if I could reach out and touch them. "Ten years. I can't believe it." But I can, of course. I know exactly how long it's been since I've stood in this spot or been near this horse.

"We all got a little older, didn't we?" He tips his cap forward to reveal a head full of gray. "I've turned into Father Christmas."

"Aw, Charlie, you look the same, just like this place. The hair only makes you look dignified."

"Dignified!" He laugh-shouts the word and a horse in the paddock whinnies a response. "Don't think that's quite the right word for me, but I'll try to keep impressing you." He turns and watches Star thoughtfully for a moment, then looks toward me and tilts his head.

"You still ride?"

"Not since I was here."

"You know what they say, right? 'It's just like riding a horse.' You never forget."

I laugh. "I'm pretty sure the saying is 'It's just like riding a bike.'"

"Same thing."

"Oh, right," I say, laughing again. "Thousand-pound animal with a mind of its own, thirty-pound metal frame with hand brakes. Exact same."

Star is still prancing in the distance, glancing our way every few seconds, as if she's a kid showing off. "Well, she sure does seem to want your attention. Want to take her inside, give her a good grooming?"

"Yes," I say, the answer automatic, the idea of getting close to Star impossible to resist.

He grins. "All right, then. Let's go."

Seven

harlie and I let ourselves into the paddock to
fetch Star. We lead her into the stable, where we
attach her to crossties, which clip to each side of
her halter, in the aisle. Charlie turns up the radiant
heaters above our heads, and soon it's warm and cozy.

"Hey, girl," I say, stroking my fingers across her soft
nose, then up over her shiny-coated neck. She snorts
and nods.

One of the barn hands comes to ask Charlie a question, and Star and I are alone. I loosen the bits of mud
stuck to her coat with a currycomb, moving it in wide
circles she seems to enjoy. As I work, I talk to her, asking her what she did to get herself so dirty. After the
mud is gone, I pick up the dandy brush, and this gets
rid of the dust and dander left in her coat. Soon, it's
shining and Star seems completely relaxed, nickering
gently every time I leave to get another brush in the
tack room, greeting me with soft, contented noises
when I return.

I'm stroking her face with the softest brush I can

find when Charlie returns. "She's a sweet girl," he says. "And she's clearly happy to see you."

"Do you use her for the trails or the riding school?" I ask him, and something passes across his face, but then it's gone and I wonder if maybe I imagined it.

Either way, whatever it is, it's interrupted by a vibrating noise from his jacket pocket. He looks confused by the sound, then mutters under his breath, "This damn contraption Tate makes me carry, probably that silly group chat again."

He pulls a battered cell phone from the pocket of his oilskin coat. His *hello* is followed by a series of *mmmhmm*s and a *you sure about that*.

"Tomorrow morning, first thing, though?" he says.

I really hope he's not talking about my car.

"Thank you, Meredith. Bye, now."

Damn it.

He hangs up and looks at me. "She says they've had a power outage at the shop because the snow knocked a tree branch onto the power line closest to their garage. Haven't been able to get your tires on yet. They're going to have to call it a night. Hydro is insisting they'll be back in business first thing, if not sooner—and Meredith is insisting it's not personal this time. It really was a tree branch. I believe her."

I try to swallow my dismay.

"Any hotels nearby other than the Evergreen Inn? Because I'm pretty sure I'm banned there," I say.

"You don't need to worry about that," Charlie says. "You'll stay here. Like I said, Tate's out of town. His cabin is just sitting there empty."

"*No.* I couldn't." And I really believe this.

"We had a flood up in the main house and I'm afraid it's a mess of construction right now," Charlie says. "Tate won't mind if you stay at his place, I promise you."

How do you know that? I want to ask. Does Tate know he broke my heart worse than anyone ever has?

Except I can't say any of that. Charlie is being so kind to me. And where else am I supposed to go? A stall? A snowbank?

"I appreciate it," I manage.

"Christmas is the time of year for making room for weary travelers, don't you think?" he says gruffly. "Although I'd never turn you away. Hope you know that."

"Can I at least earn my keep?" I ask. "I'm sure there are evening chores you need to do, right?"

He nods. "Barn hand's headed home because of the storm."

"And with Tate out of town, you'll need help."

"Not going to say no to that," he says, his eyes now cleared of whatever was bothering him. "Thank you, Emory."

. . . .

Charlie and I pass a few pleasant hours bringing horses in from their various paddocks, feeding them, cleaning stalls. It's straightforward, satisfying work, and I forget my worries in the steady process of measuring grain, pitchforking sweet hay into feed bins, sweeping aisles.

When we're done, Charlie tells me he's microwaved us some potpies for dinner, and we can eat them in the office.

"That sounds perfect," I tell him—and I mean it. I haven't eaten since dinner last night and I'm starving.

In the small, dim bathroom I wash the barn from my hands with the herbaceous soap that causes my heart to thump with painful nostalgia as its spicy scent hits my nostrils. *Tate.* I wrote a magazine article on scent and memory, so I know exactly what's happening to my brain right now, which centers are being lit up by the smell of this soap. But just because there's a scientific explanation for the way I'm feeling doesn't make the ache any less intense. I stand still for a moment and let it wash over me, hoping the feelings might run their course. It won't be long now, I tell myself. One more night and I'll be gone again.

I look away from my pale, tired reflection in the mirror and head down a narrow hallway back to the ranch's office. Charlie passes me a paper plate, then a mug filled with steaming-hot tea.

As we eat and chat about the stables, the horses, life on the ranch, I am careful not to ask directly about Tate. I'm not sure my ravaged heart can take it, as calming as I found the barn work. But still, my eyes drift around the room. Eventually, they land on a photograph tacked to a bulletin board behind the desk. It's of Tate standing with a teenage boy and a horse. The horse's bridle is bedecked with blue ribbons. The boy is smiling proudly, and so is Tate.

"That's Tate and his star pupil at the riding school," Charlie says. Then he puts down his fork. "It was going real well. But there have been some challenges."

"I'm sorry to hear that," I say. I want to ask what the challenges are, but Charlie hasn't offered any more information, and I'm hesitant to pry.

Charlie sighs, but then shrugs. "That's life when you're running a business. Now, you must be exhausted. I'll walk you out to the cabin."

My last bite of dinner sticks in my throat. *I'm not ready*, I want to say. *I need more time.* Everything around here already reminds me of him. How am I going to feel actually stepping into his place?

I can't voice any of these thoughts or feelings. Instead, I swallow hard, then throw away my paper plate and follow Charlie.

By the time we've passed all the stables and followed the path through the trees to Tate's cabin, my apprehension has made my chest feel so tight it's hard to breathe.

When Charlie unlocks the cabin door, opens it, steps aside, and invites me in, my voice is a sudden yelp. "I just need a minute!" I move away, farther into the night instead of the warmth of the cabin. I can't go in there. I can't even look.

Charlie backtracks, peers out at me in surprise before stepping back onto the porch.

"I'd like to . . . look at the stars," I say. "Get some fresh air. Then I'll go in." There's a Muskoka chair on the deck beside the door. I brush it off and sit, then look levelly at Charlie. "I'll be a few minutes, you go on home."

"Still snowing," Charlie remarks, putting his hands in his pockets and looking up at the sky. "Aren't really any stars out tonight. Sure you want to be staying outside?"

"Absolutely," I say. "I don't get a lot of fresh air, living in the city and all."

He raises an eyebrow but lets me be. "All right. Just as long as you promise me you will go inside eventually, not sit out here all night and freeze."

"Promise."

"I'll let you be with your thoughts, then."

He nods, then disappears into the night. When he's gone, I lean back in the chair and stare upward.

Charlie's right: There are no stars, just a blanket of clouds, heavy with snow. The flakes swirl down, reminding me of ash from a bonfire. They hit my face, melt on my skin. I sigh. It's still hard to admit, even to myself, how many times I've fantasized about seeing Tate again. And now he's not here and I'm about to sleep in his cabin. Alone. Frankly, I'd rather do anything else. I have a sinking feeling this is not going to give me closure. Instead, it's going to open wounds.

But what choice do I have? I stand, take a deep, agonized breath, turn toward the door, and stare it down like we're in a ring and it's my opponent. All at once, words are flowing into my mind—ones I wrote, a decade ago. I kept a moment-by-moment account of our time together in my diary, then threw the entire notebook in the trash at the rental cabin before leaving Evergreen for what I thought was going to be forever. And yet, I can still remember every sentence, every memory that flowed from my pen.

Which is how I know that this place is exactly how he said it would be.

Eight

I push open the door. And he's there, even though he's not. Tate Wilder. Everywhere.

Woodsmoke, leather, saddle soap, pine needles. His cabin is made entirely of logs, in wood stained the softest, warmest brown. There are beams overhead with the same patina. I turn on a lamp, and the living room and open-concept kitchen are bathed in a gentle glow. It's like stepping into a magazine spread. There's a stone fireplace, a Navajo rug, a salvaged wood coffee table, books stacked on top. I walk over and pick them up, one by one. A copy of Bob Dylan's *Chronicles*; *Moneyball* by Michael Lewis; bell hooks. I pick up *All About Love* and stare down at the red cover. It's one of my all-time favorites, and I often give it to friends as a holiday gift.

Which gives me pause. I flip open the cover. And there it is: my name, Emory Oakes, written on the inside flap. I gave Tate my own copy of the book when I was here that Christmas. Does the fact that he kept it, leaves it sitting on his coffee table, mean something?

I sit down on the couch—which is caramel leather,

cozy and deep, loaded with pillows and blankets. Still holding the book, I stare ahead into the cold, empty maw of Tate's fireplace. The tears that have dogged me all day are on my cheeks now, nothing I can do. I sniffle, sit still, let the pain and loneliness wash over me.

It's not just being here, in this place, without Tate. Not just that a long-ago hurt has been reopened, as I knew it would be the moment I walked in here. There's more behind my tears: the fresh wound of my family's disgrace, equal parts worry and anger. I've been running away from my feelings about my father's arrest, and now that I've stopped moving, those feelings have caught up.

I'm *so* mad at him, *so* disappointed. But he's my father, and I really hope he's okay. My relationship with my parents has been strained for more than a decade. After high school, I left home for university and didn't really look back. My parents were both mystified and hurt by the independent way I've chosen to live my life, which did nothing but prove to me that they never really knew me at all.

But they're still my family—and they're all the family I have.

I should call my mom. I should rip off the Band-Aid and find out more about the charges, where my father is being held, what's next.

But I can't do it. Not yet. I leave my cell phone in my gym bag, put down the book I'm holding, and stand to continue my solitary tour of Tate's house of dreams.

Beyond the living room is a bedroom with windows along one wall, the fireplace on the other, a chair beside that. A log-framed bed covered in a dark green duvet, red-and-green-plaid blankets piled at its foot. An end table is stacked with more books, mostly novels: Zadie Smith, Barbara Kingsolver, Lauren Fox. There are equine and agricultural magazines, too, a few notebooks. No pictures, nothing personal aside from the books. A Wilder Ranch hat discarded on the dresser, a T-shirt discarded on a chair, a flannel jacket hanging on a hook on the back of the door that looks so close to the one he wore when we first met I wonder if it could be the very same.

His smell is everywhere, the pine needles and saddle soap, woodsmoke and winter.

I can't sleep in his room, I realize. There's no way.

I turn off his bedroom light with a click so decisive it makes me wish the closure I seek could be that simple. But still, I find I'm not ready for sleep. I need a shower after my long day and my time in the barn.

I undress quickly in his bathroom, avoiding the mirror so being naked at Tate Wilder's house will feel less real. I turn on the shower, hold my face in the steamy water for a long time, turn and let it fall on the back of my neck, feel it begin to loosen the tension a little. There's a bottle of Old Spice all-in-one wash for hair and body. I look at the label and marvel at the fact that a man can have one product marketed toward him, claiming to do what I use a minimum of three products to accomplish. But when I shampoo my hair with it, I question whether it really is all-purpose; my hair feels as squeaky-clean as a freshly washed floor, and I smell like a pine-scented air freshener.

But also, I smell like Tate. He's all around me, even if he isn't here.

I let the hot water sluice over me a little longer, trying to think of something other than Tate. It's been a strange day, but a good one, too. I got to see Charlie and spend time with Star. I close my eyes, and I can picture the night she was born—except Tate was there, too, so now I'm thinking of him again, as hard as I'm trying not to. I turn off the shower, towel myself dry. I pull the Fit-mas Tree gym T-shirt over my head, spread the blankets out on the couch, lie down, and pick up my phone. I stare at its dark screen as if there will be answers there. It's late, and my mom won't be awake anyway. Tomorrow, I tell myself. I'll call her first thing.

I'm thirsty, so I stand and walk to the kitchen to get a glass of water. I pause to look out the window. It's quiet out there in the woods, just as peaceful as I remember. I could be the only person in the world. Then I hear a car on the road and I feel less alone. I find a large tumbler in one of the cupboards and fill it.

Which is when I hear a rattling sound at the door.

I freeze. More rattling. I realize it's the sound of a key in the lock. Burglars don't have keys, do they? I'm frozen in the middle of the kitchen, terrified.

When the door opens, I scream and throw the glass I'm holding.

"What the hell!" shouts the intruder as the water glass bounces off him and hits the kitchen floor tiles, exploding into countless shards at my feet.

I look up from the mess of broken glass—straight into Tate Wilder's amber eyes, which are wide with surprise. He's standing in the doorway of his kitchen, his coat splashed with water I threw at him, the shock in his expression turning to bemusement as he takes me in, and I tug the T-shirt down as far as it will go.

"I can explain," I say, even though I really can't. My mind feels like it's short-circuiting. Because Tate Wilder is standing in front of me, and it's almost too much for me to process.

I force myself to really look at him. Be a journalist, I tell myself. Be objective. *Observe.*

He's taller. His already broad shoulders have filled out. His hair is somehow the same: still a little too long, partially covered by a beat-up brown Stetson, with sun-kissed ends that look like leftovers from summer. He has a beard. He didn't before. I can still see the way his bottom lip is fuller than the top one. He looks like he's about to ask me what the hell I'm doing here, so I make another attempt to explain.

"Your dad said you were away," I start. "My car is in the shop, and he wouldn't take no for an answer. I never would have come here if I thought you'd be home tonight."

"Yeah, well, I came back early," he says quietly, taking off his Stetson, then his coat, placing them both on a chair. He's wearing a Wilder Ranch T-shirt, heather gray with the swooping red logo. His Levi's are a pale, faded blue.

"Tate," I say. And then I don't know what to add. He seems upset—and who could blame him? He arrived home to what he assumed would be an empty cabin to find a distant ex-girlfriend half naked in his kitchen.

But when I say his name, he seems to snap out of his daze. He looks down at the water on the floor, the broken glass everywhere.

"Don't move," he says intently. "Let me clean this up so you don't get hurt."

I have no choice but to stay perfectly still. As he picks up the broken glass, I say, "I'm sorry. This must be so weird for you."

He looks at me. Ten years gone, and all at once, it feels like no time has passed. I'm eighteen again, and catching his gaze still makes me feel like I'm an ember in his bonfire. *Get it together, Emory.*

"Your dad said you were gone until Wednesday. I didn't think I'd see you . . . I wouldn't have stayed here if I thought . . ." I can't seem to stop talking, but I'm also too flustered to put together full sentences. I trail off, mortified.

He dumps the broken glass into the garbage under the sink before turning back to me.

"It's okay," he says. "Really."

I breathe in, then out. I try hard to seem pulled together and reasonable—like someone who is wearing pants instead of just a T-shirt that reads "Do you have the balls to try the Fit-mas Tree?" in jolly red letters.

But I can't. I'm not ready for this. This is the guy I once loved, who broke my heart into tiny pieces, exactly like the glass I just threw at him. We were kids, but right now it feels like it happened yesterday.

"Let's just deal with what's happening here," he says. He's holding a mop now, gliding it across the floor.

But what *is* happening here? I feel like I'm living

through one of those dreams where you realize you're onstage and forgot to put pants on. When Tate leaves the room without a word, I stand, still and awkward, until he returns with a Shop-Vac. The loud whirring of the machine makes it possible for me to take a few shuddering breaths. My head clears a little from the increased oxygen.

But my body is a different story. Every inch of my exposed skin is covered in goosebumps he will hopefully attribute to the cold—and not my rebellious body, so full of sudden and inexplicable want. I have to clasp my arms around my torso, keeping up the pretense of being cold, so I don't reach for him. I close my eyes, but that doesn't help; I'm swept with a vertiginous sense of falling. All I can do is watch as he vacuums up the glass, his gray Wilder Ranch T-shirt straining against his biceps, riding up when he bends over. I drag my eyes away from his body—but then I'm just watching his reflection in the windows, which gives me a view of his muscled back, how good he looks in his jeans. Not at all helpful.

Eventually, he shuts off the vacuum. "You're okay?" he asks, taking a few steps back. This feels like a safer distance.

We stand still, looking at each other, the silence between us somehow even louder than the roar of the vacuum was. But as the stillness settles around us, I realize what was happening before, the visceral reaction I was having to his nearness, was probably just some sort of scent, or emotional, memory. We have nothing to say to each other, I realize. We're different people now.

"I'm just going to go and . . ." I back away, grab my gym bag from where I left it on the floor beside his couch, and walk toward the bathroom as gracefully as it's possible to walk while wearing no pants in a situation where pants are definitely required.

Once the door is closed and locked, I pull on my only pair of jeans, then check myself out in the mirror. Totally hopeless. My hair has dried in tangled clumps, and when I take my brush out of my bag to drag it through the snarls, it doesn't help. Finally, I just scrape my hair back into a ponytail, pulling on it so hard it feels like a punishment, before venturing out again to face Tate.

He's standing in the middle of his living room, staring at the couch, a look on his face that is impossible for me to decode. He's a stranger to me, I remind myself. The ghost of the teenage girl who still seems to live inside me thinks he means something to her. But he doesn't. Not anymore.

He turns, swallows, rubs a hand over his angular jaw with its unfamiliar beard. He's not smiling now, but there are smile lines around his eyes. Ten years' worth.

"What made you come here?" he asks quietly.

Doesn't he already know about my father, about all of it? Maybe not. I can't help but assume he's not the group chat type—or really the chatty type at all. So I lie.

"It was for work. I'm a journalist. I had issues with my car, and I happened to run into your dad. He helped me out. I'm really . . ." There are too many words to describe what I am right now. "Embarrassed," I finish, and this, at least, makes sense. "I didn't think you'd be coming home."

But a shadow passes across his face now. "You mentioned that," he says, looking away. Then he glances down at the couch I had planned to sleep on before he unexpectedly arrived. "I'll take the couch." I open my mouth to protest, but he shakes his head. "Stay in my room. I'll be up early anyway for morning chores, so you probably won't see me before you leave."

"Okay," I say haltingly. "So that's that, I guess."

"I guess so. Yeah." I still can't read his expression. And I'm done trying.

I turn away. "Thank you," I say over my shoulder. "Good night."

A long silence. I think he's not even going to answer me. I hear him click off the lamp beside the couch.

And then, "Good night, Emory," he says softly into the darkness.

I step into his bedroom alone and close the door, suddenly glad humans don't have that same sense horses do, the one that allows them to feel heartbeats from several feet away. It's a small mercy I cling to as I climb into his bed with a galloping heart, the smell of him settling all around me.

❄ ❄ ❄ ❄ ❄

Dear Diary,

This morning, I walked over to the stable because Tate and I had planned an early trail ride—but the vet was there, checking up on Mistletoe, and so Tate was busy inside. I walked out to the south paddock to say hello to Walt and give him a carrot while I waited for Tate. Charlie, Tate's dad, was out there, fixing a fence post—and we met formally for the first time.

He looks a lot like Tate, but taller, older, of course. He has the same smile, the same way of speaking, but in a gruffer sort of voice. "So, you're the famous City Girl," he said, which made me blush. And I wasn't sure how he meant it, calling me City Girl. Was he thinking I was just some tourist, using his son for a good time? But Charlie was watching me closely—again, reminding me of his son—and he added, "He speaks very highly of you, Emory. And I trust my son's judgment on a person. Even if they are from the city." He winked. Then he took off his work gloves and shook my hand. It was just like with Tate; he felt so familiar. Like an old friend, not someone I had just met.

I helped him for a while, first with the fence post and then with bringing some of the other horses out to their paddocks for the day. I was closing one of the gates when I heard a familiar voice.

"I thought you said you were taking riding lessons over here—not working." It was my mom, and I could tell she was horrified to see me covered in dirt, looking like a stable hand.

At that moment, Tate came out of the barn, smiling, so happy to see me, the way he always is. "Hey, City Girl . . ." He hadn't noticed my mom yet. I smiled right back and probably started blushing. If I could have played it cool, I would have. I have no power over myself when Tate is around, though.

My feelings were obvious. My mom looked at Tate, then at me, and pursed her lips as if she had just tasted something too sour. "Well, then," she said under her breath. "This explains your sudden reinterest in horses."

I could tell she was hurt I had kept this from her. She's always trying to get us to be closer, mostly by us going and doing things she likes to do, like salon visits or shopping trips, but it wasn't just that. Tate, with his dusty boots and beat-up Stetson, his plaid flannel jacket and his work-calloused hands, wasn't up to her standards.

I regret this, but I stepped away from him then. It was just one step, but it felt like I put miles between us.

I said, "This is Tate, my new friend," and could see hurt flicker across his expression.

Charlie was glancing back and forth between me, in my mud-spattered jeans, and my mother in her Hunter boots and Burberry puffer, as if searching for a resemblance, and finding it.

I wished I could tell them both that even though I look like my mother, I'm not like her at all. That I stepped away from Tate so her senses would go off high alert and she'd leave us be. That I just needed the moment to be over.

"What are you doing here, Mom?" I asked her.

She said Bitsy wasn't feeling well today—not a surprise to me; drinking a half dozen martinis a night must be catching up with her—and she had thought she'd come over and see if she and I could go for a trail ride together.

I didn't want to share Tate, or Wilder's, with anyone. But I knew I couldn't say that out loud, either. Meanwhile, my mom was asking Charlie if he had any "well-bred horses" she could ride, one eyebrow skeptically cocked, as if she expected him to say they had only mules. Charlie seemed impervious to the snobbish undercurrent of her voice. He led her off toward a paddock, pointing out Jax and a horse named Stormy, both Thoroughbreds, and a big beautiful Dutch warmblood named Inez, with a dappled gray coat.

"I'm sorry," I said to Tate.

"For what?" Tate said.

"We had plans."

He just shrugged, said, "It's fine," suddenly sounding distant and not meeting my eye. "If it's all the same to you, I might pass on the ride now," he went on. "Let Charlie take you two out on the trails, while I stay back and keep an eye on Mistletoe."

I tried to think of ways to explain why I had seemed embarrassed by him, when really it was my mother who had embarrassed me. But it suddenly felt like a wall had gone up between us, like even if I thought of the right words, he didn't want to hear them right now. "What did the vet say?" I ventured.

He shook his head. "I'll tell you later. I need to get back to Mistletoe."

Then he walked away without saying goodbye, and all I could do was watch him go.

During the trail ride, I was impervious to the gorgeous, snowy trails, the blue sky, the peaceful setting.

My mother went on and on about what a surprisingly lovely place this was, and when I asked her why she was so surprised, she said, "Well, you know, darling. We're out in the middle of nowhere." As if small-town standards could never measure up to hers. I was counting the seconds until I could get back, see Tate, find a way to apologize that would get through to him, and find out what was wrong with Mistletoe.

When we finally returned, Tate came out to greet us, though his expression was strained, and I became more worried than ever about his horse. And about us. My mother dismounted and handed her horse's reins to Tate like he was a hired hand. I wanted to call her on it, but I also didn't want her to stick around and help get her own horse untacked. She then tried to hand Charlie a few hundreds, but he wouldn't take them.

"Emory's been so helpful," he said, while my mother glanced at my muddy, disheveled state and said under her breath, "Clearly."

Charlie pretended not to hear. "We owe her. Ride's on the house, and come back anytime."

When my mother was gone, I turned to Tate. "Mistletoe," I began. "Is she . . ." But he shook his head and looked away. I stepped closer to him. And he finally looked at me—which is when I remembered: I can tell him anything. So, I did.

I took a deep breath and told him how I felt within my family. Like an imposter, an outsider. I told him that here at Wilder Ranch, I finally felt at home—and that my reaction when my mother was here was not because I was ashamed of him or this place, but because it felt to me like my mother had no place here. But that I did. I wanted to. And I was desperate to know if Mistletoe was going to be okay.

He listened to me so carefully, the way he always does. His expression slowly relaxed—then became agonized. "I'm sorry, too," he said, interrupting me. "You don't have to keep explaining. I know I overreacted. I was being a jerk." He sighed and ran one hand through his soft, messy hair; his Stetson was off, he was holding it in his other hand. "It's just, I like you so much."

"I like you, too," I began, but he shook his head, kept going.

"I feel like I'm the one who is an outsider in your life. Like I don't belong in it. Like after this holiday is over I'll wake up and you'll just . . . be gone."

"No," I said. "I promise. Tate, we're going to find a way."

We were standing close again, and then his hands were on my waist and I felt so relieved to be back where I belonged. "Tell me about Mistletoe," I whispered. "Please." He explained that she'd been restless all day and the night before, raising her tail a lot, too—all signs of her potentially fixing to go into labor too early, the vet said. He didn't find any issue with the foal inside her, not that he could tell everything by feeling her flank and using an equine fetal heart monitor, but he wants to be extra cautious. So now Mistletoe can't be turned out with the other horses in the paddock. She has to stay in her stall.

We went to see her and found her absolutely miserable. Just standing and staring out her tiny stall window.

"She's going to be okay," I told Tate, and he turned to me.

"What is it about you that makes me believe that could be true?" he said.

"Why wouldn't you believe it?"

He shook his head sadly. "It's just that sometimes, you can really love someone and want them to stay, or be all right, and no amount of wishing or praying is going to change what's meant to happen."

I realized he wasn't just talking about Mistletoe; he was also talking about his mom's death. I stepped closer to him, wrapped my arms around him. "Just because one bad thing happened, doesn't mean more will," I said.

"You make it sound so simple, City Girl," he murmured, but he was smiling again, faintly, but there.

I looked up into his eyes and still saw sadness. "You miss her so much, don't you?" He leaned into me, put his face on my shoulder. "Yeah," he whispered. "I never talk about it."

"You can talk to me."

A long pause. "I know. That's one of the things I like so much about you." I held him closer, rubbed his back gently. "I miss having my mom around. This time of year especially."

"I bet she was wonderful," I said.

"She really was." His voice was so soft now, I could barely hear him, almost a whisper when he said, "I wish you could have met her."

"I wish I could have, too," I said, holding him tighter.

Then he pulled away. His eyes were shining. "So, hey,

are you too tired from your ride with your mom, or do you want to come out on the trail with me and help hang up the rest of the lanterns for the Starlight Ride? We can double on Walt."

I told him of course I wasn't too tired. We got Walt ready and then headed out. I sat behind Tate, my head leaning against his back, my cheek against the soft flannel of his jacket. Our breathing began to match in pace as our bodies adjusted to Walt's gait as one. We forgot about any sadness we had been feeling earlier, any insecurity about what was going to happen with us after the holidays. About our families—about there being any such thing in the world as heartache.

I could feel his mood lift even more as we headed deeper into the woods. Mine did, too. How could anything go wrong in a place like this? How could it not be true that we were being bound together by magic, by alchemy? I listened to the beat of his heart, slow and steady. It felt like mine began to beat in rhythm with his. Like our hearts were connected, somehow. It made me think that no matter what happens after I leave, I'll still feel this way and so will he. That we're going to be together, no matter what. For always.

Nine

It's barely dawn but I know I can't stay at Wilder Ranch a moment longer. Last night is coming back to me.

Tate returning unexpectedly. Me, half naked in his kitchen. The spilled water, the broken glass. His voice in the darkness, saying good night. I stayed up late texting with Lani, telling her everything that happened, step by step, play by play.

So, he's out there on his couch and you're in his bed? she wrote. The guy you've thought of and dreamed about for over a decade?? And you're not out there talking things through with him because . . . ?

I told her Tate and I had already talked, and it had been stilted and strange. That there was no way I was going out into his living room to try to speak with him again. There's nothing left to say, and that's final. You need to get to sleep. I'm sorry I kept you up so long.

Are you kidding?? I'm leaving my phone beside me all night. Text if ANYTHING happens.

But nothing happened except that I tossed and turned until close to dawn, and the sleep I did get was fitful.

I make his bed carefully, so it will look like I was never here. I wish there was a way to erase all traces of last night from his memory, too, but I'm not a magician. I take a last look out his window, at the forest of hardwoods, the snowy dawn. It's beautiful here, just as I remember it. But if I stay, I'll get lost in the past. I need to go.

I push open the bedroom door and listen. Silence. When I walk out into the living room, the couch is empty, the pillows stacked neatly, the blankets folded—as if Tate, too, has tried to erase all traces of the night before.

I assume he's already down at the stables doing morning chores with Charlie. At this, I feel a pang. I think of father and son working in tandem. I remember the peace of that—how good it felt to join in. I also think of Star, in her stall or maybe out in the paddock by now. How happy I had felt to see her, how nice it would be to say farewell. But I can't go down there. I have to get out of here. It's well past time I did.

On my phone, I search for a taxi service in the vicinity, and am grateful to find Evergreen Enterprise Taxi & Food Delivery Service. I call the number; a man answers who sounds like I've woken him, but he still groggily agrees to come pick me up and take me to town.

I dress and pack up all my stuff. I walk quickly through Tate's home, determined not to leave any more traces, close the front door, and breathe in the cold, crisp morning air. I pause on his front steps and look into the distance, at the ranch. I know I'll never forget the red-painted stables, the Christmas lights on them still glowing in the dark of the winter morning, because I never have.

I hear voices in the distant stables, low rumbles I know are Tate and Charlie. A horse's whinny, then Kevin's indignant *hee-haw* in response. It makes me smile—and all at once, the words "you are home" arrive in my mind unbidden. But no. This is not home. Evergreen is an easy place to turn rose-colored, and so is Wilder Ranch. It exists in a perfect winter wonderland, with twinkling lights on stable eaves, horses in snowy fields wearing red-and-green-checked blankets, a father and son amicably doing morning chores together in a red-painted barn, a horse named Star who had a mother named Mistletoe.

But things change. This place is not as frozen in time as it seems. Tate and I aren't teenagers anymore, and we don't mean anything to each other.

I see the taxi bumping up the driveway, a battered, forest-green SUV. I'm sneaking out of here like a criminal, which is going to guarantee I can never come back. Criminal behavior must run in the family, I think grimly as I run across the snow toward the car. I wave him down so he doesn't go all the way to the stables, hoping Tate and Charlie won't spot us.

"Never had a call out to Wilder's before," the driver says. He's a middle-aged man with a long, gray ponytail. "I'm Frank."

His gaze is curious, and I'm sure the Evergreen

grapevine will soon be filled with gossipy chatter about a woman taking a taxi from Wilder Ranch, from Tate's cabin, so early in the morning. But by the time the news is out, I'll be long gone.

Twenty minutes later, the taxi pulls up in front of the mechanic's. I pay Frank with the last twenty in my wallet. When I approach the garage, I see a **closed** sign on the door—but then, almost miraculously, a hand appears and spins the sign to **open**. Things are starting to go my way, finally.

"All ready for you," Meredith says when I walk in, handing me my keys and an invoice. Yesterday's disapproval seems to be forgotten. I pay with my credit card, which thankfully isn't declined. All these things, I tell myself, are positive signs that I'm heading in the right direction. Away from here.

I back my car out of the parking lot and turn right. Out of Evergreen. In the opposite direction of my past.

The snow tires make all the difference. Soon, I'm driving easily along the rural roads that will lead to the highway, past the frozen lakes and rivers whose pristine beauty struck me on my way here. I force myself to ignore the scenery, just focus on the road, on my journey out. I know I'm speeding a little, but I don't slow down. My need to flee is as strong as the impulse that brought me north to Evergreen in the first place. I turn on the radio and am rewarded with Kayak FM's quirky holiday playlist—first "Dominick the Donkey" by Lou Monte, then "Rudolph the Red-Nosed Reindeer" performed by Destiny's Child.

I'm belting it out along with Beyoncé when the radio station fizzles. I've lost the signal as I approach the border of the Haliburton region. I don't want silence because then I'll be alone with my thoughts, so I fiddle with the radio, in search of another festive song.

I've only taken my eyes from the road for a second. But when I look back up again, I'm in trouble.

Up ahead: spindly legs, dark fur, massive antlers, unwieldy body.

A moose has leapt in front of my car. It's the biggest animal I've ever seen in my life, larger than any of the horses at Wilder's. I swerve, squeezing my eyes shut as my car slides off the road and tumbles down a ditch. I open my eyes just in time to spin my steering wheel and narrowly avoid a tree. There's a cracking sound before my car staggers to a stop.

I gasp as the moose crashes through the trees in front of my windshield, disappearing, unscathed, into the forest. I'm shaking. I think I'm in shock. I reach for my cell phone to call for help, but there's no cell signal out here. So I open my car door and get out, testing my legs, making sure I'm not hurt. I seem to be fine, except for the shaking, which gets worse when I turn to my car and see the damage.

One wheel is gone, rolled away into the woods, and the vehicle sits at a strange angle against a fallen log. I won't be driving out of these woods. I'm stuck. I walk up to the road and stand still, my head turned north. Back toward Evergreen.

"I give up!" I shout, my voice a strange comfort in the vast silence, proof that I'm alive, at least, even if I'm alone. "Fine, I'll stay!"

Ten

"C an I offer you a hot buttered rum?" The bartender's eyes are filled with kind concern. "I just saw your car get towed into M&M's Autobody. Heard you hit a moose out on the 118. Must have been terrifying, hey? I've lived here all my life and only ever seen one moose on the road."

"Wow, the grapevine in this town . . ." I mutter.

Her empathetic smile deepens. She's mid-forties with long dark hair, straight as sudden rain, falling almost to her waist. Her nametag reads GWEN. "It's *very* robust. Anyway, you're lucky to be alive, and probably pretty shaken up. I'll get you that rum. First one's on me, after what you've been through."

"That does sound nice," I say.

And it is. The red pottery mug she hands me is warm against my still-shivering hands. The liquid inside is sweet with hints of vanilla and a little kick of festive spice. Comforting. After a few more bracing sips, I open my phone to look for a car rental agency. There's one in Minden, about forty minutes away. I could get Frank, the taxi driver who picked me up this morning, to drive me there. Except after what happened with the moose, the idea of getting in a car and going back out on those roads turns my bones to jelly. I take another sip of the rum drink instead. And any fight I had left retreats. I accept it. I'm stuck in Evergreen, again.

I look around. The Watering Hole pub is quiet at this time on a weekday afternoon. There are a few patrons finishing their lunches at the homey wooden tables, mostly centered around a large fireplace with cheerful red and green stockings hung across its mantel. The pub's walls are covered in vintage framed posters—ads for baking powder, bread yeast, shampoo—that look like they've been collected from thrift stores and yard sales over the years. Christmas garlands are wound around the wooden beams and rafters above. Over the speakers, Bruce Springsteen is wishing his baby a Merry Christmas.

Gwen has appeared again, holding a bowl of soup. "This will help, too," she says with her gentle smile. I'm touched by the gesture. I stir it. Minestrone, topped with a cloud of freshly grated parmesan and flecks of parsley. It's delicious. For some reason, the taste of it, the way it warms my chest, the kindness of Gwen feeding me a steady stream of warm liquids to help me recover from the shock I just had, makes me want to cry. Or maybe the feeling welling up inside me right now is something else. Maybe it's not sadness at all. I eat slowly, trying to process my emotions.

"So," Gwen says later, wiping the bar top in front of me with a cloth embroidered with little snowmen. "Your car's pretty wrecked, huh?"

"You tell me," I say. "What did Meredith write in the group chat?"

Gwen laughs. "It's a broken axle," she says, shooting me a rueful look. "Possibly unfixable, but they'll know more tomorrow."

"That sounds expensive," I say, morose.

"Since I know you're not driving, how about another one?" She doesn't even wait for my response before taking my mug away for a refill. I thank her before she goes off to serve more bar patrons. When she's gone, I open my phone again. I text Lani, deciding to leave out the worrying details and just tell her I'm having car trouble and will be delayed in my return to the city. Then I scroll to my bank account, which does not have good news for me. Next, I check my emails, which are even worse. It's clear I can't just casually email a pitch to an editor without addressing the huge red flag: that I'm the daughter of a hot item in the current news cycle. An Emory Oakes byline is likely not the most appealing thing in the world right now. An interview might be, but there's no way I'm giving one.

As the afternoon sun sinks low in the sky, I sip my drink and think about calling my mother, the way I had resolved to last night. But after the near-death experience of almost hitting the moose, I feel even more fragile than before. I know I need to talk to her—but not yet.

"Why are you being so nice to me?" I ask Gwen when she returns to clear my empty soup bowl away. "Even though you know who I am?"

"Because I'm not the kind of person who judges people by their family," she says simply. "And because you were so shaken up when you came in here." Then she looks away, addresses someone behind me. I think it's another customer until she says, "Oh, hello, Tate."

She's so casual, I almost don't process it—because Tate is not a name I use casually at all. But then, I smell him. Pine needles, bonfire smoke. A voice like maple syrup on snow, saying, "I've been looking for you."

I turn, and there he is. Amber eyes, that full bottom lip, pulled tight in a slight grimace of concern. Plaid flannel jacket, Stetson, too-long dark blond hair peeking out from beneath it. His new beard. Or not new, but new to me. I realize this moment of me staring at him, taking him in, has lasted too long when his frown deepens and he glances at Gwen. "Is she okay?"

"I think she's still in shock," Gwen says, and I feel embarrassed that I seem so feeble they have to talk about me as if I'm not even there.

"I'm fine, really," I say, but my voice wobbles as I say it, revealing the truth. *I am not at all fine.* From the looks now on Tate's and Gwen's faces, I realize I've said those last words aloud, too. I push the mug of rum away and Gwen, my guardian angel, quickly replaces it with a glass of water, then leaves us to talk. "I heard about the accident," Tate says. "It makes sense you'd be shaken up. Almost hitting a moose—that's a big deal. You could've been . . ." But he doesn't finish his sentence.

"But I wasn't," I say—except, in an effort to keep my voice steady, the words come out belligerent. "I'm fine."

"You aren't fine," Tate says quietly, and begins to list the reasons for this on one hand. "I found you in my kitchen last night, standing in a puddle of water and a pile of broken glass—"

"Please, don't remind me."

"Then you just took off."

"Without even thanking your dad," I say, now joining in on the list of the reasons I'm a mess. "I'm sorry for that."

He ignores me, keeps going. "You almost hit a moose. Wrecked your car. You were already the number one topic on the group chat, but now—"

"I'm the town pariah and I don't even live here. You shouldn't be seen with me. Bad for business."

"I'm not going anywhere," he says, pulling up a stool—and something about the tone of his voice causes my heart to do a *boom, boom, boom, clap*. Great. Now I'm thinking in Charli xcx lyrics. "Even if this isn't what . . ." But then he trails off.

He doesn't have to finish the sentence, though. I can see myself through his eyes. I know what he's thinking.

Even if this isn't what I want to be doing. We are nothing to each other. My mind knows this, but my heart doesn't seem to have caught up to this fact. I saw it in his eyes last night, and it's all too clear today. He doesn't want to see me. Sitting in a bar with a distant ex who has blown into town like hell on wheels is not his idea of a good time. But he's a good guy, and he heard I had an accident, so he needed to check if I was okay.

I excuse myself and run off to the bathroom to splash water on my face and try to compose myself. When I return, a steaming mug of coffee sits beside my water glass. I pick up the mug and blow on it, grateful for something to do with my hands.

"Could you please tell Charlie I'm sorry?" I ask him. "He was so kind, and I didn't even thank him."

"Don't worry about Charlie, he gets it. We're just worried about you."

I can't look at him. It's too embarrassing. I'm a subject of concern, a tragic figure. All the times I imagined seeing Tate again—and I did imagine it, I can't deny that—it was always in a perfect scenario where I was having a great hair day and wearing my favorite outfit and had just won a National Newspaper Award. I turn my head away from him slightly so the intoxicating blend of pine needles and woodsmoke and saddle soap and leather doesn't light up quite so many core memory points in my brain and make me feel even worse.

"What really brought you here?" he says, his voice low in my ear. And now my heart sinks. Does he think I came back here chasing after a memory of him?

I clutch the coffee cup, stare into it, looking for a way to answer. Maybe I just need to do it. Tell him everything. What do I have to lose? *I drove here because I needed to. Because it's the first place I thought of. The only place that has ever felt like home.*

"I think I know," he says before I can speak. "Charlie told me that you wanted to apologize to Gill."

"*Oh.* Right." I close my eyes briefly.

"That's not a good idea. I heard Gill is pretty upset."

"He must be devastated."

"Actually, I think he's more embarrassed. He wants everyone to drop it. Which we won't, of course. No one is going to let him lose the restaurant."

"I couldn't stand it if that happened," I say, genuinely anguished.

"I know that," he says. He's staring at me, the moment stretching into something that feels far too intense for mid-afternoon in a local dive bar. It's almost as if he's saying, *I remember you. There was a time you told me everything.* Then he looks away, and I can breathe again.

"Almost done with your coffee?" he says, still not looking at me.

"Close."

"Good. Because I'm under strict instructions from Charlie to bring you back to the ranch and not let you leave again until you have a legitimately safe way to return to the city."

"Tell Charlie thank you, but I'll be fine. I can get myself back to the city." This isn't true, but he doesn't need to know that.

"He figured you'd say that, so he wants to know exactly what the plan is. Is someone coming to get you?"

I think of Lani, with her twin babies. I could never

ask her to come get me. I don't want to ask my mother, either, because I'm still not ready to talk to her. Facing the rest of my friends or colleagues feels overwhelming. And I don't have enough money to call a driver.

"The bus," I venture. "And I'll come back and get my car when it's ready."

"The bus route that used to run between here and the city got cut last year. And you know how Charlie is when he gets something in his head. Just come back, Emory."

A feeling of lightness fills my chest—fleeting, almost slipping away as soon as I grasp at its edges, but there. I chase it. It's a memory.

I turn to him. "Remember on Christmas Eve, when Charlie insisted that if he kept stirring his lumpy fondue with a whisk and adding flour, it was going to work?"

Tate laughs at this recollection, too. A reward. The happiness stays.

"And then he had to start over, and he pretended that had been his plan all along."

"Do you still do that?" I ask.

"Do what, the Christmas Eve fondue? Yeah."

"And listen to Bing Crosby's reading of 'The Small One' while you eat?"

Another nod. Then he leans closer. "But now he just buys those premade packs of fondue at the grocery store and pretends to have made it himself. And *I* pretend not to see the packages in the garbage when I take it out later."

I smile down into my coffee mug, suddenly lost in

nostalgia—and wondering if it's possible Tate feels the same. Or if he just feels sorry for me. If he's just following his father's instructions to be kind to a person in distress at Christmas.

I look back up at him. "Tate?" But any words dry up in my throat. I have so much to say, and nothing to say at all. It's as if Tate and I exist on two planes: what's real, and what's all just memory.

His gaze is like a searchlight across my face. I don't know what he's looking for, or if he finds it.

He just says, "Come back to the ranch. It's not a big deal."

Which is possibly the understatement of the century. Then, he's signaling to Gwen for the bill and she's shaking her head and mouthing, "It's on the house." When I stand, Tate puts his hand on the small of my back, guiding me toward the door. There are two layers of clothing between his hand and my skin, yet the heat of his touch feels like it could burn a hole in my coat. My knees go weak and I almost stumble, which makes him loop his arm around my waist to hold me steady. I want to lean into him, but I don't. I shore myself up and keep walking, gently pulling away from him because in his arms is not, I remind myself, the safe place it used to be.

I glance at him sidelong to see if any of this experience is having the same effect on him, but his expression betrays nothing except perfect calm. Tate is fine. He has no weakness when it comes to me. *Come back to the ranch*, he said earlier. *It's not a big deal.* And I need to stop making it one, because this is all circumstantial.

I get to the door of the bar before Tate does, pushing it open myself and welcoming the feel of the cold winter air on my hot cheeks, surprised to find it's almost dark out, this strange day nearly over already.

"Not a big deal," I whisper to myself. Maybe if I keep saying it, it will finally become true.

Eleven

I hop up into the cab of Tate's truck and try to steel myself against the scent of pine needles and bonfire smoke, leather and saddle soap, but it's even stronger in here.

He turns on the radio. It's tuned to Kayak FM; as we drive, a DJ with a breathy voice details all the holiday "goings-on about town." "There's the holiday hoedown tomorrow night at Cormac's Community Garden," she says. "A special turkey supper at the Rotary Club, and, of course, the Starlight Ride, a week from today. That's always a local highlight, and this year will be no different . . ."

I glance at him. "The Starlight Ride still happens?"

He turns up the speed of his windshield wipers against the thickening of the falling snow before he answers. "Evergreen tradition. You remember?"

Stevie Nicks's version of "Silent Night" begins on the radio. "Of course. How could I forget?"

A long pause. I listen to Stevie's smoky voice, the rush of the road under the truck tires, the shushing of the windshield wipers against the snow. And try to deal with a sudden surge of longing on my part, for starry nights and snowy trails.

For the way we were, once.

This *not a big deal* mantra is not working at all.

"Yeah. It's a good time" is all he says.

And we leave it at that.

. . . .

Tate pulls up in front of his cabin and I thank him. "You're being really generous with your place."

He just shrugs. "Of course," he says. "You need somewhere to stay. And I'm fine bunking with Charlie. There's stew in the fridge, some salad stuff, fruit and coffee and bread for the morning. Help yourself. You know where everything is?"

"Think so," I say, trying to mirror his casual tone.

"Then . . ." He leans over me to pop open the passenger door, and I know it's just Tate being Tate, that Charlie raised him to be mannerly. He would lean over and open the door for anyone. And yet, having him so close, even just for a few seconds, fills me with more of that confused longing. "Take care of yourself," he says. I nod, hop down, land gently in the snow. For some reason, I salute as I stand there, and he smiles as if he's not surprised at my awkward behavior, because he still knows me. I find myself smiling back.

But when I turn toward his front door and the sound of his truck fades down the lane, a wave of loneliness threatens to destabilize me again. This *is* a big deal. I'm at Tate Wilder's cabin, alone, yet again. I pause and look up to the sky. Like last night, there are just snow clouds. No stars to wish on. Nothing for me to do but let myself inside and try to get some rest.

....

The next morning, I call Lani. She is, as I predicted, horrified about the moose and my near-death experience, and I have to spend several minutes reassuring her I really am unhurt. But she seems almost delighted that I'm back in Tate's cabin. "I knew this wasn't over," she says, her voice taking on the same dreamy quality it gets when she's discussing the happy ending of one of her favorite movies. Which are, by the way, *Notting Hill* and *Sleepless in Seattle*. Lani is a romantic at heart, but it's never quite rubbed off on me.

"Oh, trust me," I say, turning on the coffee maker. "It's over. He's just being polite. There's nothing left between us." A knock at the front door punctuates this sentence.

"Is that *him*?" Lani whispers.

"I'll call you back," I promise, for just a moment feeling like Anna in *Notting Hill* as I fix my hair self-consciously in a mirror before rushing to answer the door. But it's not Tate.

"She's alive," Charlie says, his tone wry but his eyes dancing as he leans against the doorframe. I blink against the sunlight. The snow has finally stopped.

"I'm so sorry I left yesterday without saying goodbye," I begin.

"No apology needed," he says. "You didn't expect to have Tate come crashing in, in the middle of the night."

"I think I'm the one who did the crashing," I say ruefully, but he just shakes his head and smiles while I wonder exactly what Tate told him.

"I put a call in to the mechanic, just to make sure they didn't plan to mess you around again. They need a bit of time to figure out what it'll take." I can only nod as he lifts his Stetson from his head, mashes it in his hand as he regards me thoughtfully. "And you'll stay here," he concludes, his voice now firm. "Until it's fixed."

"That's kind of you. And Tate," I manage. "Hopefully, it won't be long."

Charlie nods, then puts his hat back on. "Do you think you might do me a favor?" he asks.

"Of course. Anything, Charlie."

"Star seemed so happy to see you yesterday, and she really took to you being close to her. And remember what I said about how you never forget how to ride a horse?" I nod. "Would you be interested in riding her?"

I remember how it felt as I groomed her. Like we belonged together. The truth is, I'd like nothing more than to try riding Star—and so I tell Charlie that.

He grins. "Meet me at the north barn, where her stall is, once you've had some breakfast."

He tips his hat and turns to leave while I stand at Tate's door watching him walk away down the path toward the stables, a sense of joyful anticipation bubbling up in my chest like fizzy liquid in a holiday party punch bowl.

. . . .

When I'm ready, I head outside and walk down the snowy path, through the snow-clad trees, toward the ranch. Inside the north barn, Charlie already has Star in crossties, and I start grooming her. As I do, I can't help but glance around, looking for Tate. Charlie has tracked my gaze and lifts an eyebrow.

"He's out for a trail ride with a friend."

"Who is?" I say, shrugging my shoulders, turning away. I pick up a currycomb from Star's grooming kit, rub it against her coat in gentle circles, loosening the dirt. Once I finish that, I reach for the hoof pick.

"I can do that if you want," Charlie says. "Her hooves are pretty muddy."

"I want to see if I can still manage it," I say, determined.

Star resists me at first, but I lean my weight against her, nudge her shoulder with mine. Finally, she lifts her front foot for me. Charlie is right: The insides of her hooves are packed tight with mud, but I work at it and succeed. Soon, all four of her hooves are done and I'm in possession of a deep sense of satisfaction. It's so easy to be happy around here, I find myself thinking. That confused sense of longing returns.

Charlie has gone off to find me a helmet and a pair of riding boots, and once I have those on, we make short work of tacking her up together. I place her ebony leather saddle gently atop a white fluffy saddle pad on her back, slide her bit between her teeth, and the straps of her bridle over her ears.

"You ready?" Charlie asks me. I secure my helmet, and even though my heart has started knocking against my chest like it wants to be let in from the cold, I nod and say yes, trying to sound more confident than I feel.

Just like riding a horse, I say softly to myself as we walk toward the arena.

I step up onto the mounting block, holding Star's reins in one hand and the saddle pommel in the other, then lift my left foot into the stirrup so I can swing myself up into the seat.

"What'd I tell ya, kid?" Charlie calls out. "You never forget!"

I laugh. "I'm just sitting in the saddle! We haven't gone anywhere yet!"

But I know what to do. I nudge Star's flanks gently with the bottoms of my heels, take the reins tighter in my hands, and direct her out onto the track. Charlie is right; you don't forget how to do this. The simple signals between horse and rider are still second nature to me.

As we walk the arena track, our pace leisurely, I gaze out the small windows we pass, take in the fresh layers of snow on the distant hills and evergreens of the Haliburton Forest. I can just picture it: Because of all the snow still falling outside, the fields and trails will be fresh and white. I suddenly long to go out there with Star, to ride those trails I still remember so well on this horse. After I've walked Star around the track a few more times, Charlie instructs me to ask her for a trot.

Again, I nudge her flanks with my heels—a little harder than before—while tightening up the reins to signal to her that it's time to move faster. As I begin posting—rising and falling in the saddle seat along with her stride—Charlie calls out, "You two look great!" I'm practically beaming with pride at his compliments as he directs me to make some circles and figure eights with Star on either end of the arena, then asks if I feel up to cantering, which is the gait one speed lower than gallop.

"I'm ready!" I call.

"You know what to do," he answers—and again, he's right. I shift my hips so my seat is lower in the saddle, slide one heel just in front of the girth and one just behind. I squeeze, and we're off.

Some horses have a smooth canter, some a bumpy one. Some are in between. Star's canter feels like riding a cloud. I never want it to stop, but eventually, I know I have to slow her down. The frosty plumes of air from her nostrils fill the air and she's working up a sweat. Exhilarated, I pat her shoulder enthusiastically then slow her to a walk again.

I can tell Charlie's also thrilled. He approaches Star to pat her shoulder, too, while she tosses her head, clearly pleased.

"What would you think of cooling her down a bit more outside?" he asks me, a thoughtful expression on his face. My heart feels like it's soaring.

"I'd love to ride her in the snow," I say.

"Let me just go grab my guy, Hank, and we'll all walk outside together."

Within moments, Charlie is back with his horse. There's a garage-style door at one end of the arena, and Charlie opens it, then gets on Hank easily, no need for a mounting block. I follow them out into the sunny morning, into a scene as picture-perfect as any holiday card I've ever seen: the stables, the paddocks, the horses, the rolling hills in the distance and the Haliburton Forest beyond, all of the scenery covered with the purest white snow. It's nothing like the snow in the city, which looks beautiful during the first few hours but soon becomes gray with exhaust fumes. I breathe deep; the air is so much cleaner and clearer here, too.

Star and I walk slowly along the lane, Hank and Charlie just behind us, past the north barn, then the south, toward the woods. My eyes hungrily take in the scenery. The way the snow has settled on the branches of the evergreens, how the sun makes the top coat of the snow glitter like stardust. I see movement in the trees, and realize it's two riders, walking their horses along the forest trail and out into the open. I recognize the Stetson, the red-and-white-checked plaid of Tate's jacket. His head is tilted toward his companion. He's laughing—and so is she.

She.

The woman has a long blond braid snaking out from beneath her riding helmet, flipped over one shoulder. Her jacket is emerald green, the perfect contrast to Tate's red plaid. She's laughing, too. Even from a distance, I can see how happy she is. And I can feel it, too. Because I know exactly what it's like to feel that joyful on horseback beside Tate, walking along a snowy trail. There's nothing like it.

In my distraction, I realize I've stopped paying attention to Star. She's prancing sideways, and my reins are too loose to stop her. I pull at the leather straps, nudge my legs against her sides to try to get her to move forward again, but I've lost her. And the yanking of the reins is just upsetting her. Her ears are flat against her head—a sign that she's distressed. She jolts forward.

I hear Charlie behind me saying, "Whoa there, hey there. Come on, Star."

I try to tell her to *whoa*, too, but I know my voice sounds scared and shaky. Not good. Horses are sensitive to fear. And now everything I thought I remembered about riding is gone. I'm nothing but frightened as Star kicks her legs out behind her in a buck, then takes off at a gallop. All I can do is hold on for dear life until, seconds later, I'm flying through the air. I land with a soft thump in a snowbank and lie there for a moment, staring up at the blue sky, gasping for air because the wind has been knocked out of me.

When I can breathe again, I lean up, relieved that nothing feels broken, just bruised. I need to catch Star before she runs off.

Only, someone else has already caught her. It's Tate, a thunderous expression on his face as he hands her off to Charlie, who has hopped off Hank. I notice the woman Tate had been out on the trail with standing behind him, holding their two horses by the reins.

As Tate approaches me, his expression softens into one of concern. He kneels down in the snow beside me.

"Are you okay? You shouldn't be standing up yet," he says as I try to scramble to my feet.

"Really, I'm fine."

"We don't know that yet. Just wait to get up. Please. Are you feeling pain? Tell me where."

I'm embarrassed for a number of reasons, but the main one is that the only place that hurts is my backside. And I'm not about to say that.

"I'm *okay*," I say again. "Nothing hurts, except my pride."

"Can I see your helmet?" I take it off and he checks it over for any cracks or damage. Satisfied there is none, he reaches for me—and it feels like the wind has been knocked out of me again. His fingers move gently along the base of my neck. I try to ignore the way my heart gets away from me when he does this, racing so suddenly and so fast it reminds me of how it felt when Star took off from beneath me. I realize I've let out a little gasp. Tate looks alarmed.

"Does that hurt?"

"No. Truly, Tate. I'm fine. The snow broke my fall. I'm just sorry it happened. Is Star okay?"

"She's perfectly all right." This is Charlie, approaching with Star's reins in one hand, Hank's in the other. "But I owe you an apology. Both of you."

I stand, and this time, Tate doesn't stop me. When Star gets close enough, she butts her head against me, as if she wants to apologize.

"It's okay, girl," I say, rubbing her nose.

"But it's not," Tate says, sounding agonized. More like the teenager I remember than the man he's become. "Dad, did you even tell her?"

"Tell me what?"

Charlie clears his throat. "Star got hurt this summer," he says. "Spooked by a coyote during a trail ride, stumbled and cut her leg. Even though it didn't take much time to rehab the injury, it affected her. Sometimes horses who are born prematurely carry it with them—an inability to let things go, I guess you could say. A problem with processing. She hadn't been taking well to being ridden, especially outdoors—and I wondered if you might be the solution. I didn't want to tell you about the issues she'd been having because it would have just added to your nerves. Which wouldn't have been good for either of you."

"And you think Emory getting tossed into a snowbank was good for anyone? You're a great horse trainer, Dad, but I just don't think this was the right call."

Charlie sighs. "You're right. I'm sorry, son. It seemed like the right thing to do at the time, but it wasn't. Not at all."

There's something in the air all around us that feels charged, fraught. I've never seen Tate and Charlie at odds, and I hate that I'm the reason.

"I wasn't paying attention the way I should have been," I say. "I got distracted. I let her down. It was me."

But Tate shakes his head. "You shouldn't have been riding her in the first place."

Charlie turns to his son. "Mariella is waiting for you. You should get back to her."

Mariella. It's a pretty name that matches her perfectly. Tate looks at her, all flustered, showing me that Mariella and I being here at the same time is not what he wants at all.

"It's fine," Charlie says. "Emory and I will go into the arena and she'll get back on Star for a few minutes. Right, Emory?"

The idea makes me nervous, but I know he's right to ask it of me. The saying is true: You really do need to get back on the horse—both for your own confidence and for the horse's training. Because a horse who is untacked and put back in her paddock or stall to eat, play, or rest after a rider has been thrown off will do so again to get out of working. Soon, the horse won't be rideable at all.

"Of course," I say. "Anything for Star."

For a moment, I actually think Tate might argue with Charlie, with me, about my getting back on Star—but he doesn't.

He just says to Charlie, under his breath, "Make sure she's really okay, please. That they both are."

Then he walks away, toward the beautiful woman waiting for him.

Mariella, with her blond braid shining in the sunlight, her blue eyes bright with an anticipation I know all too well.

Twelve

F eeling good up there? Nothing hurts?"

"Only thing that's wounded is my pride," I say to Charlie, my new refrain. But that's not quite true. In addition to my sore backside, which will definitely bruise, there's a dull pain in my chest I know isn't related to the fall.

I'm worried about Star—and about Tate, too.

"At least she had the good grace to dump you off in a snowbank, though. She's a lovely girl at heart, just dealing with some stuff."

"Aren't we all," I mutter.

I try to focus on finishing off my ride, making sure Star knows tossing riders off will not be tolerated, building back my own confidence, for whatever that's going to be worth. As Star and I walk around the arena track, I pat her shoulder, say her name, tell her what a good girl she is.

She slows, then stops at a window and looks out, lets out a sigh before lowering her head.

"You know you can do it, right?"

She tosses her head, stamps one foot, as though she's understood me. My heart aches for her, and I wish I knew how to help.

Charlie approaches. "You're right," he says. "She *can* do it." He looks up at me. "Tate's not going to like this, but I think you two should keep trying."

Tate's not going to like this. I wonder why but can't ask. And maybe I don't have to wonder. Maybe I just need to accept the truth. Tate is fine, living his life, helping his dad run the ranch, spending time with his gorgeous girlfriend, Mariella. He never expected to see me and definitely does not want me here.

Except I *am* here. And Star needs help. "If you want me to try again with her, of course I will. I'm not afraid," I say. "I just want to help her."

"You *are* helping her," Charlie says, then pauses. "And—" Star nuzzles his shoulder and I wonder what he's about to add.

But then, a voice at the arena door interrupts us. It's a tall man in a cranberry-hued tuque greeting Charlie, who glances at his watch. "That would be the farrier," he says to me, then calls out, "Good morning, Seb! Be right with you."

Charlie waits while I dismount, then tells me we'll talk later before he heads off in one direction and I in another, to untack Star and put her back in her stall. I set her up in crossties, remove her saddle and bridle, and lightly brush her, talking to her softly all the while. Before I return her to her stall, I pilfer a carrot from Kevin's stash, promising I'll find her some mints for next time as she crunches the carrot.

I'm walking out of the tack room when I hear voices in the aisle. I pull back into the shadows in time to see Tate walk past beside Mariella.

"It's so great here," Mariella says, her voice appealingly husky, in a just-rolled-out-of-bed sort of way. Then she lets out a happy little sigh, and I grimace. She's sexy *and* adorable. "You're so lucky, Tate, to get to ride out on those trails whenever you want."

"You could ride out there whenever you want, too," Tate says. "I mean . . . if you decide . . ."

What he says next is muffled by the sound of Kevin braying loudly, perhaps wise to the fact that one of his carrots is now missing. Delighted laughter from Mariella, and I suddenly feel so bitterly jealous I can practically taste it in my mouth. But then I'm startled from my thoughts by a sound. Tate has entered the tack room, carrying two bridles.

He jumps when he sees me. "Emory! I didn't know you were still here."

"Sorry," I find myself saying, even though I'm not quite sure what I'm apologizing for. My existence? I turn away from him, pick up a sponge, and pretend to be scrubbing Star's already clean bridle.

Behind me, Tate clears his throat. "You're okay?" he says. "Absolutely positive nothing is hurt from the fall?"

"I'm fine," I say, with more force than I intended. Then I turn to him. "Really," I say more gently. "You don't have to worry about me."

But his amber eyes are clouded with concern, and now that my gaze has met his, I find I can't look away.

I wish I could suddenly develop mind-reading powers. His expression is a puzzle. He bites his lip, then lets out a long puff of air.

"Could you wait here a sec?" he asks. "There's something I need you to do."

He's back within moments, holding a clipboard, which he hands to me.

"It's a waiver," he says.

It seems straightforward, just a document indemnifying the ranch of liability should I get hurt while riding here. But there's more to it than that, and I know it. I look back up at him, not bothering to disguise the hurt I feel.

"You think I'd sue," I say.

"Everyone who rides here has to sign one," he says. "But Charlie always forgets. I have to protect the ranch."

Every fiber of my being wants to protect the ranch, too. I love this place. But how do I say this to him when he never believed it before? He's certainly not going to believe it now. I realize as I stare at his unreadable expression that he's always expected the worst of me. Even ten years later, this hasn't changed.

"Does she have to sign one?" I find myself asking.

"Who do you mean?" he says. I tilt my head toward the door, my heart feeling heavy.

"Oh. You mean Mariella." He says her name gently, like the treasure he probably sees it as. "Well, that's different," he begins. "She—"

But I don't want to hear it. I don't think I can take it. "Forget it, please. It's none of my business. I'll just sign it."

I take the pen and clipboard from him, sign my name, hand them both back. "All done."

Our eyes meet again, but this time, there's no destabilizing sensation of cosmic connection I thought was there last night. Those rum drinks must have been stronger than I thought. Now his stare is completely blank. *All done.*

"Goodbye, Tate."

I walk out of the tack room, head down the stable aisle as fast as I can, past Mariella, who I try not to look at, but then can't stop myself. She's even more beautiful up close, and her laugh as she hands Kevin a carrot is like a Christmas Eve church bell.

I'm almost out the stable door when I stop walking and turn. Star is standing at her stall door, watching me leave, nickering softly, as if calling me back. But Star is not my horse. She belongs to Tate, to Charlie. Earlier, Charlie asked me to help with Star—and I said yes. But I can't do this anymore.

"Goodbye, Star," I say, and she snorts at me, then retreats to the back of her stall.

I turn away and begin to walk, each step away deepening the ache in my heart that I desperately need to find a way to heal. But healing is not going to happen for me at Wilder Ranch. This place has only ever hurt me. I need to walk away and leave all my memories, the good and the bad, exactly where they began.

Except that, as hard as I try to tell myself my memories of this place aren't as good as I think they are, they follow me as I walk away, whispering in my ear, refusing to stop trying to convince me of what once was.

❊ ❊ ❊ ❊ ❊

Dear Diary,

Last night, as the vet had feared she might, Mistletoe went into labor. Tate and I were in the hayloft together when we heard a sharp banging below us in the barn.

Although she had calmed down after being put on rest in the bigger stall, she seemed to have become worked up again. She was kicking, even rearing up. Frankly, it was scary.

Charlie called the vet, and things got worse. The vet was at another foaling, an hour away. We were on our own for now. I could tell Charlie and Tate were really worried—and I found out why, at least partially: It turns out, Mistletoe was Tate's mom's horse. Charlie told me quietly, but Tate overheard him. He walked away from me, and it surprised me that he just wanted to be alone. I started to feel afraid then that we weren't becoming as close as I believed—but I had to put my emotions aside, because we had to focus on taking care of Mistletoe, all of us.

Charlie asked me to go get the plug-in kettle from the main house so we could boil water to sterilize things. I ran there, and when I was coming back, Tate was waiting for me outside the barn. I grabbed him, hugged him. He held on to me for what felt like dear life. I promised him Mistletoe was going to be okay. And the foal, too.

At this, Tate pulled away and looked into my eyes. He said, "I know you mean well, Emory—but you can't promise me that. You don't know how this is going to end."

That scared feeling was back, but I pushed it aside again. I held up the kettle and said we'd just better get inside to help Charlie.

In her stall, Mistletoe was lying down, looking weak. But when she saw Tate, she stood and started pacing, making strange, agitated noises. It was as if she just couldn't get comfortable, no matter what she did. I felt for her. She seemed to be in such pain. All at once, her water broke, and Charlie said there was no stopping it now: The foal was going to be born, two weeks early.

Even though I had no idea what I was doing or how to help with a foal's birth, I knew I was going to have to learn on the fly. I kept thinking that I wanted to be able to keep my promise to Tate, even if I had no control over the world. I wanted Mistletoe and her baby to be okay, so badly. But Mistletoe really seemed to be struggling. She was sweating and weak, clearly wanting to get up and change position, but now unable to even stand. When she rolled onto her side, Tate and Charlie looked terrified. Charlie explained that she was already in the final stages of labor, with the vet still half an hour away.

He told Tate and me to back away from her, even though I know Tate wanted to stay close, soothing her with his words, talking in her ear. But, Charlie explained, if a mare is distracted or agitated by anything during labor, she may try to delay things. In this case, with a premature foal, and with the water already broken, it was important to avoid any holdup in the birth canal or the foal could die. We did as we were told, but I knew it was torture for Tate not to be able to be close to his horse. I held his hand, but his was limp. He barely even seemed to be breathing.

Time slowed. Every second felt like an hour, every moment Mistletoe was in pain, that we spent wondering if her foal was going to come out okay, felt like an eternity. And then, all at once, everything began to happen fast. Mistletoe seemed to get a burst of strength, first standing, then crouching. I'd never seen a horse do anything like this. She was almost human in the way she was behaving, as if she knew exactly what was best for herself and her foal. Charlie spread out a clean tarp for the foal to land on, and had us all put on rubber gloves that went up to our shoulders, just in case he needed to reach in and help the foal out. I'll admit, this idea made me feel a bit sick—but anyway, we didn't have to do it.

First, we saw little hooves—and held our breath until Charlie made sure they were front feet and not back. Mistletoe labored and pushed, and at the very moment the vet came running in, the foal was born, encased in a blue membrane sac, but visible through it—impossibly small but, the vet said, breathing well. We waited for the foal to break the sac itself. When that didn't happen, I felt so heartsick. Until the vet broke the sac, and there she was. A filly. The tiniest, most perfect creature I had ever seen. Covered in amniotic fluid, but we could still tell her color: palomino blond with a platinum tail. She looked like an angel.

Meanwhile, something was going wrong with Mistletoe. She appeared to be in great pain, and the vet said that was because she was having trouble expelling the placenta. He gave her an injection to help it along. Tate sat by her head, talked to her. All we could do was wait. For the placenta to be expelled, for the foal to stand on her own and start to drink, the only way she was going to be guaranteed to survive without major medical intervention. Tate grasped my hand now, held it so tight it hurt. But I didn't want him to let go.

Outside of Mistletoe's large stall window I could see it was getting dark, that the first star was out—the North Star, so bright and pure. I closed my eyes and made a wish, for whatever it was worth. *Please let Mistletoe be okay. Please let the foal be okay.*

The injection worked. Mistletoe's fever broke, she expelled the placenta, she stood up. And then, the foal struggled to her feet, too. Her skinny legs didn't look strong enough to hold her, but somehow, they did. She wavered for a moment while we all held our breath, then stepped toward her mother, nuzzled below her flank, looking for milk.

"This is a miracle," the vet said. "For a premature foal to already be standing, already be feeding—honestly, I didn't think there was any chance of this tonight. I thought I'd be taking her with me to the intensive care unit at my animal hospital."

I realized I was crying, but I think we all were. We watched the foal nuzzling against Mistletoe as she leaned down her head and began to lick away the amniotic fluid from her foal's gorgeous, sunbeam-colored coat. Once the foal had finished drinking, she turned her head and looked at us, blinking, dazed, perfectly adorable, taking in everything about this new world she was in.

"Look at that," I said. "She has a blaze on her forehead, just like Mistletoe does." It shone white against her golden coat. I stepped closer, careful not to get too close and upset Mistletoe, but she didn't seem to mind. She nickered at me as if to say, *Look how beautiful my foal is.* "It looks just like a shooting star," I said, pointing to the marking.

And that's how Star got her name.

Thirteen

I t doesn't matter to me that I have nowhere to go. It doesn't matter that I'm going to be letting Charlie down again. I need to leave. I call Frank the taxi driver to ask for a pickup as I walk to Tate's cabin to get my bag. "I'll be there in ten minutes," Frank assures me.

Inside the cabin, I force myself to be quick. But I can't help it: My bag now in hand, I pause in the living room and take it all in, one last time. It's perfect, this place. It's just what he wanted. And I don't belong here. And yet, I still find it hard to leave. I walk to the living room and pick up the bell hooks book I gave him back then. *All About Love.* I almost scoff at the title now. What did I ever learn about love, after my days here? But it looks like *he* learned something. At least one of us is happy.

A sound at the door. Tate has opened it and stepped inside. He holds up two hands in surrender.

"Don't throw anything. It's just me." He's trying to make a joke about my first night here, but I can't work up a smile.

"I was just getting my things," I say, and realize I'm still holding the book. He looks at the cover, then at me. He bites his full lower lip.

"You can have that back, if you want," he says. "It's yours, after all."

"Right. Why would you want it?" I shove it into the outer pocket of my gym bag. "I called a taxi," I say. "I need to go."

His brow furrows. "Where are you going?"

"To town, to talk to the mechanic about my car. I need to find out how long it's going to be."

"You know you can stay here until it's fixed. That's what I came to tell you. I heard you saying goodbye to Star, and it sounded so final." His voice is husky, but I must be imagining that it's filled with emotion. I move toward the door, but this just brings me closer to Tate. To his still-familiar smell, the saddle soap and leather, the woodsy tang of pine needles. I find I need to steady myself by putting my hand on the smooth wood beam of the wall.

"Emory," he says. My name on his lips, the sound of his voice, sends a jolt through me that feels a lot like electricity. "You don't need to leave."

I shake my head. A lump in my throat is making it hard for me to speak, but I know I need to. That I need to explain to him why this has to be so final.

"I don't know why I came here," I begin. "It was a mistake. I only stayed because Charlie said you weren't here." A flicker of hurt passes over his expression, but I keep going because that flicker is nothing compared to what I'm feeling. "Then, somehow, I ended up stuck here. I don't want to be stuck anymore. Our past is just that: the past. Today you showed me that nothing has changed. You still think I'm somehow out to get you, to ruin things here at the ranch." I allow myself to remember and feel what it did to me back then when I realized how little he thought of me, what he'd presumed about my intentions. I can feel the tears gathering and fight them hard.

"I didn't—" he starts. I haven't said anything to interrupt him, but he stops speaking as if I have. He tries again. "I know you didn't have bad intentions. I knew it the second you left town."

His voice seems full of anguish—but I find myself backing away. If he knew all this time, why did he never reach out? He had my phone number, my address. We exchanged all that during our first days together. But when I think about his final words to me ten years ago, I know exactly why. I can hear them as if they were yesterday: *I thought I knew you, but I have no idea who you are, or what you're capable of.*

A car horn sounds out in the driveway. "Frank is here," I say. "I have to go." I don't wait for Tate to respond, just step past him and leave.

. . . .

Meredith isn't around when I reach the mechanic's; it's her brother, Mario, who comes out of the repair bay to greet me today, on my fourth day here in Evergreen—and hopefully, my last. His coveralls are forest green and his smile, to my relief, doesn't come coated with a layer of frost. In fact, he seems downright excited to see me.

"Only a *truly* qualified mechanic can repair a broken axle," he tells me. "I've been training for this my whole career." He goes on to explain what exactly this repair job will entail while I try to focus on his words instead of remembering Tate's anguished expression. When I finally bring myself to ask how much this is going to cost, he gives me an approximate number that's not as staggering as I imagined, but still high enough to make me nervous. My bank balance is currently as low as my emotions.

"It's definitely worth fixing," he says. His eyes are hopeful, like he's afraid I'll take this dream job away from him.

"Oh, I'm fixing it," I assure him. "How long will it take? A few hours?"

"A few days, more like. Hard to say exactly how many," he replies, and I bite my lip, dismayed. *Days?* "But I *can* promise you the car will be ready by Christmas Eve at the latest. A week from yesterday."

This causes my heart to plummet even lower. "A week," I say. "I can't stay here a week. Do you know of a car rental place? I'll have to go back to the city and come get the car another time."

He hands me a card for a car rental place, and I thank him and leave.

....

I spot a bench up ahead and take out my phone, thinking I'll call Lani—but find myself pulling up the contact info for my mom. I stare down at it, take a deep breath, then hit the CALL button.

She answers on the first ring. "Emory, hello."

It's only been a few days, but it feels like a lifetime to me. I've been holding everything at bay, but when I hear her voice, it all rushes in.

"How's Dad?" I find myself blurting out. "Is he okay? Where is he being held?"

"At the Toronto South Detention Centre," she says, her voice breaking, too. "The bail hearing was yesterday. He's considered a flight risk, can you believe that?"

Actually, I can absolutely see my parents hopping on a flight to some remote island with a lax extradition policy to avoid all this. But I don't say that. I let her go on.

"Anyway, the bail is too much. We don't—" Her voice breaks again. "With everything we need to keep aside for legal fees, we don't have it. Your father has a few ideas, but for now, it looks like he'll be spending Christmas . . . there."

I know she can't say it. *In jail.* That would make it real.

"And you've seen him?" I manage.

"I've visited every day since he's been in," she says. "Four days. But it feels like forever. He looks so tired, and I worry . . ." She trails off, and I can tell she's trying to put on a brave face for me. "But his legal team is on it, and he is assuring me this will all be behind us soon."

"When will the trial happen?"

"I don't know. Sometime in the new year."

"And he's going to plead . . ."

"Not guilty," she says firmly.

I don't know what to say to this, but I know what my gut is telling me. That he really doesn't think he did anything wrong, and neither does my mother. I look around me, at the snowy town of Evergreen. A place that contains a man named Gill who has lost everything because of my family. That's real. My parents shouldn't be denying it.

"I should go," I find myself saying.

"So soon? Where are you? When are you coming home? You haven't told me anything."

"I'm . . ." I look around me, at the shops hung with holiday lights, their windows festooned with garlands. I'm in a place that feels so far from the city that none of what's happening there seems real. But it is. "I'm sorry I'm not there for you. I just . . . I can't be there right now." When I say it, I realize it's true—I can't return to the city yet. The idea of renting a car to drive back fills me with dread. I feel completely directionless, stuck in a place I don't belong—but unable to go back to the city and face what waits for me there. Not yet. "I wish I could help you, Mom."

"You've helped me," my mother says, her voice suddenly soft. But she doesn't go further than this, doesn't mention the trust fund. I wonder if she ever will. She has always been so good at maintaining a façade. Maybe we'll just never talk about it. Maybe one day, when my father's legal team has somehow managed to get him out of this, she'll just refer to it as *that nasty business with the law* and move on.

"But I'll see you on Christmas?" my mother is asking me, and I feel a deep pang of guilt. I know where I want to be on Christmas, where I should be—and it's with my best friend and her warm, welcoming family. But my mother's going to be alone. My father is in jail.

And yet, I still can't tell her I'll come home for Christmas. Right now, it feels like I have no idea where home even is.

"I'll see, Mom" is all I can say. "I have to go. I'll check in again soon."

. . . .

I walk slowly through Evergreen's downtown, past all the quaint, familiar shops. As I walk by a gray Victorian, slightly set back from the road, I nearly bump into a white-haired, bespectacled, and mustachioed man carrying a stack of newspapers so high they almost obscure his face. I step aside too late. We collide, and the newspapers begin to slide from his grip.

"Oh, no! I'm so sorry!" I've managed to catch the newspapers just before they fall to the sidewalk, but a few escape, fluttering off in the snowy breeze. Once I've secured his stack back in his arms, I race to catch the other newspapers before they blow onto the street.

It's the local newspaper, *The Evergreen Enquirer*. "May I buy one?" I ask the man.

"Oh, it's free," he says. "But these are all for subscribers. And I need to get them out today." He seems extremely harried—which is when I notice he's wearing an air-boot cast on his left foot.

"Can I help you deliver them?" I ask.

"A kind stranger," the man says with a genuine smile. "I'm Bruce McLaren. Chief reporter for *The Evergreen Enquirer*. Publisher, too." He pauses. "Come to think of it, I do all the jobs at the *Enquirer* these days— including newspaper carrier, which isn't easy considering I slipped on the ice last week and ended up with this." He lifts his air-booted leg with a rueful smile.

"Here," I say, taking the stack of newspapers from him. "I can do this for you. Do you have a list of addresses?"

"Oh, I couldn't ask that of you," he says. "Honestly, you're too kind . . ." He trails off, waiting for me to say my name. I hesitate.

"Emory," I finally say, and wait for a flash of unfriendly recognition. But despite the fact that he's the town's only news reporter, he appears to have no clue who I am.

"Guess you aren't in the Evergreen Business Owners' group chat," I say under my breath—but he hears me and looks horrified.

"Are you kidding me? I don't have time for group chats! I have *news* to report on, and a paper to print, and then newspapers to deliver. It's exhausting." He pushes up his glasses, which are sliding down his nose. "Maybe I *will* take you up on your kind offer. No addresses needed. Every house and business in the town proper gets one. Shouldn't take you more than an hour. You're sure you don't mind helping me with this?"

"I'm positive," I say.

"Well, then, meet me back here when you're done, and I'll make you a nice pot of tea as a thank-you."

....

I feel the same way I did while helping Charlie with the chores at the ranch yesterday: Having a straightforward task passes the time, and I don't spiral into worry over my parents, over how I'm going to find a place to stay or when I'm going to get back to Toronto. I enjoy walking through Evergreen with a purpose, taking in the holiday decorations. People here go all out, and decorations run the gamut from elaborately tacky tableaus featuring life-size blow-up Frosty the Snowmen to traditional cedar garlands, fairy lights, and elaborate pine wreaths hanging from door knockers. I slide newspapers into letter boxes and through door handles, lay them on front porches, wish everyone I see "happy holidays" and receive the greeting back. I read the headlines on the cover, and they all make me smile. "Holiday Hoedown Set to Be a Huge Success!" "Classic Christmas Recipes from Grandma Shirley." "Owner of Overturned Golf Cart on 118 Found."

On my way back to the newspaper office, I see a couple up ahead on the sidewalk, heading toward Carrie's Café, talking and laughing. With the snow falling gently around them, they look picture-perfect, walking side by side—but then the man turns and I realize who it is.

He's not wearing his plaid barn jacket; he's got on a navy parka. And it's Mariella beside him, her long blond hair unbraided, gliding down her back like a glacial waterfall. She's wearing a cute little red beret and looks like the main character in a holiday romance movie. He seemed so upset when I saw him a few hours ago—but all that's gone now.

It's fine, I tell myself. It's good that Tate has a beautiful girlfriend who clearly makes him very happy. I can't forever regret the way things ended between us when we were young. But still, I stand frozen watching as he holds the door of the café open for her. He doesn't turn; he doesn't see me at all.

When he's inside, I cross the street and approach the Victorian house, all the joyful, festive feelings I was having while delivering the newspapers evaporating.

. . . .

Bruce opens the door with a smile, which cheers me up a bit.

"I really do appreciate you," he tells me when he lets me in, leading me through a dusty, papery smelling newspaper office that is, I note, completely empty of any staff. He clears some space on a messy desk and sets down a teakettle and invites me to sit. I look around at the framed front pages lining the walls, at the stacks of paper everywhere. The place is messy but also homey and warm.

"Is your staff on Christmas holiday?" I ask him.

"I used to have a reporter, but she decided journalism wasn't for her and went to med school," he says sadly.

"Smart," I say. "I have a journalism degree, actually. Sometimes I wish I had decided to do something else."

"But journalism is one of the most honorable professions!" he says, aghast. "'A good newspaper, I suppose, is a nation talking to itself.' Arthur Miller said that. 'The quality of democracy and the quality of journalism are deeply entwined.' Bill Moyers."

"'A journalist is a person who has mistaken their calling,'" I retort. "Otto von Bismarck."

He laughs. "Ah, so young to be so jaded!" He regards me over his teacup. "So, you don't work as a journalist anymore?"

"Well, I don't have an actual job. I freelance."

"And whom have you freelanced for?"

I list off publications, then realize he's writing them down.

"Wait," I say. "Is this a job interview?"

"You seem to be at a loss for things to do, considering you just volunteered to deliver my newspapers for me. And you've already noticed how short-staffed I am at the moment." He stops writing, waves his pen around at the empty room, then puts it down. I can see that all he's written on the page is *VERY EXPERIENCED*, which is then underlined three times. "In fact, the matter is settled. I'm offering you a job."

"But . . . I don't even live in Evergreen," I say.

"Then what are you doing here?"

"I'm stuck here until my car gets fixed. I almost hit a moose out on the 118 last night." Again, he looks shocked—and I marvel at the fact that the town's newspaper reporter and publisher seems to be woefully behind on town gossip.

"How long will you be here?"

"A week, probably."

"And where are you staying?"

I bite my lip. "I haven't figured that out yet," I say.

"I have an apartment for rent upstairs," he says, tilting his head toward the window, where I see an **Apartment for Rent** sign I hadn't noticed before. "It's been vacant for a while, so is a bit dusty, but it's furnished and cozy. You could stay there."

"Really?"

He smiles. "Of course!"

"How about I work in exchange for board?"

"Considering the paper doesn't actually turn a profit so I wasn't sure how I was going to pay you, work for board it is! Can you start right now? I'm working on a special restaurant review section for the Christmas Eve edition of the paper. Let's go out for a working lunch, shall we?"

He stands and gets his jacket while I put my parka

back on. Then I walk with him out into the snowy Evergreen afternoon, suddenly a journalist again— the rush of happiness inside me over this fact as delicate as an heirloom Christmas ornament that surely will break if I'm not careful with it.

Fourteen

Bruce and I move at a leisurely pace down Main Street, Evergreen. My heart still feels light at the idea of a journalism job, no matter how temporary or humble it is, and my stomach is still growling with hunger. But I'm on high alert—especially when he stops in front of Carrie's Café.

"Here we are!" he says.

I glance nervously through the window but I don't see Tate and Mariella inside—although I'm sure I catch a leftover whiff of pine needles and woodsmoke as I open the door and hold it for Bruce to limp through.

The memories hit me as soon as I walk in. Tate and I came here one afternoon to meet two of his friends for hot chocolate and cookies. I remember how nervous I was, as we held hands across a Formica tabletop, to meet people from his real life, separate from the romantic world of two we had been inhabiting. But when his friends Mya and J.T. came in, they made me feel welcome and comfortable right away. I remember sharing giant caramel chip cookies the size of our heads as we laughed and chatted easily. Mya talked about her family's restaurant in town, how slow it was in winter, but how at least it gave her the chance to study for med school admissions tests; J.T. talked about how he was hoping for a new dirt bike for Christmas. I remembered Tate's eyes, so warm; his touch, so distracting. The way all I could think was that I wanted to go somewhere and kiss him, kiss him, kiss him. That was all I ever wanted back then. But I also felt so happy that day, with him and his friends.

I had no idea it would be so fleeting.

"You all right there, Emory?"

I blink the memories away and return to reality, to the present—which never seems to be an easy task. "I'm fine."

"You look lost in memories. Have you been to Evergreen before?"

"A long time ago," I say. "I was a teenager. My family spent one Christmas here. It was . . . really nice." Understatement of the year. It was perfect and it was horrible. It was the best and it was the worst. It was everything and nothing. But Bruce can't tell how conflicted I am. He's simply smiling that now-familiar kind smile of his.

"Evergreen does many things right," he says. "Christmas being just one of them—but an important one. It's such a beautifully festive town at this time of year, isn't it? I think it's perfect here." A slight change in his expression now. He seems distracted, saddened by something. The corners of his moustache are pulled down by his frown, so he looks like a slightly dejected hound dog. "I just wish we could get more tourists through here. Some of these businesses are really struggling. I always feel like I should be helping more—even though I'm probably the most old-fashioned out of anyone, still running a newspaper and all. Who reads newspapers anymore?"

I don't like to see him so morose. "Apparently, community newspapers are more important and more popular than ever," I say.

He sighs. "I did hear that. I just wonder if the tourists who come through town read any of it." He brightens up a bit. "Either way, I'm trying out a new restaurant review section. My valiant attempt to get these places some recognition, even if it's just amongst those who already know them. Sometimes, you can't really see what's right in front of you, you know?" I nod and he smiles at me. "You came along at the perfect time, Emory. You can breathe some city life into things around here. Can't you?" But his words press me back into the past. City life. City girl. *Hey, City Girl.* He pauses, tilts his head. "Although, not *too* much city. I think what makes Evergreen so perfect is its small-town charm, don't you?"

"I couldn't agree more," I say.

But I'm taken aback when I look around more closely. Instead of the homey, inviting café I remember —with butter-yellow-painted walls, knotty pine shelves filled with books and board games for patrons to read or play as they enjoyed their food, and mismatched cups and saucers set on equally mismatched tables and chairs—Carrie's is now painted white on white on white. All the tables and chairs match. And so, I note, do all the mugs. White. I shiver a little because it feels cold inside. And I see Bruce beside me shake his head.

"I heard she was freshening things up in here. Can't say I agree with the paint choice."

"I thought it was just me," I murmur. "But look." I point across the room to the counter display. "Cookies! If I recall correctly, they are amazing here."

There are stacks of them under glass domes. We stand and wait for just a moment before a woman comes out from the back kitchen to greet us. Her gray eyes widen when she sees us. She has blond curly hair, streaked with vivid white, tied up in a messy bun and topped with a red kerchief decorated with little white snowmen. "Bruce! You're up and about again! Wonderful to see! But don't stand there any longer, go, sit, take any table you like! Who's your friend?"

"This is my brand-new employee, Emory," Bruce says proudly. "She'll be helping me out at the *Enquirer* for the holidays. My very own Christmas angel, just when I needed her."

Carrie smiles warmly at me, but I can't help thinking that I'm no angel. If Carrie is at all active in the Evergreen Business Owners' group chat, she'll know that. But she doesn't seem to make any connections when she looks at me or hears my name. She simply points again at the gaggle of empty tables. "Please, grab a seat and I'll be right with you," she says.

We take a two-top near the window, looking out at Evergreen's snowy Main Street. Bruce settles into his chair with a contented sigh. Soon, Carrie is at our table again, a smile on her face, her eyes bright and excited.

"I heard you were doing restaurant reviews now," she says, while Bruce murmurs, "Honestly, the rumor mill in this town," and I wonder why a newspaperman isn't more up with local gossip. "And that's wonderful timing, since I'm trying to perk things up around here, modernize it a little, see if I can drum up some more business even during the offseason."

"Now, Carrie," Bruce says with mock dismay. "If you know it's a review, doesn't that defeat the whole purpose?" But then he laughs and says, "As if anyone could go incognito in this town, right? Indeed, I'm planning a restaurant review section for the special Christmas Eve issue, and you're my first restaurant. Now, what have you got to tell us about today?"

"Why don't you forget the menu and just let me bring you some of our new stuff."

"Will there be cookies?" I ask hopefully.

She looks at me like I've asked a truly absurd question. "Of course there will be cookies, dear."

She hustles over to the counter, then returns quickly with a large tray. "Since you mentioned the cookies, why don't you start with those," she says, pointing to a small pile of what I think are the caramel chip cookies of my dreams. I almost swoon at the sight of them, then take one from the tray and bite into it enthusiastically. Bruce brings out a notebook and pen, then gingerly takes a cookie as well.

For the first few seconds, the cookie is as I recall it: dense, chewy, with generous chunks of caramel. But

the walnuts seem weird. Another bite, and I feel sure
they aren't walnuts.

"What am I tasting here?" I ask Carrie, hoping my
expression doesn't give away my alarm.

"New addition to the menu! Candied beef brisket
chip!"

Bruce spits his bite into his napkin as casually as
possible and stares at me, wide-eyed, across the table.
"I'm a pescatarian," he mouths.

"Mmmm!" I say, but I put my cookie down. "*Brisket*
caramel chip. Wow."

"*Candied* brisket," Carrie corrects. "I'm glad you
love it."

"'Love' is not the right word, Carrie," Bruce says,
and I have to take a sip of water to hide my smile.

"Oh, I am just so glad to see someone enjoying this
new recipe of mine. I can't seem to get any of my regulars to branch out." She looks down at me. "So, where's
your hometown?" she asks.

"Toronto," I say, nervous now, hoping she doesn't
ask any more questions about why I'm in Evergreen.

"You must have fancy, inventive cookies like this in
the Big Smoke, eh? And now we have them here in
Evergreen."

"Well, these are just so . . . unique," I say, to what I
hope is believable effect.

"You never had anything you needed to improve
on, though," Bruce says thoughtfully. "Do you still
make the original cookies?"

"Oh, sure, but those are sold out—all my regulars
come in and buy those up first thing, along with my

apple fritters. I gave the last of those to Tate and his Mariella. Since she's considering moving to Evergreen, I think he wanted to win her over with the classics." Bruce has a confused expression on his face, clearly way behind on the small-town tea about Tate and his girlfriend. If the words "his Mariella" felt like little papercuts on my soul, the idea of them moving in together is even worse.

"Your apple fritters are truly heavenly," Bruce says.

"Sure, but what's left here"—she nods down at the rest of the food she's holding on her tray—"is truly special. We just need to get people to be adventurous and try them. Which is where you come in."

"Well, then, tell us what else you have there," Bruce says. "Anything without meat?"

"Of course. We've got Yellow-Iced Snownuts. Name speaks for itself," she says, while I hear Bruce murmur something along the lines of "mon dieu." "The Ring of Fire donut," she continues. "Obviously, that one's spicy. A dill pickle fritter, because apple is just boring"—at this, my stomach swoops—"and I now serve donut breakfast sandwiches, too. Well, I *will* serve them if anyone ever orders one. Just need to get more out-of-towners in here and I'm sure it'll happen. Like you, Emory. I'm sure you'd love to try a dill pickle fritter." I suddenly wonder if she knows exactly who I am and I'm being punked.

"Where do you get your culinary inspiration from, Carrie?" I ask in an attempt to delay actually having to try the pickle fritter.

"My husband and I went to the Canadian National

Exhibition last fall," she says. "Where all the great chefs try out their new flavors."

I don't have the heart to tell her that's not at all true, that the food at the CNE, a popular fall fair held in downtown Toronto every year, is known for being wild, weird, and not always palatable, the entire point being to come up with unique dishes and strange ingredient combinations—none of which would ever make it onto actual restaurant menus. For very good reason.

I smile and nod instead. "Wow," I manage.

"Why don't you get started on what you have here, and I'll go get some donut breakfast sandwiches going."

"Good lord, Carrie," Bruce says, and I can tell he's trying hard to control his facial expressions, which verge on horrified. "That sounds like it's going to be a lot of food for just the two of us!"

"I'll be rolling you out of here, Bruce," she says over her shoulder.

When she's gone, he stares at me, wide-eyed.

"Please don't quit on me on your first day," he says.

I laugh. "I promise," I say. "Maybe when she comes back, we should order something simple—coffee?"

His eyes light up. "What a great idea. You're a genius."

When Carrie returns, he asks her about coffee.

"Sure, what would you like? Oat-Milk Olive-Oil Macchiato? Pistachio Cortado?"

"Do you still have just . . . plain coffee?" I ask, and she looks so crestfallen I regret it.

"What's the point of reviewing just plain coffee?"

"No, absolutely, you're right, Carrie," Bruce says. "I have an idea. Bring us one of each of those coffees you mentioned but make them to go. Make everything to go if you don't mind. Bring us some boxes for all this, please. We have so much material here, I think the best thing for us to do is take all this food back to the newspaper office so we can type glowing adjectives *as* we eat."

"Oh, wonderful!" she exclaims.

We head to the register to pay, but Carrie won't hear of it. She's cramming boxes full of donuts, cookies, sandwiches, looking almost panicked that we might miss out on trying something. She comes around the counter and clutches at Bruce's arm. "The review's going to be positive, right?"

"Of course, Carrie," Bruce says. "Not to worry. With this much to work with, you can bet we'll have a lot to say—*all* of it good. I promise."

I carry the boxes, and Bruce takes a bag. Once we're out on the snowy street again, down the road a bit from Carrie's, Bruce turns to me, his eyes still as big as the saucers at the café.

"That was not good," he says. "It turns out you can't do restaurant reviews in a small town unless you plan to go to places in secret. I should never have promised a positive review, where's my journalistic integrity?"

"You did what you had to, Bruce," I say, patting his shoulder.

He glances over his other shoulder as if he's afraid Carrie will come out and pursue us, more of her strange baked goods on offer. But no one is following.

"Come on, let's go," he says, beginning to move down the sidewalk as quickly as he can with his boot cast. "Let's get back to the office. I'll get out my *Merriam-Webster Thesaurus* and we'll get creative. We can use words like . . . 'edible.' 'Palatable.' '*Rare*.'"

"Sounds good," I say, happy that trying to figure out how to describe Carrie's new baked goods in a favorable light is sure to distract me from my feelings about Tate and Mariella moving in together.

But when we reach the front door of the old Victorian that houses the newspaper office, he turns to me, a thoughtful expression on his face.

"You know, we can't really think of all the creative adjectives we need to, erm, do this food justice if we don't have some actual calories in our systems. And there's a place in town I can guarantee has good food."

"I truly am starving," I admit. "Where are you thinking?"

"Gill's Fish n Chips n Bait n Tackle. The best fish-and-chips you'll ever have in your life. No funny business." My mouth has gone dry. I don't know how to respond. "You haven't lived until you've tried his lake-caught pickerel and chips. What do you say?"

Fifteen

I feel terrible. And not just because I'm pretending to be sick on my first day on the job at *The Evergreen Enquirer*. I'm the worst. When Bruce suggested we go over to Gill's for lunch, my stomach dropped so quickly I almost felt motion sick.

Bruce immediately asked if I was feeling unwell—if it was brought on by the candied brisket chunks in the cookie I'd eaten earlier—and I nodded instead of telling him who I am and why I'm persona non grata in some establishments in town. He looked deeply worried, which of course just made it all worse. Bruce is a kind person who is helping me out. He deserves more than for me to be faking sick when I've barely even started the job.

I flop down on the bed and take in my surroundings. It's a little dusty up here, but otherwise quite charming. The apartment consists of a bedroom at the front, with pink-and-white tea rose–patterned wallpaper and two gabled windows looking down at the street. There's a walnut bedroom set with Ikea bedding on top of the mattress, the bedding still in its packaging.

I open my gym bag and unpack my few belongings into the walnut dresser. There are little potpourri sachets tucked inside the drawers; they smell of cinnamon and cloves. I make the bed as I ruminate further on my situation. I feel awful about lying to Bruce, even if I'm sure showing my face in Gill's would have felt worse. Charlie specifically told me not to go there and so did Tate. When Bruce suggested it, I think I just panicked. Still, it's no excuse. I should have told him the truth.

With the bed finished, I walk out into the living room. There's a pink settee, a small TV with a dust-furred screen, and a coffee table in the same walnut wood as the bedroom set. The fridge in the kitchen is olive green, and so are the tub, sink, and toilet in the bathroom. I can hear the light drip of the tap in the kitchen, the buzz of the refrigerator running. I open it, and it's empty. My stomach delivers a low growl as I stare at the fridge's clean, bare shelves.

I go back downstairs into the newspaper office, wondering if perhaps there are some granola bars down there. The office is dim and silent. Dust motes float in the weak sunlight that filters through the windows. After going to Gill's for lunch, Bruce returned to work a little and then headed home. He said we could start our restaurant review series up again tomorrow if I was feeling well enough.

The cookies and donuts from Carrie's are sitting in

their boxes on Bruce's desk, beside a piece of paper scrawled with words like "scrumptious"—crossed out—and "unparalleled." That one is underlined three times. I smile. Bruce might be onto something there.

I then see a note about Gill's, and this causes my heart to sink again. *Haliburton Gold,* he has written. *Special of the Week—absolutely delicious!!* Then beside that, a heading that says, *Fundraiser for Gill, ideas. Crowd-fund???* This is underlined five times and makes me suddenly want to weep. I imagine poor Gill, practically destitute so close to the holidays, still lovingly preparing his weekly special for his loyal customers—all the while worrying that he might not be able to keep his restaurant open for much longer. What has my family done?

I put on my parka and head outside. This time of year, the light is so fleeting. It's only three o'clock in the afternoon, but the sun is already getting low. Clouds are gathering, too, muting the winter light even more. The clouds are swollen with snow and I wonder if we're in for another blizzard. But as the snow begins to fall, the flakes are soft and gentle, swirling easily down from the sky.

I walk down Main Street until I reach Gill's. There are a few customers inside, finishing their late lunches. And I can see a large man who must be Gill behind the counter, smiling as someone says something to him. But even from here, I can see that he looks tired.

I find that my feet are rooted to the sidewalk. I want to go in, but I can't. I don't know what to say, how I could ever offer to help or make up for what my family has done. I feel like Scrooge, looking in through a window at all the things he should have changed. But this is not a Charles Dickens tale, which means there are no ghosts of Christmas past, present, or future to make things right. I back away from the window before anyone sees me and continue to walk. *One foot in front of the other*, as my dad would say.

....

As I pass Carrie's, I see her behind the counter. I duck my head, but she doesn't spot me. I breathe a sigh of relief. If I had to eat any more of her carnival-inspired dishes, I feel sure I actually would be sick.

Up ahead, I spot a flashing **open** sign in the window of Young's Chinese Cuisine. Of course, yet again, this place holds memories: Tate's friend Mya's family owned it. We had dinner here just before everything went wrong. *But don't think about that,* I remind myself, trying to wrench my mind away from the memory of Tate's gaze across the table in the dimly lit restaurant. The paper placemats detailing cocktails we both agreed probably no one had ever ordered. The laminated menus no one looked at, because everyone in town had their usual. Mya sitting with us and chatting whenever she got a break from waiting tables or ringing up takeout.

Suddenly, I'm craving fried rice, egg rolls, lemon chicken. I'm absolutely famished and this, at least, exorcises Tate from my mind. For now.

When I enter the restaurant, I note that although

there have been a few updates—bigger windows, brighter lights, whiter walls—I can smell the tang of the lemon sauce for the chicken I remember, the garlic and peppers for the vegetable fried rice. My mouth waters as I pick up the menu—except just as I do, there's a popping sound from behind the kitchen door, and all the lights in the restaurant go out. I stand still in the total darkness, startled. But in seconds, the lights are back on again.

A woman emerges from the kitchen area, calling out an apology. "Sorry, sorry! I didn't know anyone was here!" She's tall and slender, her straight dark hair pulled back in a low ponytail. She has a textbook held up: *Canadian Electrical Code, Part 1.* "Just working on a school project."

"Training to be an electrician?"

She nods and smiles, and I realize it's Mya. I wonder if she recognizes me, too. "Trying to get ahead of things during the Christmas holidays. Fuses are not yet my strong suit. Are you dining in or taking out?"

I'm so hungry, I don't think I can wait until I get back to the apartment to eat, so I tell her I'll be dining in. She waves her hand around the empty restaurant as behind her, the phone rings.

"Dinner rush hasn't started yet," she says to me. "Pick any table you'd like."

She answers the phone, takes an order, calls it back into the kitchen, then approaches my table. I'm reading through all the options, feeling overwhelmed.

She raises an eyebrow. "I think you've had a recent food trauma and probably need a total reset, right?"

I look up from the menu, surprised.

"How did you . . ."

"Carrie and her 'special' donuts, right? You have that look."

I laugh. "Come on. Do I really?"

"It was all over the Evergreen Business Owners' group chat . . ." she begins, and I put down my menu, feeling dismayed.

"Then you must know who I am."

"Emory Oakes. I remember you."

"I remember you, too," I say. "Weren't you studying for med school when I met you?"

"Tried that." She smiles ruefully. "Turns out blood makes me faint. But I find electricity fascinating, and light electrical shock just makes me stronger." I laugh.

She puts down the textbook she's still holding so it perches at the edge of my table.

"And you're now working for Bruce, which means it's *our* turn for a restaurant review in the *Enquirer,* right? So, I'd like to give you a proper meal. Sound okay? We've been working on something new." She doesn't wait for me to answer, just reaches into her shirt pocket and pulls out a piece of paper covered in simple black typing, hands it to me. It reads "Young's Secret Menu" across the top. When I put it down on the table to read it, she taps it with a long, pale-pink-painted fingernail. "*Real* Chinese food. Not the fried rice and chicken balls you white people like."

I laugh. "Hey, in my own defense, I remember your fried rice and chicken balls being *so* good," I say—but I still read the secret menu with interest. There's lychee pork, an array of dumplings, mapo tofu, fish poached in chili oil, and more. "Mya, this all sounds *amazing.*"

"I'll go back and tell my parents you're here. We can make you a sampler," she says. She pauses—and I wonder if she's going to say something about Tate. "*And* some chicken balls, promise," is all she says. "You're right, they're very good here. Like potato chips."

She walks away and I watch her for a moment, lost once more in the memory of meeting her for the first time. Then I look down and keep perusing the secret menu. I hear the front door of the restaurant open, the tinkle of the little bells above it, feel the blast of cool, wintry air behind. And then, something breaks through all the delicious cooking smells. It's a scent that suddenly fills me with yearning and a different sort of hunger.

Saddle soap, leather, pine needles, woodsmoke.

I don't need to turn around to know that the customer who just came in brought not only a gust of cold winter air, but also a blast from my past. Yet again.

Tate Wilder.

Sixteen

*O*f all the restaurants, I think as I stare down at the secret menu and the words before me lose all meaning. But of course, this is one of the only restaurants in town, and it's owned and run by his friend and her family. I should have known there was a chance I'd run into him here. And what if he's not alone?

I can't avoid it any longer. I look up. But despite the fact that Tate's mere presence has turned me into the equivalent of one of Mya's electrical projects, at risk of shorting out from emotional overload, he doesn't appear to have noticed me. He's standing at the counter, his back toward me. He's wearing that red plaid jacket, has his Stetson pulled low over his too-long, brown-blond hair. Mariella isn't with him, which adds confusing relief to the cavalcade of emotions inside me.

I watch as Mya comes out of the kitchen and greets him warmly. Then she says something in a low voice and I know she's telling him I'm here. I wish I could see his reaction, his face—but when he turns around,

I find I can't look. I pretend to be absorbed in the secret menu. But I can feel his gaze landing on me like it's a tangible thing.

I look up, and our eyes meeting feels tangible, too. Almost like a connection between us clicking into place. A long moment passes with us just staring at each other across the restaurant. There's enough time for the electricity to fizzle and for me to remember how we parted ways this morning. And to firmly recall the image of him and "his Mariella" walking through town.

But then, as he begins to head my way, I lose control once more. My body floods with nerves, anticipation, and that treacherous, traitorous longing left over from another era. My hand, holding the secret menu, shakes; the paper flutters like the last leaf on a tree in late autumn, about to fall to the ground. I put it down on the table, then place my trembling hands on my lap so he won't see the effect he has on me.

"May I sit?" he asks.

I can't speak. All I can do is shrug, not a yes, not a no. He sits.

Seconds later, Mr. and Mrs. Young burst through the kitchen's swinging door, their arms open wide, as if greeting an old friend. They say hello to Tate, then to me. "A newspaper reporter, here!" They're greeting me like I'm a celebrity, and I can see Tate's bemused expression. "You'll stay and eat, too, Tate," they say.

"Oh. I'm not staying. I'm just . . ."

They don't let him finish. "Dine with your old friend. It's settled."

I feel embarrassed, because this is clearly the last

thing Tate wants to do—he probably needs to get back to Mariella—but I also know he's far too polite to decline.

He looks across the table at me again.

"What's this all about?" he asks. "You're the new town newspaper reporter?"

"I got a job," I say. "With Bruce. In exchange for a place to stay while my car gets fixed. So, I officially don't need to stay with you."

"Right. Yeah, you mentioned this morning you really didn't want to do that."

He looks away from me, sighs, and picks up the paper placemat cocktail menu in front of him, begins ripping pieces off the corner as if he's nervous. Or maybe he's just trying to endure sitting here with me.

Then, Mya is back. She raises an eyebrow at the placemat he's destroying, says, "Want to order one of those or are you just going to wreck the menu?"

"Sorry, Mya," he says, but he doesn't stop.

"No worries. We've got a stack of them in the back. But seriously, can I get you something, Tate?"

He hesitates. Then, "Sure," he says. "I'll have a . . ." He points at a random drink, which happens to be something called a Zombie Punch.

Mya raises an eyebrow. "Tate, no one orders most of these drinks, but no one ever orders that one. I think it contains like . . . five types of alcohol and three kinds of soda."

"It's fine," Tate says. "I didn't drive. Mariella dropped me off in town on her way to Minden." I feel a pang at the mention of this.

She glances at me. "Should I make that two?"

I think I could use the drink. "Sure, I'm walking, too. My car is broken."

She heads off to the bar to prepare them, and Tate continues with his paper-shredding mission as we sit there in silence.

Finally, I can't help but ask him, "Are you okay, Tate?"

"Sure, I'm fine," he says.

But then he drops the menu and places his hand beside the little mountain of shredded paper. "Okay, no. I'm not. We need to talk. This can't wait any longer."

Seventeen

We're interrupted by Mya setting down our drinks. "Two Zombie Punches. And two pints of water. Proceed with caution."

Tate takes a sip and winces slightly. "It's not bad," he says.

I follow suit and nearly spit mine across the table.

"Are you kidding? It tastes like paint thinner!"

"That would be the hundred proof rum," Mya calls playfully from across the restaurant, and we both push our drinks away at the same time, as if we're having the same thought: that it isn't safe to lose control in front of each other, the way these drinks would doubtless cause us to.

I'm about to ask Tate to tell me whatever it is that's bothering him so much when Mya's parents show up, each bearing a plate of dumplings. "Time for the first course!"

When Tate looks at me again, I don't see anything but helplessness in his expression. I have no idea how

he feels, or what he was about to say. I don't know if he
wants to be joining me for dinner, or if he hoped to just
say what was on his mind and leave, to officially never
see me again. But either way, it's too late. The Youngs
are placing food in front of us that, despite my tortured
emotional state, makes my mouth water and my stomach grumble with hunger.

"Three kinds of dumplings," Mr. Young announces.
"The first are filled with ground lamb and spices."
These are surrounded in their bowl by steamed greens.
"Next," he says. "The Three Umami dumplings, which
have ground pork, shrimp, and dill." These have white
and green dumpling wrappers and look very festive.
"Finally, Hot and Sour Dumpling Soup. This is my
mother's very secret recipe." He says this with pride.

"He won't even tell me what's in it," Mrs. Young
chimes in. The soup is in small white bowls filled to
the brim with liquid as red as a Christmas gift ribbon.
Little flecks of sesame seeds and scallions float on top,
and it smells delicious. It is a testament to my hunger,
and to the enticing display, that even while I'm sitting
across from Tate Wilder all I can do is reach for a
spoon.

"This is so good," I breathe—and see with relief
that Tate is spooning it up as eagerly as I am. Once he
has a bite of the soup, he, too, lets out an involuntary
sound of pleasure that strikes a chord deep inside me,
unlocks a memory as steamy as the soup.

"*So* good," he agrees. "This definitely makes the
fried rice and beef with broccoli Charlie insists on get-

ting pretty boring. I'm ordering from the secret menu from now on."

We're barely finished with the dumplings and soup when the Young family arrives at our table again, this time with platters they describe with love as each dish lands before us: fresh, hand-pulled noodles that Mr. Young beams over. The bowl of noodles is studded with stir-fried vegetables, jeweled with meat. There's also mapo tofu, in a bright gravy as vivid as the hot and sour soup broth; steamed eggplant topped with aromatics and a black vinegar sauce; and a "Chinese hamburger," which is a pita-like bun filled with tender braised pork, chopped green herbs, and sauce. Mrs. Young explains that this was her favorite street food, growing up in Shanxi.

There are also rolls of Pingyao beef—"like a Chinese corned beef"—and Shanxi crispy duck, which is first steamed and then fried, Mrs. Young tells us, making it "so crispy and delicious you'll forget about Peking duck forever." The duck is served with what she calls "bings": like pancake wraps, savory, mixed with Chinese chives and spices.

"I have no idea how we're going to eat all this," I say to Tate.

"I have a feeling we'll manage," he says.

"True, the last time I ate properly was at the Watering Hole. I'm famished." I realize I don't care that I'm talking with my mouth full.

For a while, all we do is chat lightly as we eat, skimming across the surface of our lives as if we are just two old friends catching up. The food has somehow thawed things between us, the warmth of sharing a meal so strong it even works on us. We talk about the horses, about Evergreen life, about my working at the *Enquirer* for the week. We exclaim over how great the food is. I take notes on a steno pad Mya gives me, and Tate helps me out with ways to describe it all. *Succulent. Heavenly. Ambrosial. Exquisite.*

But eventually, he puts down his fork. The agonized look returns.

"What is it, Tate?" I say.

"If you're going to be staying in town, even just for another week, I don't want it to be weird every time we see each other. Because"—he gestures around him—"in Evergreen, you can't throw a stone without hitting someone you don't want to see."

Someone you don't want to see. I look away from him and shovel a bite of duck into my mouth in an attempt to eat my stung feelings—but it doesn't help.

"So, you don't want to see me," I say. "And you keep running into me. I'm sorry. I wish I weren't here just as much as you wish I weren't here, okay?"

Now he looks surprised. "That's not what I—"

"Oh, I get what you mean."

"Emory." His voice is low, his eyes suddenly fierce. "Please. It's not that I don't want you here. That's not it at all. And it's no coincidence that I came in here. I was out looking for you. I'd been to every place in town."

I stop chewing. I don't know how I manage to get the last bite down, because my mouth has gone completely dry.

"Why were you looking for me?"

"Because we need to talk. I can see why you're up-set with me." He rubs his beard-fuzzed chin with his hand. "The last time we saw each other, I wasn't very nice. Maybe that's an understatement. And when you fell off Star, I . . ." He clears his throat. "I was worried about you. Really worried." There's pain in his eyes. "And when I asked you to sign the waiver, I know it came off as me being a dick, thinking you might sue—but things have been really hard at the ranch. And I didn't know . . ." He shakes his head. "I'm sorry, but it has been ten years. I couldn't let my feelings get in the way of doing what was right for the ranch." He looks up at me again. "Except it's you," he says. "I know you would never sue. I should have given you the benefit of the doubt, finally. I'm sorry about that."

I'm not sure what to do with everything he has just said to me. The fact that he was looking for me. The way he just said *Except it's you*. But I can't let my heart get away from me. He's stumbling over his words, prob-ably doesn't even really know what he's saying. I focus on the words that felt the most ominous. "What do you mean, 'things have been really hard at the ranch'?"

He sighs. "It's never been easy. You know that. But for a few years recently, things got especially challeng-ing. I tried to start up a training and show facility, and it just increased our overhead way too much. We ended up in a lot of debt we're still digging out of." He looks into his glass, takes a sip, puts it down. I know, perhaps better than anyone, that this is hard for him to tell me. "The town rallied together to keep us from going under.

There was a big holiday fundraiser last year. It was difficult, to take money from people. Charlie fought so hard against it—and I wanted to fight, too. You know about my pride, maybe better than anyone." I can't help but nod. "But I knew we had no other choice. Either we took the help, or we were going to have to start selling horses."

He looks at me now and his words hang between us. I know there isn't a single horse in the Wilder Ranch herd that Tate and Charlie would be able to let go of without regret.

"Did things get better?"

He shakes his head. "It's what happened with Star. When she got hurt, this past summer—it wasn't just her who was hurt. A group booked a trail ride. None of them had ever been near a horse before, even though they said they had experience. That's when Star got spooked by the coyote. Unfortunately, the guy fell off and broke his leg."

Tate takes a sip of his drink, grimaces, swallows hard, and puts it down. "We got him to the hospital as fast as we could, and it wasn't a complicated break; they set it easily. But turns out he was a lawyer."

I feel stricken. But then something clicks. It still hurts that earlier today he made it seem like he couldn't trust me. But I can see how all this might be a little raw. "No waiver?"

"There was one, but it was just something I'd found on the internet and printed off. It didn't cover all the bases, it turns out. And the guy, he really scared us with all his legalese and threats. I started to think maybe we'd lose everything if we went to trial. So, we settled out of court—but it was a lot of money. We're slowly regrouping, but it feels sometimes like it's day by day at the ranch. It's been stressful. But things are getting better."

Mya is at the table again, beginning to clear our plates. Her father, behind her, drops off a platter of lo mai chi, little cakes that resemble mochi, and a pot of tea. I reach for a cake and stare down at its pale pink, sugar-dusted surface. It makes sense that Tate would be so nervous about my fall, about all riders signing waivers—even someone he knows.

"I wish I could help," I find myself saying. "With Wilder's. Your situation." I realize too late that this isn't the right thing to say—it's what broke us apart in the first place.

Tate looks away. "That's not why I told you," he says, and his tone has cooled a few degrees. "I just wanted you to understand why I reacted that way to your fall, why I asked you to sign a waiver. I didn't want you to think I was still like I was back then, always assuming the worst of you."

"It was a long time ago," I say. My tone makes it sound like I haven't agonized over it, not just for the past four days, but for all the years before. Like seeing him again hasn't brought it all back—like being at the ranch hasn't made the old wound sting. I didn't realize I was such a good actress.

I stare across the table at him, feeling our past hanging all around us like a ghost.

Maybe it's a ghost I can't ignore anymore.

The control I've had over my emotions melts away like snow in sunshine. "Hey," I say. "Don't treat me like it's *back then*. It's not, and we both know it. Of course I don't want to swoop in and try to save the day with my family's money. I know that's not what you would want, and as you probably know, my family doesn't have any money anymore. I said I want to help you because I *love* Wilder's. I love Star. I was there when she was born, and I'll never forget that. It's a place that means something to me, too."

His hand is on his chin again, rubbing across his jaw in agitation. "Okay," he says. "You're right. We have a lot of"—he waves his hand around in the air—"baggage, I guess you could say. Maybe because we were teenagers when we knew each other."

"Just kids," I agree. "And now we're adults. We need to figure out a way to put whatever judgments we made about each other behind us. We hurt each other—but it was a long time ago. Can we agree on a statute of limitations?"

I should be used to it by now, the way being caught in the snare of Tate's intense gaze can suddenly make me feel like I'm falling, but it still knocks me sideways. I practically have to cling to my chair.

"That's what you want?" he says in a low voice. "To forget?"

"I don't think I said 'forget' . . ." I begin, but I don't know how to finish that sentence.

What *do* I want? I have never understood that when it comes to Tate Wilder.

But now, today, in the present, he has nothing to give me. He has Mariella. He has the ranch, which needs his full attention. What I want, whether I'm fully aware of it or not, doesn't matter.

He releases me from his gaze and I exhale with relief. He looks out the window at the darkening street. I look, too, at the snow caught in the lamplight, and a shop owner across the street hanging Christmas lights on the eaves of his store with great care. The man climbs down the ladder and stands back to observe his handiwork, nodding with pride before going inside.

"There is a way you can help, okay?" Tate says, snapping me out of my reverie. "Charlie's right. You were good on Star. She took to you. She wasn't perfect, obviously. I mean, she threw you in a snowbank." Now he smiles that crooked smile and it sparks a warmth in my core. "But she hasn't been that calm with anyone in ages. It would be great to get Star back to the way she once was, with your help."

"You mean, you actually want me to ride her again?"

"With certain parameters, yes."

"Such as?"

"Me as your riding coach. Could you handle that?"

"You telling me what to do?" I laugh. "Probably not. But I'd love to help Star."

I say this sincerely. I feel so relieved to be able to say it at all—and realize the relief is also coming from the knowledge that I get to go back to Wilder Ranch. I want to see Star again. Charlie, too. And Tate. I can't help it. Even if he's not mine, and never will be.

"I really would," I say. "Maybe I could even get her ready enough for the Starlight Ride next week."

"Now, that would probably take a Christmas miracle," Tate says, shaking his head. "Christmas Eve is less than a week away. And Star is a unique case. Prematurely born horses may seem perfectly healthy— and she is, don't get me wrong. But her processing isn't quite the same as other horses'."

"Charlie told me," I murmur.

"Yeah. I've noticed this with her before, only it's never been this bad. But you can at least help get her started on the right track again before you leave town."

Before you leave town. Those words hurt, for reasons I don't let myself explore. I try to focus on the positives. I focus on Star.

"There's nothing I'd rather do than help Star." I know I mean this, at least.

"Then it's settled," Tate says. "You'll come back to Wilder's a few times while you're here. To ride Star."

"To ride Star," I repeat.

He glances down at his watch. "Charlie was out picking something up in my truck, but he's coming through town to get me in a few minutes. I have to go."

He pulls out his wallet, but Mya calls for him to put his money away before her parents catch him trying to pay for a meal that was supposed to be their holiday treat.

"Does tomorrow afternoon work? Three-ish?"

"I'll be there," I tell him.

He stands and crosses the room, trying once more to pay as Mya laughs and waves him off. "Stop being such a gentleman all the time, Tate Wilder!"

He laughs and leaves the restaurant. A part of me thinks he'll look back at me through the window. But he doesn't.

❄ ❄ ❄ ❄ ❄

Dear Diary,

Tate.

TATE.

TATE!!!

I'm . . . I don't know if I can say this, let alone write it. But I will anyway, because it's you: I think I'm in love with him. So many times, I've come close to saying it. Can you imagine? We've only known each other a week, but it feels like a lifetime. And what a lifetime it has been. Especially with Star being born, having that incredible experience together, I just feel so close to him . . .

I'm scared, of course. What do I know about love?

I've tried to learn about it by reading books. My favorite is <u>All About Love</u> by bell hooks. I have it with me here, but I opened it to a passage that scared me even more, one about how the practice of love offers no place of safety. It means opening oneself up to the possibility of loss, hurt, pain.

But he does make me feel safe. He makes me feel special, he makes me feel seen. He makes me feel like I'm exactly where I belong now. When he looks at me, the world stops spinning, I swear. When we touch, I feel like I'm . . . an actual firework or something. I can't imagine not feeling this way about him. It feels like a part of who I am, who I'll always be. And if it causes pain, so be it. I can take it, to be with him.

But of course, I still have reality to contend with, even if I feel like I'm living in a dream. For example, yesterday, my dad and Cousin Reuben went into town and came back talking about some business venture they're planning. They had been out at some restaurant called Gill's, they said. A fish place. And the owner had given them some boxes of free fish-and-chips to take home for the group. They dumped the boxes on the counter and said the housekeeper would come in and throw them away later before the chef started to cook us some "real food." Which I just thought was such a rotten thing to say. It smelled SO good. Plus, I for one am tired of what my parents call "real food." It's either too rich or as insubstantial as a puff of air. So, I packed up some of the boxes of fish-and-chips and took them with me over to Wilder's, where Tate was waiting for me. And he was <u>thrilled</u>. He said Gill's was his favorite, and that I was going to love it, too.

But first, we went to visit Mistletoe and Star, who are both doing well. Mistletoe is a wonderful mother, and I will never get enough of watching them snuggled up together, sleeping in their stall. And Star is so cute. You'd never know she was a preemie. She's always up and about, eating well, and has the softest little nose.

After we visited the horses, we took our food up to the hayloft and had a little picnic, sitting on a cozy plaid horse blanket on top of a bunch of hay bales, which was almost a bed. (More on that later, but I'm already blushing.) The food was so good, even cold, so I can see why Tate loves it so much. I sucked on a lemon after, because I said I wanted to kiss him but didn't want to taste like tartar sauce—and he said he didn't care, that I was perfect always, no matter what.

It went beyond kissing. Before I knew it, we were both half naked on top of the blanket and I didn't want to stop. Do you get what I mean? <u>I didn't want to stop.</u> It probably goes without saying that I've never done it before. I assume he has. J.T. said something about a previous girlfriend the afternoon we all hung out. It was just a passing mention, not designed to make me uncomfortable, but Tate just seems so assured about everything. I'm sure he has experience. Still, I was afraid to ask. And eventually, he was the one who said to slow down. I honestly don't think I would have. But then again, we were in a hayloft and maybe that's not the right spot. Except . . . where? I'm serious. Because I think I want to. Actually, I <u>know</u> I want to. Because I feel sure that no matter where it is, or when it is, it's going to be perfect.

What isn't perfect is when I got back, my mom and Aunt Bitsy didn't hear me come in. They were in the kitchen talking about me. And about Tate.

"I wouldn't worry, Cass," Bitsy was saying. "She's just having a little bit of holiday fun with a local. She won't look back once she's in the city again." My mom said something about how I'm not the type to have fun, which almost made me laugh—except it's true, I'm not.

I snuck up the back steps, feeling determined to prove them wrong. I am not going to leave Tate behind. And I will never care that my snobbish family thinks he isn't good enough. I feel more comfortable with Tate, at Wilder's, than I ever have anywhere in my life. I already know that feeling is not something I'm just going to be able to walk away from.

Eighteen

The next morning, my fifth in Evergreen, when Bruce arrives at the newspaper office, I'm downstairs early, waiting for him with a freshly brewed pot of coffee.

"Before we can go on, we need to talk," I tell him.

"Oh, *no*," he exclaims. "I was afraid this would happen. You got food poisoning on your first day! Please, don't quit on me. One last chance?"

I laugh. "It wasn't the terrible cookies," I say. But then my expression grows serious again.

I ask him to come sit with me at my desk. I turn on my computer and do a search on my dad. I open the news items and explain as I click through them that this is my family—and that Gill of Gill's Fish n Chips n Bait n Tackle is in financial ruin because of us.

"You really do need to check in on the Evergreen Business Owners' group chat every once in a while," I conclude. "There are definitely some news leads there, Bruce."

Bruce leans over me and reads the article about my

father and his corporate fraud crimes, then sits down in the chair beside me and lets out a long sigh. He's deep in thought for so long I wonder if he's going to ask me to leave or say anything at all.

When he finally does speak, all he says is, "This is unfortunate." My heart sinks. "But not for the reasons you think it is. I feel for you, Emory. This is a tough burden to carry."

He nods his head at my computer, then x's out of the story. "My grandfather was the mayor of this town years ago, and he embezzled money from a local treasury. Especially in a community this small, it was a lot to live down. But I made a name for myself because *I am not* my grandfather. I imagine you are not your father. Either way, I plan to judge for myself."

"Even though I faked sick on my first day?"

"You had your reasons and came clean at the first opportunity. As far as I'm concerned, there's nothing more to discuss. All is forgiven."

We spend the rest of the morning working on our review of Carrie's, settling on "inventive" and "surprising" for the spicy Ring of Fire donut, and "unique" and "savory" for the meat cookie—which we agree in both cases is the truth, leaving our journalistic integrity intact.

When I tell him about my dinner at Young's Chinese, Bruce is delighted. "Why don't you give me eight hundred words on the secret menu and its origins by lunchtime? It sounds like the Youngs gave you a lot to work with."

I've almost forgotten how exciting it is to be working on deadline in a newsroom. I know *The Ever-green Enquirer* is a long way from *The Globe and Mail* newsroom—both literally and figuratively—but I still feel that same sense of purpose and urgency.

I have an hour-long fact-checking conversation with Mrs. Young, who is more than happy to expound at length about her favorite foods, and the inspirations behind the secret menu. She also tells me about a holiday special they're running for those who may not want to cook their own Christmas meal. I transcribe my notes, then start to write—and before I know it, a first draft is finished, and it's noon.

I stand up from my desk and stretch my arms above my head. "Bruce?" He looks up from his computer. "I think I'm going to go over and pick us up some lunch," I say. "From Gill's."

He nods and says, "Best of luck, Emory." And then he goes back to his work.

. . . .

The sign for Gill's Fish n Chips n Bait n Tackle is still the same as I remember: an old tin fishing boat featuring a hand-painted rendering of a speckled lake trout. When I walk in, I can't help but expect to find the fish-and-chips shop just as it was the decade before—but, I remind myself, Evergreen has moved on.

Time hasn't been standing still, even if it did in my mind. So many things here have changed. Including Tate. Including me.

But even so, Gill's does end up matching my memory

of the time Tate and I came here together, after the first time I tried the fish-and-chips with him in the hayloft. The walls are still decorated with old-timey fishing lures and hung with netting. This time of year, there are little red and green Christmas balls strung through the netting, too. It still smells like freshly gutted fish, which you would think would be a bad thing, but really isn't; in here, it's fresh and briny. There's still a fridge with containers of bait, shelves lined with tackle for sale.

Gill comes out of the kitchen at the sound of the tinkling fishing lure mobile that hangs above the door. He's wearing a starched white apron, and his blue eyes crinkle up with a welcoming smile.

"How may I help you?" he asks me.

My heart feels like it's breaking already. How could my father and Reuben take money from this man? This is his family business, his heart and soul. I can tell. And it's all just so unfair.

"I'm, uh, from the newspaper," I say. I shouldn't. But I *want* him to know we're writing a review. He deserves every advantage he can get. Plus, maybe he'll figure out who I am and I won't have to come out and say it—which I'm finding myself far too nervous to do. "I'm picking up lunch for Bruce and me—and *we'll* be sure to give it a glowing write-up in our special holiday restaurant review section."

This isn't how it's supposed to work, and I know it. And it also wasn't my intent when I came here. My plan was to tell him who I am and apologize on behalf of my family. But being here, seeing him in person, is making me realize it isn't that simple. Meanwhile, Gill keeps smiling, but there's a weariness behind his eyes that makes me feel even worse about everything.

Still, "Oh, that would be nice," he says. "A boost would be good. So, lunch for the two of you? We do have our regular pickerel and chips, but I've also got something special I've been offering lately."

My heart sinks at the "something special"; I'm still traumatized by Carrie's. But he's gone back into the kitchen before I can ask for the regular fish-n-chips meal his place is so famous for.

In a little while, he emerges with two take-out containers in hand. "This is my pan-fried Haliburton Gold," he says. "And parsnip frites. I'll be really interested to hear what you think."

"What is Haliburton Gold?" I ask him.

"A special kind of trout you can only get in this lake region," he says. "It's especially good this time of year, when the ice is new and the trout are up in the shallows. Like bobbing for apples with shark teeth."

He winks at me and I want to finally blurt out my apology, but I find myself unable to say anything except to thank him for the food. He doesn't want me to pay for it, but I insist. I thank him again, then leave, determined that of all the reviews I write for Bruce's special holiday restaurant section, this will be the best one. Even better than the one I wrote for Young's. But I still wish there was more I could do for Gill—and wonder if I'll ever stop feeling this way, or if I'm destined to carry the burden of my father's crimes wherever I go from now on.

Nineteen

rank, the Evergreen taxi driver, drops me off at Wilder Ranch and tells me he'll be back to get me later.

"This is better than Uber!" I tell him as I get out of the car, but he shoots me a confused look. "Never mind," I say, paying him through the window before walking toward the ranch buildings.

Just then my phone chimes. It's Lani: She's sent a photo of the babies snuggled up together sleeping, little half smiles on their angelic faces. Then another image of her mother and aunts, still hard at work cooking for the holidays—today, it's caldereta, a slow-cooked beef stew with peppers and onions, and ube halaya, which is a purple yam jam, plus stacks and stacks of pandesal, fluffy, soft bread rolls. We've talked and texted a few times over the past few days—but she keeps insisting I need to open up more to Tate about how I've felt all these years, the existence of Mariella be damned. And I just can't do that. I "heart" both images, then lift my phone to take a picture of the setting I'm in: the snow, the red stables, the herds of horses in the distant paddocks, in their red-and-green-plaid Wilder Ranch blankets.

I lower my phone and see that Tate is in the shot, in the distance, bringing some horses inside, holding two lead ropes in each hand, like he's a dog walker, not a horse wrangler. He doesn't see me. He walks toward the back of the south barn's doors while I watch him go. Then I look down at my phone again, at the photo I didn't know I was taking of him. I keep it, but I don't send it to Lani. I don't know why.

I walk toward the north barn, the closer one. Inside, it's warm, the air heavy with the smell of horses, their hay and grain, the leather of their saddles. Star is already in her stall, back in from the paddock and ready to be groomed. I don't wait for Tate; I know what I'm doing. I lead her from the stall into the aisle and set her up in crossties. There's a box of brushes and other grooming tools on the floor outside her stall. I take out a currycomb and loosen the dirt in her coat, flick it off with the dandy brush, then set about smoothing her golden coat to a sheen with the body brush. She seems happy to see me, but that could just be because she smells the mints in my pocket, I tell myself, smiling as she nickers and snorts gently, taps one hoof then the other on the interlocking brick of the aisle floor, wanting her treat early.

I speak to her softly, telling her what a good girl she is, asking about her day. I feel like she understands me. And I'm just so happy to be near her. I bury my face in her neck for a moment, wrap my fingers in her mane.

A throat clears, and I pull away, embarrassed to see Tate approaching down the aisle.

"I see you two are getting reacquainted," he says with a gentle smile as I blush. But he's all business and moves right on. "You good getting her tacked up?"

I nod. "I know where her tack is from last time."

"Okay. Meet you in the arena in five minutes," he says, as if he really is just my riding instructor and I'm just a student. As if my palms haven't started to sweat and my heart hasn't started to race. As if, as he walks away, I don't find myself staring at the way he looks in his plaid jacket and dark Levi's, the way his muscled thighs fill out the well-worn denim.

I thought after our conversation last night I might have successfully exorcised any feelings I still seem to have for him. We both said it: We're adults now, not teenagers. We're trying, for the brief time I'm here in Evergreen, to be friends—or at least, friend*ly*. And, of course, there's the fact that he has a pretty girlfriend, with her long blond braid and preppy riding clothes— meanwhile, I'm wearing clothes I hand-washed and hung to dry in the bathroom of my temporary apart- ment, and they still feel slightly damp. Glamorous city girl, I am not.

I couldn't have turned out the way he imagined I might—if he ever thought of me at all over the years. And I have to allow that not to matter. I'm here for a different purpose. For Star.

Soon, I have her saddled up and am leading her to

the arena. Tate is waiting, as promised. He shoots me a smile from the center of the ring. "Hey, City Girl," he says, and I can't help it; despite my resolve, my heart flutters at his use of that old nickname. For just a moment, my knees are weak, but then I remember what I'm here to do. This is about Star. Helping her, that's all. I lead her to the mounting block and hoist myself into her saddle. I look over at Tate, who is leaning against a jump standard, his Stetson low, his hair peeking out from beneath it. I tell myself he's just a riding instructor. He isn't the first person I ever kissed. He isn't someone who, without even trying, I can still remember the exact taste of. Mints and lemon. I swear I can feel a tingle on my lips, like the ghost of his kiss. I drag my thoughts back to the present as he calls out to me again.

"Okay, just a walk for now. Let's take it nice and slow."

I do as he suggests, and then, after two laps of the ring, he instructs me to ask her for a trot. I find I'm nervous, still, and it's not because of any doubts I have about my riding skills. With Charlie, it was easier to just focus on riding Star. Now my mind is also on Tate.

"Wrong diagonal," he says with a raised eyebrow and a half smile—referring to the fact that I'm supposed to lift my body out of the saddle in time with Star's inside, not outside, leg. "Do I need to teach you the same phrase my beginners have to learn?"

"Oh, yeah?" I call out. "What's that?"

He says it in a singsong voice. "Rise-and-fall-with-the-leg-on-the-wall. We make a little poem out of it. They never forget."

"I haven't forgotten, either," I retort. "I just . . ." But I don't finish the sentence. I can't admit that it's because I'm distracted by thoughts of us, limbs entwined in the loft above.

"Okay, change direction now," he says, and I do—then stick my tongue out at him when I correct my diagonal in the middle of the arena.

"Hey!" he says, laughing. "Don't make me put you on the ranch school's naughty list."

"What happens to the students who get put on the naughty list?" I ask.

"Stall-mucking duty for a week," he replies. "Okay, slow her to a walk now, please. I know you probably want to canter now, and I don't blame you—that would be the logical next step, and this horse has a gait like a rocking chair," he says. I nod my agreement. "But I was thinking . . ." He takes a few steps closer and looks up at me.

Even from this height, this distance, even with a thousand pounds of horse between us, I feel it—that connection, that flash of electricity. Discomfited, I break his gaze and reach down to pretend I need to check the tightness of Star's girth.

Tate's voice is softer now, but I can still hear him. "I'd love to get her back out on the trail," he says. "I really would. What you said about the Starlight Ride . . . it's improbable, but it would be so great to have her there again. Still, if it's not what she wants,

I'm not going to force it. I need to be really sure, though. So I want to listen to her, to watch her. And I want to do that while someone else is riding her. Someone I trust."

Someone I trust. It shouldn't mean so much that he has said this, but I find myself grabbing on to those words and holding them in my heart like a Christmas gift I had been fervently hoping for, but not expecting to receive.

"What if we go for a walk on the trail and I lead her?" he continues. "It would mean you're not in control. I'd take off her bridle and use a halter and lead rope. But it also means I can be close to her, watch her. I can try to listen to her. Determine what she really wants, what she really needs. And then I can decide if I'll keep forcing it, or if she'll just become one of our horses who we don't use on the trail."

"I'd be fine with that," I say. "I trust you, too."

He looks up at me, but just for a split second, so there's not enough time for me to fall into that electrical minefield. He nods, once, decisively, then says, "Okay, I'll be right back."

He returns quickly, holding Star's halter and a lead rope, which is striped red and white like a candy cane. I wait as he removes her bridle and hangs it on the jump standard, then puts on her halter and attaches the lead rope to the little brass ring at her chin. "Ready, girl?" he says to her.

Then he looks up at me, his expression serious. "I'll do my absolute best to keep her from rearing," he says. "I'll hold her head tight and keep her down if anything happens. I'm not going to let her get away from me. We'll turn around and head straight back here if she seems too upset."

I nod. "I know. It's going to be okay."

"Are you nervous?" he asks.

"No," I say. "It wouldn't be fair to her to be nervous. She'd feel it."

He nods. "She would."

"She can do this," I say. *For Star*, I tell myself.

"I know she can," he says, looking me straight in the eye. But then he looks away and leads us outside, into the wintry late afternoon.

Twenty

With me on Star, and Tate walking along beside us, there will be no more moments when our gazes meet—and this is a good thing. Because it's important for me to keep my heart rate steady so Star can do the same for herself. Now I can only see the top of Tate's head, covered in his Stetson, the sun-bleached ends of his always-in-need-of-a-cut hair peeking out from beneath it.

The air is cold and crisp; all I can smell is the almost minty tang of snow—and then, as we reach the forest trail, cedar, pine, some distant woodsmoke. It's Tate, but not Tate. It doesn't have the same effect. So far, so good.

"So," Tate says as we walk, "how've you been all these years?" Then he laughs at himself, and I find myself laughing, too. "Big question, I guess. But seriously— you went to journalism school, the way you wanted?"

"I did," I say. "And I worked at *The Globe and Mail*, in the newsroom, for five years."

"Your dream," he says, and I feel surprise at this—the way he still remembers my dreams. But then, I still remember his. "And you're not there now?"

"Layoffs," I say. Star butts her head softly against Tate's shoulder as we walk. With him close, she has been completely calm since he led her from the arena. He murmurs softly to her. So gently, his voice full of care.

"That's a bummer."

"It was. But I've been freelancing since last year. That's going pretty well. Or, at least, it was."

"Oh, really? Who do you write for?"

I name some of the publications, and he lets out a low whistle. "Impressive. I'll have to look up some of your work."

I find myself blushing, thinking of him reading my articles online—but then feel a little disappointed at the idea that he's never once googled me.

"Why do you say your freelancing was going well?" he asks me. "Past tense?"

I sigh. "With what's happened with my dad, I'm just not sure about approaching editors. Some of them might want me to give them the inside scoop. Others just might not be interested in my work, given my family name."

"Do you really think that? That people will judge you by what your dad did?"

With no reins to hold on to, I've settled my hands on the saddle pommel, and now I twist them together.

"I do think that," I find myself saying. "I feel really . . . well, to be honest, I feel ashamed. Like I should have done something. My dad wanted me to work with him, and I didn't. Maybe if I had, things would have been different."

"It isn't your fault," Tate says. "I met your dad. He didn't exactly seem like a guy who was . . ." He pauses, thinks. "Open to suggestions that weren't his."

Despite the fact that this topic makes me feel morose, I find myself laughing quietly. "You nailed it," I say.

"So, then, why blame yourself when you know you never would have been able to stop him? And, even if you could have, it was his company. His responsibility to do right."

"You have a point," I say, and it surprises me how much better this conversation with Tate is making me feel. As if I'm talking to someone who understands me, and my life, deeply. The sun filters through the snow-covered tree branches. There's the distant call of a crow, the crunch of Star's hooves and Tate's feet on the path, the sound of my breathing, and Star's gentle snorts.

"Thank you," I finally say. "That really helps."

"I hope you know I'll—" Tate clears his throat. "I'll always be happy to help you, Emory," he says quietly. "I can imagine this situation is a lot to carry."

A lump rises to my throat. I don't want to cry, not here, not now, so I ask him a question instead. "Tell me what you've been up to all this time," I say, trying to lighten the mood. "Big question, but we have time, right?"

"You're looking at it," he says. "I've been here,

mostly. I did go to the University of Guelph, for stable management. Two years. Charlie insisted, said it would be good for me to get away, but mostly I just missed it here, and learned stuff I already knew."

I laugh. "Ever occur to you that you're just a know-it-all?"

He laughs back. "Well, I come by it honestly, I guess. Pretty sure Charlie knows all there is to know about most things."

"He's taught you well."

Just then, up ahead, a pile of snow falls from a branch. Star freezes, snorts nervously, begins to back away.

"It's okay, girl," I say, my fingers tight on the pommel now as I work hard to stay calm, to trust both myself and this horse—and Tate, who is leading us, and promised it would all be okay. He's got his hand firmly on the lead rope, holds it under Star, speaks soothing words. She balks twice, and I'm afraid she might rear. But he's got her, I can tell. I can feel the calm flow through both of us. Soon, Star walks forward again, as if nothing happened. Tate looks up at me.

"You're good?"

"I'm fine," I say. "Thanks to you."

"Ah, it wasn't anything I did. It's all Star. She's doing great. She handled that so well. That was a good test for her."

We walk on for a moment in silence, and then he looks up at me again. "And so are you, by the way. You're doing great. She would have been able to tell if you were scared. You weren't."

"I wasn't," I agree. And I don't add, *Because you were here with me.*

Star is now walking confidently forward again. We pass the tree that dumped its snow moments before and she hardly reacts, keeps walking ahead as the sunlight starts to fade completely and night begins to approach. Tate is talking to her again, telling her what a good girl she is, and I'm listening to his voice, a little mesmerized. Then I realize he's asked me a question.

"Do you remember our first trail ride out here? You were on Walt." There's a smile in his voice. I can picture that smile in my mind, even though I can't see his face. "He was the best. Probably our most reliable trail horse. We'd had him from when I was a really little kid, when my parents first bought this place."

I'm grateful that it seems his question about if I remember our trail ride is rhetorical. Because how would I answer it? *Of course I remember. I try to forget, but I can't. I remember every single moment we spent together. I still feel it in my bones.*

"Was?" I find myself saying. "He's gone?"

"Died last year," Tate says. "He made it to thirty years old, which is pretty amazing. Most of the horses we have are younger now, not quite as settled into themselves the way he was. Definitely not as reliable for the trails. It's why I'm trying so hard with Star, even if it could be a mistake."

"It's not a mistake," I say firmly. "She needs this. She's so happy out here."

And it's true. She's walking forward with confidence,

her head raised, her ears pricked forward. Eager, not nervous. But still, I hear Tate sigh.

"Yeah, but it's on me, some of what's happening here at the ranch. I focused on getting younger horses, Thoroughbreds, because I wanted to try to put together a show team. Then, we went into debt." Another sigh. "And lessons slowed down. Now it seems that mostly what people want is just to go on trail rides in the summer. People from out of town. No one who lives nearby can afford to put their kids in shows these days; the fees are just way too expensive. I need to get back to basics, regular lessons, but . . ." He trails off. "Sorry. This is not your problem. And we should be focusing on Star."

"No," I say. "You can talk to me. I remember your dream of having a show team. I'm sorry that's been derailed these past few years, but don't beat yourself up over pursuing your dream, over focusing on show horses rather than trail horses. You haven't done anything wrong."

"It hasn't exactly been great for business," he says. "But I've got some other ideas."

"Oh, yeah? Like what?"

"I'm trying to hire a riding instructor, for a more basic, kid-focused riding school. And I think Charlie and I could do well if we could put a bit more into horse training."

"Oh, that's perfect," I find myself exclaiming. "Remember how much you used to love watching *Heartland*?"

He laughs softly, surprised. "I think you're the only

person who knows that about me," he says. "I freaking *loved* that show."

"You're kind of reminding me of Amy right now," I say. Amy was one of the main characters, a talented and intuitive horse trainer on the popular CBC show. "You're like a horse whisperer, here with Star."

He looks up at me again, and I'm grateful the sun is almost set, that I can't see the exact shade of his eyes, the intensity of them that is sure to derail my central nervous system.

"Well, I wouldn't go that far," he says, his voice bashful now. "You're the one who is riding her, so give yourself some credit. But I do hope I can start building up my horse-training skills, and our client list. I was thinking if I could move all the school and boarder horses into the larger south stable, with someone hired to take care of that end of things, and turn the north building into a training, conditioning, and rehabilitation barn, we could be onto something. I have a few clients lined up already, from some of the trade shows I've gone to. I just need to hire a new riding instructor to help us manage the school, because we need to keep it going. The hiring has been a bit of a process. But I'm close to finalizing that."

A crow swoops down from a tree, and Star is surprised, but she doesn't spook. Again, Tate praises her, then looks up at me, smiling proudly, as if to say, *Look at you two now.* I smile, too, and pat her shoulder gently.

"Your plans sound amazing. I'm so impressed," I say.

"Yes, well, right now they're just that. Plans. But I feel closer every day to bringing them to fruition."

"I knew you when all this was just a dream, you running this place. I know it might sound weird of me to say this, but I'm proud of you, Tate."

He looks up at me, thoughtful—and then suddenly, as if he can't resist it, he grins.

"Thanks, Emory," he says. "I really mean that. Your opinion means a lot to me."

We walk on in silence for a little while. Then, he says, "Okay, I think this is enough for today. I don't want to push her, or you, too far. But I'm glad we did this."

He leans his head down and speaks softly to Star. "You did so well, girl. You have to keep it up, keep trying," he says, as if she's human and can understand. And from the way she nickers at him, I really think she can.

I'm touched by his words—not him thanking me, or not just that, but the way he's speaking to Star. His love of her is almost palpable, like something I could reach out and hold, soft against my chest. He doesn't fully understand her, because she can't talk back to him. But, oh, how hard he tries.

"You're going to be such a great horse trainer," I say.

"You might be giving me too much credit today. You're the one who was riding her."

"More like, I was along for the ride."

"No," he says firmly. "That's not all this is and you

know it. Not just anyone could be riding her right now. You were there when she was born. You helped. You care about her, and I'm sure she can feel that. You've stayed calm with her, even though she threw you off two days ago. Even after you knew there was a risk to this, that there still is, you still wanted to come out here."

For a second, it feels like he's talking about something else—about us. I think of my old bell hooks book, and the words about the risk of love. The risk of pain. And I know exactly what he means. I realize that my reaction to his gaze, to the sound of his voice, to my memories of us, spook me the way Star gets spooked. I'm terrified of getting hurt again.

And I should be.

Because Mariella exists. For the past few hours, it's been as if she doesn't. But she does. He has someone. Tate does not belong to me. After this week, I'll probably never see him again. I'll never ride Star again. I'll never be back on this trail.

I grip the saddle pommel and look straight ahead at the forest path in front of us: the trees and the sunset's orange glow through their branches. The snow and the beauty of it all. I try to lose myself and my emotions in that.

"Emory?" Tate's voice breaks through the noise in my head. "You okay?"

Can he sense it, I wonder, can he feel my heart the way a horse can? Does he know what I'm feeling, still?

It's not possible. "I'm okay," I manage, but my voice

is hoarse with sudden emotion. "It's just a really pretty time of day, is all. I'm enjoying the scenery."

"Yeah, it's gorgeous out here," he agrees. Then he pulls Star to a gentle stop and looks up at me. "My mom and I used to always go for trail rides at this time of day, in winter. To catch the way the sun looks as it starts to set over the snowy world." He nods toward the forest and hills spread out before us, the lake in the distance, the shadows falling across it: orange, pink, the softest yellow.

"It's so perfect," I breathe, taking it in, any sadness I was feeling lifting as Tate shares this memory of his mother, his connection to this place, with me. I look down at him. "Eleven years without your mom," I begin. "I'm sure you miss her still."

He nods. "I do. It's gotten easier over the years. But I've never felt her any less—if that makes sense. If anything, I've just learned to live with the loss better."

It does make sense. It's not the same, but I feel like I've been living with the loss of him, too. I can't say this, though.

We walk forward again, back toward the ranch. Our silence now feels charged, full of all sorts of things left unsaid—because they have to be, I tell myself. There is no place for me here, not after this week. And there is no place for these feelings.

Almost as if this thought needs emphasizing, I see a car on its way up the driveway. It's her. Mariella.

She gets out of her car, and I can see the bright shine of her long blond ponytail, even in the falling darkness.

I can sense a change in him, too. "Shoot, I forgot," he says. "I have another appointment." *Appointment.* I feel embarrassed, a bit resentful, too. Like he's trying to protect my feelings by calling it that.

"You don't have to say it's an appointment," I say, while he looks at me, confused.

When we reach the back door of the closest barn, Tate steps back so I can dismount.

"Are you okay getting her—"

I interrupt him. "Of course I can untack her. Does she need anything else?"

He shakes his head. "I've got a night hand coming in later, he'll do all the turnouts." He looks nervous now, ill at ease. Maybe he doesn't want his girlfriend to see us together, doesn't want to have to explain me. I hold my hand out for the lead rope and he hesitates before he hands it to me—but still, he's got me, on his line like a fish, caught in his gaze yet again.

"Thank you, Emory," he says, holding me fast with his amber eyes, as much as I want to resist. "I said it before, but I mean it. Star needed this. And I think she needed it to be with *you.*"

I look away from him, at Star. I run a hand along her velvety nose, then reach into my pocket and take out a mint, which I hold flat on my palm so she can snap it up.

"You remembered," he says with a smile.

I remember all of it.

I don't say this. All I say is, "You really don't have to thank me. I was happy to do this for her."

Mariella is approaching, walking up the small hill

that leads from the parking lot, waving at Tate. I don't
want to see them together. I need to get back into the
barn and away.

"See you, Tate."

I turn away, tug gently on Star's rope. She follows
along beside me, as obedient as a puppy, and I tell Star
that I love her so much, trying to drown out the sound
of Tate greeting Mariella, saying how happy he is to
see her, and her replying the same to him.

Twenty-One

The next morning, I awake from a troubled night's sleep, filled with dreams of trail rides and dark forests. I was riding Walt, and Tate was riding Jax—but then we lost each other in the darkness. I spent what felt like hours searching for him, and when I finally found him, he was looking for me, too. We galloped our horses toward each other, and when we were close, I remember seeing such joy on his face at finding me. I felt it, too, a sense of lightness and happiness so complete that when I woke up and realized it was just a dream, I almost wept.

Now I've decided to distract myself, and surprise Bruce, by decorating the *Evergreen Enquirer* offices for Christmas, something I realize he hasn't been able to do because of his injury. I go downstairs early and hunt for boxes of decorations, which I find in a closet, on a high shelf. There are wreaths and garlands, plenty of lights, and even a tree, which I set up and decorate with care. I'm on a stool, putting the star on top, when Bruce arrives.

"Aren't you a delight!" he cries. "I'd resigned myself to no decorations this year because of my foot, but you've given me a wonderful surprise, with just a few days to go until Christmas!" I'm happy he's so pleased.

"Should I put the outdoor lights on the porch, too?" I ask him.

"If it's not too much trouble. I know you didn't sign on for all of this."

I tell him it's my pleasure and bring the box of outdoor garlands and lights to the porch. Bruce stands by to make sure I'm safe on the ladder, and soon the Victorian house is looking just as festive as the rest of Evergreen.

Back inside, we make tea and get back to work on *The Evergreen Enquirer*'s special holiday restaurant review section. It's almost noon when Bruce declares us finished.

"That's it?" I ask him. "Only four restaurants?"

"Well, it's not a very big town," he says with a smile. "We'll just have to use lots of pictures to fill it out."

But I have an idea. "What about the Evergreen Inn? It's not a restaurant, exactly, but they do serve food to their guests. I stayed there on the first night I was here. Reesa's Saturday Soup was amazing."

"What a wonderful idea!" Bruce exclaims. "I need to finish my weekly column or I'd join you. Why don't you borrow my car and head out there? You can drop me at home and pick me up again tomorrow morning."

· ·

After I drop off Bruce, as I drive to Reesa's, I think about some of the ideas I'd like to suggest to Bruce, to make the *Enquirer* content more accessible to tourists when they're in Evergreen in the high season. A website would be easy enough to help him set up—though I do worry about him maintaining it. Same goes for an Instagram account. But, I decide as I turn onto the road that leads to the inn, these are all things for us to discuss tomorrow. First, I have work to do. And hopefully, a fence to mend.

I pull up to the inn, which is as lovely as I remember it, like it's been conjured straight out of a Trisha Romance painting. The eaves drip with glittering icicles, more cedar garlands have been added to the front banister, the berries on the front door wreath seem to shine as bright as Christmas lights. I park Bruce's car. When I get out, I see movement at the front window of the inn. Then Sam comes running down the stairs, excited to potentially meet a new guest—but her smile fades when she sees me. "Oh. It's you."

"Hi, Sam," I say. "Is your mom around?"

But Reesa is already standing on the top step. "Hello," she says hesitantly. "Did you forget something?"

I explain about my new job at the newspaper and tell her about the special restaurant section. Her expression stays guarded, and I wonder what I'm going to have to do to win her over. Until she comes down the steps, stands before me, and says, "I owe you an apology. I was not fair to you. Sam needs to hear this, too. I don't know anything about you personally, except that you were kind to my daughter. It isn't fair to judge people on their families. I think I was just shocked. Gill is such a great guy . . ."

"I know," I say. "It's okay, really. I understand it must have been a shock—and what happened with Gill is horrible. I wish I could fix it myself."

"Well, you're trying," Reesa says. "I've already heard about the holiday section, and who knows, maybe someone who doesn't already live in this town will pick it up. So, you're staying in town for a while?"

"Just a few more days," I say. "Until my car is fixed."

Sam steps in between us, her expression skeptical. "And you have a job? That doesn't sound like someone staying just a few days."

Reesa laughs and tells Sam to mind her own business. "Don't pry, sweetie," she murmurs. "Now, come on in. I just finished a pot of soup for lunch and baked a batch of those scones you never got to try."

....

Reesa makes tea, and we chat as she sets the table. She tells me all about how the inn fell into disrepair for years after my family rented it.

"There isn't really a market for luxury rentals out here," Reesa says. "The investors who owned it defaulted on their mortgage, the bank foreclosed, and it sat abandoned for two years. When my nan died, she left me a bit of money."

I write it all down, sure this is going to make a good article. "So, for better or for worse, I sank it all into this place," Reesa continues. "We've managed to stay afloat, but it hasn't always been easy. Summer is better, of course. But I just think it's so beautiful here in the winter. I wish we could get more tourists to see that."

While the soup warms through, and Sam busily stirs it, Reesa and I sit at the harvest table by the kitchen window. It looks out over the frozen lake, which is dotted with fishing huts. I take notes about how Reesa has single-handedly turned the place into something very different than the vast, impersonal mansion I stayed in with my family years ago. But it's so quiet, and obvious that they need more business. I hope my little article will help, and also feel more determined than ever to get Bruce and the *Enquirer* online so these establishments will all be searchable on the internet for potential visitors to Evergreen.

The soup is ready, and we're about to sit down to lunch when there's a knock at the door. Sam pops out of her chair. "It might be a guest!" she exclaims.

But when she returns, she doesn't have a guest in tow. She's leading Tate into the kitchen and looking up at him like he hung the moon. "Mama, look who's here!"

She looks thrilled, but Reesa seems guarded. "I told you we'd have to revisit lessons in the new year, Tate."

"That's not exactly why I'm here. Is it, kiddo?" Tate

smiles down at Sam, ruffles her hair, then turns his smile on me. I smile back, hoping my sudden longing for him, a feeling that's almost like a reflex, isn't written all over my face.

"I have news," he says. "A new riding instructor just accepted a job over at Wilder's. It was hard for me to find someone, but it's official now." He looks over at me and winks, and I remember our conversation out on the trail. How much he needed and wanted this.

"Wow, congratulations, Tate!"

"That's great news for you," Reesa says. "So, you'll be focusing more on horse training, you and Charlie? The way you've been talking about?"

Tate glances at me again, and I can see pride in his eyes. One of his dreams coming true. I beam back at him.

"That's correct," he says to Reesa.

And," he continues, "the new instructor needs to learn the ropes. I'm wondering if you might send Sam over as much as possible for the rest of the school holidays to do lessons with her."

As Reesa starts to protest, he says, "I won't accept payment, it's for the new instructor's training. And we can definitely talk about moving forward with lessons in the new year, okay? But you should know I'm working on a plan to have some of the students help exercise the horses in exchange for lessons."

"You can't afford to be giving free lessons," Reesa says, still uncertain. I see that Sam is gazing nervously at her mother. I remember her saying something the first day I came to stay, about them maybe finally being able to afford riding lessons again if they got some more business at the inn.

"You'd be helping me," Tate says. "I *need* Sam."

I can feel Sam practically vibrating with excitement beside me, and when her mother says yes, she starts jumping up and down. "Calm down, you'll scare the guests upstairs," her mother says, but she's happy, too, I can tell.

"Speaking of helping me," Tate says, and now he's looking at me again. "A new riding instructor, expanding Wilder Ranch, and going into horse training is probably newsworthy, right?"

"I think so, and I'm sure Bruce would agree," I say.

"Why don't you come over for a bit when you're done here? Have a coffee with me, get the scoop on what I'm up to?"

"Sure," I say, keeping my voice casual, even though the idea of spending time with him makes me feel anything but—no matter what I keep telling myself. "I'll come over when I'm done here."

"I'll see you soon, then," he says. "Mariella's waiting with the horses outside. We rode over here. I should go."

And as quickly as my spirits lifted, they're down again. *He is not yours, and he never will be,* I tell myself sternly.

Sam is observing my expression, looking confused. "You okay?" she mouths. I nod and look away, embarrassed that my emotions are so obvious even a nine-year-old can clock them.

When Tate is gone, Reesa sets out the soup and scones—still, I can't help but be drawn to the window, where Sam is standing, too. She sighs and clasps her hands together. I follow her gaze out to the woods, where Tate and Mariella are riding on horseback through the trees, along the very same path I was on, just the day before.

It had felt then like we were the only two people in the world. I force myself not to look away; I make myself watch as Tate and Mariella, against the backdrop of the setting sun, talk and laugh their way out of my line of sight.

Training my heart to remember that Tate is not mine feels harder than breaking a wild horse. But I have to keep trying, even in this place where the memories of him, of us, are all around.

✶ ✶ ✶ ✶ ✶

Dear Diary,

I am no longer a virgin.

It happened in the hayloft, which I wasn't sure about at first, but then I realized there would be no other place for us to be alone—and that I really wanted it to happen before I left. Sooner rather than later, frankly, so it could happen more than once. ☺

We've spent every possible moment together for the past two weeks, and we only have one week left. I have to believe our relationship will go beyond this time—but even if it doesn't, I have no regrets. I tried to find a way to tell him this, and he looked into my eyes—Diary, I cannot possibly express the way it feels when our eyes meet, every single time. Like I'm spinning, like I'm floating, like the world is brand-new . . .

He kept asking if I was <u>sure</u> and I kept telling him I had never been more certain of anything, ever. When I told him it was my first time, he got really quiet. I was worried he might think it was weird that I was eighteen and had never gotten this far with anyone—except at this point, I've been pretty honest with him about most things. All we do is talk and talk (and kiss) and talk. He knows I've never really liked anyone at my school. I do know he's had a few girlfriends, but no one he has felt this way about. I believe him when he says that. I try not to get too jealous, thinking about being gone in just one more week and all the girls who are probably crazy about him, because who wouldn't be?

But then he looked into my eyes and said, "It's not my first time—but it is my first time with someone I feel this way about. Someone I'm in love with. And so, in a way, it really is a first time." When I close my eyes, I can hear him say those words to me. Over and over, the most perfect words to say.

He made it really special. I came over after dinner, late, snuck out—although honestly, I don't know why I bother, no one seems to notice what I'm doing. I wonder if half of my parents' guests even know I'm around. And my mom just thinks I'm upstairs reading or over at the barn taking lessons.

I like that only Tate and I will ever know <u>exactly</u> what it was like.

He had lanterns all set up on the hay bales—like candles, but of course, those wouldn't have been safe with all the hay. The plaid horse blanket was laid out, and another blanket on top of that. I was so touched. It was so sweet.

I was so nervous. I could hardly look at him—but when I did, I knew it would be okay.

"I want this. I want you," I said to him, wrapping my arms around his neck. "This will never have been a mistake."

It did hurt, for just a minute. Then it didn't anymore, and I was worrying about what I was doing, if I was doing it right. As if reading my mind, Tate kissed me, then pulled away and looked at me, his gaze deeper, I think, than it has ever been. "Don't worry," he whispered. "You're perfect."

I believed him. Suddenly, it felt like I was perfect. The very best, most beautiful version of myself possible. I stopped being self-conscious and focused only on what I was feeling in my heart—and my body. The intensity of his kiss, the way his skin felt on mine, how I didn't just feel but knew in that moment I was closer to him than I had ever been to anyone. He was gentle, he was sweet— but also . . . well, he's so hot. It was so good. Thinking about it makes me blush—and want to do it all over again.

When it was over, he pulled the blankets over us and held me close, kissed my hair, whispered in my ear. "In case it wasn't clear before, City Girl, I wasn't just saying that because I wanted you. I mean, I did want you—I do, actually, I don't think I'll ever stop. But I love you, Emory Oakes. I really do."

"I love you, too, Tate Wilder," I said. And I felt like the happiest, luckiest girl in the world.

Twenty-Two

I'm at the inn for another two hours, chatting with Reesa after interviewing her for the article. When I eventually walk to Bruce's car in the semidarkness, stars blink to life above me, like Christmas lights on a tree. I breathe deeply, trying to quell my racing heart, my confused emotions. But no matter how unsettled I may be feeling about Tate, I can't deny it: To me, this is the most magical place in the world. Nowhere I've ever been, before or since, has compared to Evergreen. To Wilder Ranch.

I think I belong here.

And yet, there's no place for me here, not really. Tate doesn't belong to me. Our wild dreams to be together forever never came true. Our youthful declarations of love were just that: teenage dreams. I keep telling myself to get over it, that leaving it all behind again in a few days shouldn't hurt as much as I know it's going to.

I've almost reached the car, but I stop walking. Should I really go to Wilder Ranch? Or should I drive

Bruce's car back to town and tell Tate something came up? No, because that's not fair to him, or to Wilder's. Just because I'm having a hard time seeing him so happy with Mariella doesn't mean I have the right to be unkind to him, or to Charlie. I need to write this article. I need to be strong, for the Wilders and for Star, as complicated as it all is.

I get in Bruce's car and drive the short distance to the ranch. As I park, I see Mariella's hatchback pulling away. She waves at me as she passes on the driveway, and I wave back, trying hard not to grit my teeth.

I approach the north stable and pull open the door. Tate is there, outside Star's stall. He smiles when he sees me.

"You came," he says, as if he thought I might not. As if he can tell that at one point I was standing in the woods, considering turning back, making up some excuse and bailing on the article.

"Of course," I say. I hold up the notebook. "It's my journalistic duty."

"Right," he says. "Let's go to the office."

Inside the ranch office, with its messy desk and bulletin board covered haphazardly with schedules and photos, random pieces of tack on every available surface, he clears off a seat for me.

"Tea? Coffee? It's instant, and kind of terrible, but it does the trick."

"Tea is good," I say. As he plugs in the kettle I take a few deep breaths. "Okay, so, let's start with your new riding instructor. Tell me about them," I say.

"Mariella," he says, and I blink.

"What about Mariella?"

"She's Wilder's new riding instructor."

"I thought . . ." I'm too shocked to finish the sentence, but I'm a reporter right now. Tate dating his riding instructor is none of my business.

"She's great," he's saying. "It took a while, because she's from Kingston. She's going to have to move here, so we both wanted to make sure it was the right decision."

I think I'm diligently writing down all the details, but realize all I've written is, *Girlfriend??? Or coworker??*

I cross it out and write down what Tate has actually said. I look up. "You two really seem to get along," I say. "Er—I mean, what's her equestrian background?"

"She trained in the Netherlands. She has family there, and they have a big horse farm. One of her younger cousins represented Holland in the Olympics a few years ago, and she coached him. It was a great experience, but she wanted to move back here to Ontario."

I've written *Did she move back here to be with Tate??* But then I cross that out, too.

"Because her mom wasn't well," Tate continues. "But don't put that in, it's personal."

"Of course," I say, the picture of professionalism. "I'm sure you've been so caring and comforting about her mom," I say. "A real support."

He tilts his head and looks a little confused. "Well, sure," he says. "I mean, I haven't known her that long. And her mom's better now. Which is why she felt she could move towns, to be here, take the job at Wilder's."

The kettle boils, and he tells me more about his

plans for the ranch as he puts a tea bag in each cup, then pours boiling water. When he hands my mug to me, our fingers touch across his desk—and he doesn't pull away. He lets his pinkie linger against mine, and his gaze holds me, too. I'm the first to look away, but I find it harder to move my hand. As if we're drawn together by magnets. I finally manage it and pick up my pen again. But then I sigh.

I find myself thinking, all at once, about my best friend's advice over the past five days. She has texted me several times, saying I need to . . . **Tell him how you feel! What do you have to lose??**

I've told myself I can't because he's with Mariella. But I know it isn't just about her. That it's about the risk of him knowing the truth about the torch I've carried for him, one that I thought had dimmed, but was really just lying dormant, waiting to be reignited.

"Tate." I bite my lip; I have to do this. "I think it's time for me to be really honest with you."

I keep my eyes trained on his, but it's an effort not to glance at his inviting mouth. Impossible not to think about our bodies entwined up in the hayloft, on top of a plaid horse blanket. Of the stars shining down on us through the hole in the stable roof. I feel the blush rise up my neck and spread over my cheeks. I remember a time he traced the progress of my blush with his lips. And the more time I spend with him, the harder it's becoming to fight off these memories. "Emory," he says, and my name becomes something else on his lips. "What do you need to say?"

I swallow over a sudden lump in my throat. "It's

just a little hard for me, seeing you and Mariella to-gether. I know we were together a long time ago, that it's all in the past—but, for me at least, it still feels a bit intense. I'm sorry; this is so embarrassing. But I can't go on like this. It's too hard. I don't think I can keep coming here."

His expression is so hard to read. He looks shocked and confused. And then as if something is dawning on him.

"Emory, we—" He stops and clears his throat. "Mariella and I are not dating."

"Yes, you are," I say. "Carrie called her *your* Mari-ella. And said she was moving here."

Tate shakes his head in slight exasperation, then chuckles. "Carrie's always saying things like that. It's just the way she talks. And Mariella's moving here for work, not for me. I've only known her a few weeks."

"But she's gorgeous—"

"She's going to be my employee."

"And you get along so well."

"Which is a good thing. And part of why I'm hiring her." Now he's smiling, as if he can't help it.

"You were jealous," he says, raising an eyebrow.

"Please, don't make this harder than it already is."

He becomes more serious. "No, you're right. I shouldn't tease you. I don't know how I'd feel, seeing you with someone else." At those words, emotions I haven't allowed myself since I was eighteen swirl through me.

"But you're right," Tate says. "This is all a bit in-tense, isn't it? I have an idea."

"Oh, yeah?"

"Trail rides solve everything," he says with a smile. "It's getting dark now. We could take Star out with one of the Starlight Ride lanterns, see how she does? Talk while we're out there, you and me?"

"That sounds perfect," I say, my heart doing that *boom-boom-boom-clap* thing again.

"With her bridle this time," he says. "I'll walk beside you, but you take the reins."

He holds my gaze when he says this, and this time, I don't look away.

Twenty-Three

The stuff you've been using for riding is all here," Tate tells me, opening a locker in the tack room. I see the helmet and boots I used, tucked away, waiting for me—and it warms my heart, makes me smile at him. He smiles back and we linger for a moment, just staring at each other. Then we hear Star whinnying. She saw us pass her stall and is growing impatient, as if she knows what's next.

We bring Star out of her stall. She keeps her ears pricked forward, and headbutts both of us frequently and gently—as if she's happy to see us together. As we get her tacked up, I feel us fall back into that easy rhythm we used to have around the horses, Tate and I.

When our hands touch as we pull Star's bridle over her ears, I'm caught, yet again, in the snare of his gaze—but for the first time since I got here, it doesn't feel like a risk. It feels safe. It feels like something I need to explore.

Tate. I can smell him all around me: woodsmoke, pine, saddle soap, leather, *him.*

The bridle is on and now we're just standing here, the softness of Star's neck between us. I place my hand on top of Star's mane, stroke the silken strands to smooth them down. And then, Tate puts his hand there, too. Our hands are almost touching.

"I'm so glad I came here," I find myself saying. "I didn't know what else to do. Maybe it sounds strange, to have run from my parents during such a hard time for them—but I needed distance, to try to find a way to get through this. And somehow, this felt like the only place for me to go."

"I get it," he says, his tone full of understanding. "You really were so happy here. I remember it."

"I remember it, too."

"It must have been so hard, finding out about your parents," he says.

As we stand there, gently stroking Star's coat with brushes, then putting on her tack, I tell him how it felt that morning at the gym to see my dad on TV. How I was surprised but *not* surprised.

"I know you said I shouldn't carry the responsibility, but it's hard not to, still. I can't shake the feeling that if I hadn't pulled away, maybe my parents' path would be different. I don't know what's going to become of either of them, you know? I'm worried about them—but I'm also so worried about other people, too." I swallow, look away from him. "Like Gill," I say. Then, I explain that I gave my trust fund to my mother. "If I still had it, I'd use it to pay him back. Only, that feels like just the tip of the iceberg."

Our hands are still resting side by side atop Star's

mane, almost touching, whispering against each other, secrets only we know.

"You can't fix everything," Tate says softly. And I know what he means.

"I wish I hadn't tried," I say. "Before. With you. I shouldn't have done that, brought my dad into it the way I did."

He looks pained now, shakes his head.

And then, Star stamps her foot and whinnies, losing patience, at the end of her rope over our long conversation. We put on her bridle and he hands me her reins, then he goes to get a lantern.

Soon, I'm on Star's back, reins in my gloved hands, and Tate is walking beside us. As we head into the woods, I think maybe I should be scared. It's dark, she's got a history of spooking on the trail, she has a lantern around her neck but the trail isn't lit up, and we're walking into darkness. But the moon is full, lighting our way. And Tate's voice is soft, comforting as he speaks to Star, telling her how good she is, how brave she is.

We don't speak anymore as Star moves sedately through the darkness; the light from the lantern on a leather strap, hung loosely around her neck, bobs up and down, casting its light into the trees, and I find myself thinking of the night of the Starlight Ride. The memory is so bittersweet.

"Maybe she really can do the Starlight Ride," I find myself saying. "Look how well she's doing."

"Maybe," Tate says. Then he looks up at me. "How about you? Should I sign you up?"

"Oh," I say, startled. "There's nothing I want more, but the Starlight Ride is on Christmas Eve. My car will be ready. I'm supposed to go to Lani's."

Just then, something darts out of the darkness, a marten or a squirrel, I don't know. It all happens so fast I don't have time to register what it is or do anything about it; Star gets the bit in her mouth and she's off down the trail, galloping a few strides before rearing up and tossing me. There's enough snow to cushion my fall, and the moment I land—on my backside, yet again—I know I'm not hurt, I've only added another bruise to my collection. My helmet is firmly on. But still, I feel tears spring to my eyes.

I know what this means for Star. And I know it's all my fault. I was so caught up in Tate, in my feelings for him, that I forgot about her. I wasn't careful. And now, even though I'm fine, I know Star will suffer for this.

"Emory! Are you okay?"

Tate runs over, and I stay sitting in the snow, telling him that I'm fine, that he should chase after Star. I watch as he pursues her and finally catches up, grabbing her reins and holding her firmly. He speaks to her, calms her down, walks back toward me.

I need to calm myself down, too. I wipe hastily at the tears on my cheeks and stand, brushing the snow from my pants. When I get close, I see that Tate's expression is distraught.

"You're really okay?" he asks me, holding Star's reins in one hand and running his other over my neck, my back.

"I swear, I'm fine."

"You didn't hit your head?"

"No. My helmet stayed put, too. Like last time, it was nothing. You know falls happen."

"I know," he says, but there's something in his voice that feels like maybe he doesn't believe this right now. And he won't look at me.

"Maybe you should head back to town," he says. "I think I need a little time with her. On my own. I need to do some training, so this doesn't happen again. And I need to be . . . a bit calmer than I am right now."

"I can help—" I begin, but he cuts me off.

"No. You should go," he says. "You can't ride Star, not anymore. It's not safe. I'm sorry."

His words sound so final. So certain. Eventually, he looks at me—but it's not the same. It's as if, behind his eyes, and in his heart, a wall has gone up, shutting me out.

It's not safe, he said—but I know he didn't just mean riding Star. He was also talking about us. The way that, no matter what, maybe we were just always destined to hurt each other.

Twenty-Four

I wake up the next morning alone in the apartment, sore, sad, and tired. I know I'm not truly hurt from the fall off of Star. But something inside me feels broken. Last night, out on the trail and at the ranch, it started to feel like magic again with Tate. I let myself pretend that ten years hadn't passed. I let myself believe we were meant to be, that there had always been an invisible connection tethering us together. I told him things about the way I felt for him and about my life. And it backfired.

In the shower, I turn the water as hot as it will go and let it pound against my shoulders and my neck. As the water drips down my cheeks, I try to pretend I'm not crying. It hurts too much this time, even though we barely started again. Even though all we did was touch hands as we tacked up Star. Stare into each other's eyes. Talk and talk.

The way we used to.

I can't deny it anymore: Those moments last night

were everything I had ever dreamed of for ten years—and then, it was all yanked away in a startling moment I should have seen coming. One second, I was on my favorite horse with a man who was turning out, yet again, to be one of the best people I had ever known.

The next? Tossed into a snowbank—and then, the look on Tate's face. Like it was all *my* fault, somehow. I had started to hope that Tate and I had grown up, that we'd changed. But Tate is still the exact same guy I fell for too hard at eighteen, and that means it's all too easy for him to write me off, to shut me out again.

And me? Apparently, I still think fairy tales are real.

But before I leave, I will keep all the promises I made here. I will not leave any loose ends. I'll write the article on Wilder Ranch like I told Tate I would. And the story about the Evergreen Inn, for Reesa and Sam. I'll help Bruce close out this week's issue of the *Enquirer* and I'll talk to him about a website. I'll try to teach him some social media tricks he might be able to use to get the newspaper more attention and, thus, get more tourist traffic to Evergreen.

And I will apologize to Gill, for what that's worth. Because it's the right thing—and the very least—I can do.

I call the mechanic and confirm with Mario that my car will be ready tomorrow. Which means I will go to Lani's and spend the rest of the holidays with her family. And on Boxing Day, I've decided, I'll go see my mom. And we'll visit my dad together. In jail.

My phone rings, startling me. My heart seizes in

my chest as I listen to an automated voice telling me I have a collect call from an inmate at Toronto South Detention Centre, almost as if I've conjured my dad with my thoughts. The voice says to press 1 if I wish to accept the charges. I do.

"Emory?"

"Dad! Are you okay?"

A dry chuckle. "Considering where I'm calling from, not exactly."

All at once, I'm a kid again—and I'm in tears. "You know what I mean."

A pause. "I do," he says. "And I'm as okay as I can be." In the silence between us, I feel dread creeping in. Why is he calling me? The Stephen Oakes I know almost always has a game plan. Is it because he wants me to try to use some of my connections in the world of journalism to help put a spin on this mess he's in? I close my eyes, bracing for it.

"I've been doing a lot of thinking," he says. I grit my teeth. "And I'm really sorry, Emory."

I open my eyes, unsure of what I'm hearing.

"I spent some time at the start of this mess thinking of ways to get out of it—but then one of my lawyers shared a few letters and statements from some of the people who were affected by what we did. I never should have gone along with Reuben's idea. It was his, yes, but I didn't say no. I have so many regrets, Emory. I wish I could fix it."

I have no idea what to say, but the first thing that comes to mind is this: "I love you, Dad." It's true. It's complicated, yes. He definitely has a lot of making up to do. And there's a very good chance he will never fully be able to pay for his crimes. Too much has been taken away from people. But it sounds like he wants to start. And this is such a relief that I wipe away tears. "I love you," I repeat. "And I'm here for you."

Voices in the background, rising in volume. "I have to go," he says, his own voice still filled with remorse. "But we'll talk again?"

"We will," I say, suddenly feeling desperate, not wanting to break this rare connection between us. "Wait, Dad. How will I . . . how do I know you're really going to be all right?"

"One foot in front of the other, Emory. That's what I'm doing. You, too, okay?"

I swallow hard over the lump in my throat. "Bye, Dad."

"Bye, sweetheart."

I hang up and stare down at my phone, my eyes still blurred with tears. That didn't sound like the Stephen Oakes of the past decade; it sounded like the dad I used to know when I was younger. Not perfect, but honest with me, at least. I have no idea what the future holds for him. But it's a comfort to know he isn't going to fight tooth and nail to get out of this. He's taking responsibility. And that's worth something. In fact, it's a small miracle.

I go downstairs to the newspaper office to turn on the coffeepot. Bruce arrives, and we fall into our routine for the morning. Having straightforward tasks to do is a relief. I proof and fact-check his column, he does the same for a short piece I wrote about a holiday charity dinner the local Rotary Club is putting on. With those two tasks done, we sit together at my desk and I show him the news template a popular web-building site offers, how easy it would be to buy the domain name for TheEvergreenEnquirer.ca. But he looks so confused by all of it, I end up promising we'll talk when I'm back in the city, that I'll help him set up the website from home. So much for leaving Evergreen behind, I think a bit grimly. But I can't say no to Bruce. I also set up a Facebook page and an Instagram account, all of which just makes him look even more bewildered.

"But I'm really very grateful to you for helping to usher me into the twenty-first century," he says uncertainly.

When I tell him about the feature I'm planning to write on Wilder Ranch, he looks happier, on more familiar ground.

"That's yet another great idea!" he says. "That place is one of the cornerstones of our community. So glad they're expanding their business. Horse training, perfect. That Tate really does have a miraculous way with animals. Last year, our dog, Millie, got out of our yard and somehow managed to get herself stuck on the road median out on Highland Street." He shakes his head, frowns at the memory. "We were sure she was going to panic and run into traffic and get hit by a car. But Tate happened to be there, and he got out of his truck, walked over to her, and whispered something in her ear. Calmed her right down, and he was able to pick her up and carry her to safety. I'll always be grateful to him for that. Quite a lovely guy, that Tate Wilder."

My mouth has gone dry, and my heart lurches painfully. "I've heard that about him," I manage, as Bruce crosses the room and points to the wall of filing cabinets.

"I've got all the articles from our past issues filed away there. Have a look if you want. There's likely some backstory on Wilder's you could use. Filed under 'W,' easy enough to find."

I transcribe my notes from my conversation with Tate the night before, trying to keep myself emotionally above it all. It's hard, but not impossible. I'm just doing my job, I tell myself. I'm just helping out Bruce and the *Enquirer*. And Evergreen can still be a place that's dear to me. I don't have to look back and feel only sadness and regret—do I?

Once I've got all my notes in order about what's next for Wilder Ranch, I realize I need some backstory— and going through past issues of the *Enquirer* will mean I can avoid having to call the ranch and speak to Tate again. It was clear from the way Tate told me to leave last night that he doesn't have anything left to say to me. And I can't risk Charlie answering, either. I think if I heard his voice, I'd just start crying again.

Bruce announces he's going to be out for the rest of the day; he's getting his boot cast removed, and then, since he'll be in Haliburton, having an early holiday dinner with his printer.

"You sure you don't want to join us?" he asks me. "I hate to leave you here working so hard."

"I'm happy to be here working," I say, which is true. The more I work, the less I have to think about all the things that are weighing on me. "There are some loose ends I need to tie up with this article. Go, enjoy. I look forward to seeing you without your boot cast tomorrow."

"Just in time for the holidays," he says merrily, and then he's gone.

Alone, I head over to the wall of filing cabinets, open the one that's labeled *W*, and flip through the drawer until I find the "Wilder Ranch" folder.

I bring it to my desk and pick up the first article. It's dated for a week in October 1998, and the headline announces the ranch has just opened. There's a picture of a much younger Charlie, beside a woman who, I see, has Tate's same full lips and welcoming smile. Her eyes are warm, her expression one of joy. She's holding the hand of a little boy of about two or three. A young Tate. I'm unable to resist picking up one of the reading magnifiers Bruce keeps at the office and holding it to the page to get a closer look. Little Tate is adorable, of course, a miniature version of who he is now, staring intently at the camera, a half smile on his face that is somehow both playful and serious.

The article tells the story of how Charlie and Elaine Wilder bought the ranch the year before, fixed up the buildings, and are slowly assembling a herd of horses to use for trail rides. They'll also be doing some horse breeding and are looking forward to joining the Evergreen community.

A few years later, there's a December article about the first ever Starlight Ride. I see a slightly older Tate, maybe five or six now, on a horse I recognize as Walt. He's tucked into the front of the saddle, and his mother is behind him. She's looking down at him, and his head is tilted up toward her. He's gazing at her adoringly.

As hurt as I am by him right now, my heart still aches for him. I think of the first night we met, when he was out by the lake, having a bonfire alone, and he told me it had been a year without his mother. How deeply he missed her.

But he never told me what happened to her. It was the one thing we never talked about. I didn't want to press him on it; I could tell how painful it was. I just assumed she had gotten ill—but my heart seizes when I see an article dated in mid-December of 2013, the year before we met, with a shattering headline.

BELOVED LOCAL HORSEWOMAN DIES IN TRAGIC ACCIDENT

"What?" I whisper. "*No.*"

I read the article with dread in my heart now, not wanting to know what horrible thing happened and yet needing to know. There are paragraphs about the loss to the community, quotes from local residents about who she was to them and how much she would be missed—and then, just a simple paragraph at the end saying she was doing what she loved best when she died: working with horses alongside her family.

I feel tears prickling at my eyelids. I can see that in this article, Bruce decided to respect the family's privacy and Elaine's memory. No details are needed. It was a riding accident, that much is clear. Tate lost his beloved mother in a riding accident at the ranch.

❊ ❊ ❊ ❊ ❊

Dear Diary,

It was the most magical Christmas Eve of my life. The Starlight Ride was everything I imagined it would be and more. I spent the day with Tate, helping him get ready. We had lunch up at the main house, and I saw some pictures of his mom on the mantel. I told him she was beautiful and asked him to tell me a story about her. A memory. He got really quiet, and I thought maybe he didn't want to, that I'd gone too far on a painful topic. But then he started speaking, telling me about a time when he was little. It was late fall, he said, and he could hear the coyotes in the woods, a pack on the prowl, louder than usual.

"I was worried the horses were going to get scared, and no matter how many times my parents told me they were used to those sounds, and that the coyotes would never come near the paddocks and the horses, because the horses were too big, I just couldn't wrap my head around it. I couldn't sleep. And when my mom came to tuck me in, she could tell I was upset. So she lifted me up out of my bed, wrapped me in a blanket, grabbed a lantern, and took me down to the stables to check on the horses."

He told me that as they walked through the darkness, the coyotes howling and yipping was the most terrifying sound—except that all at once, in his mother's arms, he didn't feel afraid.

"Because she was so brave," he said, "I knew I could be, too." They went stall to stall, checking on all the horses, giving them a nighttime treat. "They weren't at all bothered by the howls of the coyotes, of course. Except maybe Kevin—but he was safe inside. And then we checked on the herd out in the paddock, too. My mom held up the lantern and we watched the horses in the dark. They were just shadows. I could tell they were perfectly safe. And she said to me, 'Just because something seems scary doesn't make it so. It's amazing what people, what animals, can get through.'"

He looked so sad, but then he surprised me with a smile. He told me it meant the world to him to get to talk about her. That I was the only person, other than his dad, he had ever really talked about her with . . .

For the Starlight Ride, I got to be up near the front, with Charlie and Tate. This felt like such a special honor. I'll never forget it. There were forty riders in total, some people on their own horses and some on horses from the Wilder Ranch herd. And then, dozens and dozens of townspeople walking through the woods, holding lanterns, singing Christmas carols. Felix, the horse Charlie was on, was a bit spirited, but he kept him under control.

Walt, of course, was perfectly behaved. And Tate rode Angel, who is Mistletoe's mother. She, too, is slightly more skittish than some of the other horses, but he handled it. He's such a good rider.

It was a perfect night . . .

Our horses stayed close—Walt and Angel are good friends and get turned out in the paddock together daily. They kept nudging each other and got so close at one point that Tate was able to reach for my hand. I'm sure I've never been so happy.

After, Charlie lit a bonfire at the spot where I first met Tate, and the group of Starlight riders and walkers had hot chocolate and mulled wine under the stars. There was more carol singing around the fire. It was so festive, so heartwarming. The idea of going back to the rental, even though it was Christmas Eve and I know you're supposed to be with your family, filled me with sadness. So, when Charlie asked if I wanted to stay for his traditional Christmas Eve fondue dinner after we put all the horses away, I accepted without thinking twice.

I used the phone in the ranch office to call my mom and let her know my plan. She sounded disappointed, but said it was fine. I heard Bitsy whispering in the background and tried not to think about what she would say, all the things she was going to tell my mother about how I was just going to forget Tate anyway.

I was hanging up the phone when I heard Charlie, outside the office, talking to someone. "I know," he said. "We'll take care of it."

"There's only so much more we at the bank can loan

you, Charlie. I hate to be saying this on Christmas Eve, but it's getting urgent and needs to be fully dealt with before the year ends, or it will be out of my hands."

I hung back, not wanting Charlie to know I had over-heard. Luckily, he and the person he was talking to kept walking and moved farther into the barn so I didn't hear anything more. But it bothered me, and it still does. I know it's expensive to keep this place going. Tate talks a lot about how there always seems to be something that needs fixing, or a horse that needs veterinary care. And I worry.

Sometimes—most of the time—it's mortifying to me to have parents as privileged as mine are, to live in a family with the means we have. It feels so unfair. They act like money is nothing. But maybe . . . that could be a good thing. What if my dad could help Tate and Charlie? I'm going to think about it some more tonight and maybe talk to my dad tomorrow.

Meanwhile, it's midnight, which means it's officially Christmas.

Maybe I'll have the perfect Christmas surprise for Tate—a solution to all his and his dad's problems. Maybe, for once, my family's money can be a good thing.

Twenty-Five

I put down the article about Tate's mother. My heart aches for what happened to Elaine. I think it was brave of him and Charlie to carry on, even though they suffered because of the risks that come along with their passion, their livelihood, in the most painful way possible.

A tapping at the front door of the newspaper office interrupts my thoughts. I go to answer it—and find Mya outside on the porch, holding a gift basket wrapped in cellophane and tied with a red ribbon.

"Hello," she says brightly. "I hope I'm not interrupting anything. I come bearing gifts—my parents and I wanted to thank you for the article in the *Enquirer*'s special holiday section."

"Please, that isn't necessary," I say. "That was probably the most incredible meal I've ever had in my life. I think I owe *you*."

"But we're so grateful," she says, holding out the basket. "We were wondering how to get the news about the secret menu out there, and you did such a great job. Please, accept the gift."

I step back and invite her in, taking the basket from her arms. Inside it is a jade-green pottery teapot with matching pottery cups, so delicate and lovely they make me gasp.

"This is gorgeous," I say. "It's way too much."

Mya shakes her head. "We're happy to give this to you and Bruce. My parents got it the last time they were back home visiting relatives in China—and it will mean a lot to them for it to be here at the newspaper offices. I know Bruce loves his tea, so it will be put to good use."

I feel a twinge thinking about Bruce on his own once I leave, enjoying his tea. Mya is looking at me thoughtfully, as if she can tell what I'm thinking.

"Why don't we use it now? Are you in the mood for tea?"

"Definitely." I find that I don't want to be alone after reading about Tate's mom.

I prepare the tea, then we take the pot and our cups over to one of the desks—but on the way over, she stops. She's seen the articles I was reading.

"*Oh*," she says, putting the teapot down.

"I just found out how his mother died," I say, and swallow hard over the lump in my throat. "I didn't know, before . . . it's so sad."

Mya lifts one of the articles and reads it over, then puts it down on the desk again, carefully smoothing it. When she looks up, I see her eyes are shining with emotion.

"It was so awful," she says. "I remember it like it was yesterday. Mrs. Wilder was the most wonderful woman.

We all thought she'd pull through. It was a shock to the community when she passed." She's silent for a long moment. Then she blinks a few times, picks the teapot up again, and heads over to an empty desk. "Come," she says. "Let's have this before it gets cold."

We sit down. Then she looks me in the eye and says, "So. You and Tate. What's going on?"

My mouth goes dry. "What do you mean?"

"Emory, come on. I found you in here, alone, reading articles about his mother's tragic death. When I mentioned his name just now, your face changed entirely. You two had dinner at our restaurant, and the electricity in the air nearly shorted the place out, never mind the school project I was working on. And Tate . . ." But she shakes her head. "I shouldn't."

"Shouldn't what?"

"Betray his confidences. He's one of my oldest friends. I've known him since I was five. Except . . ." She sips her tea, quietly thoughtful again. "Well, I love the guy, but I might not be able to trust him to do the right thing here."

"You mean cut me loose, right? Don't worry, he already did that. I felt like we were starting to get close again—but last night, he made it clear that we, together, have no place in the present." I swallow tea, give myself a beat to put my feelings into words. "I should have gotten over Tate a long time ago."

Mya surprises me by putting down her cup and throwing up her hands in frustration. "Are you serious? God, you're just as deluded as he is! I say this with affection, because I really do like you, but it's no wonder you two have taken nearly a decade to figure this out. You're both ridiculous." Then she clasps her hands together. "I'm sorry. I can be a bit harsh, but this needs saying. And forget loyalty to Tate. You two are clearly never going to get where you need to be on your own, without a little prodding." She takes out her phone, types something out, then puts it down again.

"What do you mean?"

She shakes her head. "You know, I really thought you were smarter than this. But let me spell it out: Tate has never gotten over you, either."

My heart stutters.

"That's not true." I deny her words even as a kernel of sunlight appears in my clouded heart.

"Are you sure about that?" she asks me.

"Positive," I say as Mya rolls her eyes.

"You two," she murmurs. "*Honestly*. Have you seen the way he's been acting since you came to town? Like no time at all has passed."

"If you mean he's still shutting me out, then you're right—it feels like no time has passed at all."

"And here my parents and I thought serving you that dinner would soften things between you. You think that was just a random assortment of food? Most of it was from the new menu, but the dumplings we served you are the exact dumplings my parents ate on their first date. They secretly call them the Falling in Love dumplings. But you two are a tough case."

"Your parents know about me and Tate?"

Mya laughs. "*Everyone* here knows that the reason Tate Wilder, the town's most handsome, kindhearted yet brooding bachelor, has never settled down with anyone is because he's been pining for some long-lost city girl for the past decade."

Now I feel my cheeks flush. "That can't be true," I say, even as the kernel of sunlight grows into a ray of light. "It's just a rumor."

"I'd think that, too, except I've known Tate nearly my whole life. He's not big on feelings talk, but there have been a few instances where he's been honest with me. I know he hurt you, okay? But he was a grieving teenager when you met."

My mind goes to the articles about his mother. I feel heartsick again.

"I know, and I was so unfair to him. We can't get past it, Mya. It's too late."

But she just keeps talking as if I haven't spoken.

"He was still grieving," she repeats. "And still trying to hold on to a business that, you now understand, took his mother away. It felt like his only connection to her. He told me what happened with you two, what the blowup was about. You asking your dad to help, him offering to buy Wilder's. And I can understand it. You thought you were being helpful, but what you wanted would have changed everything. And it probably would have still spelled the end of Wilder Ranch."

"I was naïve to try to step in," I say. "And my father wasn't fair. I should have known he'd make it about profit, not compassion."

"Sure. But Tate wasn't fair to you about it, either. There was more to it than you understood."

"I never asked what happened to his mother. I

should have. I told myself it was too painful for him to talk about, but maybe I was just afraid to know how bad the truth was, because it would be something I could never help him fix."

"You could sit here thinking of ways to blame yourself forever. Trust me, he's done the same. It was probably good you didn't ask. Back then, it was still so fresh. All anyone talked about when they talked about his mom was how tragic it was. That was hard for him—it made it almost impossible for him to remember the good times. Until you came along, and you made it safe for him to share those memories of her. You did a good thing for him. Stop trying to rewrite history and make it otherwise." Her expression softens, and then her voice. "This may be clear to you already: I'm not exactly a softie. But even I can see that what's between you two is special. It deserves a chance."

I open my mouth, but I don't know what to say. Maybe because I agree, but I'm still too afraid to admit that to myself.

Mya stands. "I've said enough. You two need to talk. And if he's smart, you're about to get the chance."

Before I can ask her what she means, she's zipped up her coat and headed out into the snowy afternoon, the front door banging shut behind her.

I sit still, dazed for a moment, then stand and rush to the door, intent on calling out to her to make sure she thanks her parents from me for the tea set.

There's a figure on the walkway—but it's not Mya.

Twenty-Six

I step outside the newspaper office and onto the porch just as a light snow begins to fall. It feels like magic. Like little white sparks falling from the sky and onto Tate, who is out there waiting for me—like a vision I conjured, or a dream I keep having, come to life.

I walk down the steps toward him, ignoring the fact that I'm in socked feet, stopping in front of him in the snow.

"Tate," I begin. "I just found out what happened to your mom. I had no idea. I'm so sorry."

"You had no idea because I never told you," he says gently.

"But I didn't ask."

"Maybe you shouldn't have had to." His amber eyes are sad but also lit up with something I think I recognize: the emotions he felt for me back then. The ones he might still feel for me now.

We stand there in the gentle snowfall, a few feet

apart, glittering flakes falling between us—and sparks flying between us, too. I feel them. I've always felt them.

Why *can't* it be possible that some things are just meant to be?

"Do you want to come inside?" I ask him. He nods and then follows me up the steps.

Inside the newspaper office, I feel suddenly shy. I put on the kettle again to have something to do with my hands. When I turn back around, he's standing beside my desk. I see him pick up the article about his mom. He starts to read, and I stay still, not wanting to disturb him.

"I never read this," he finally says. "At the time I was so grief-stricken, I just couldn't. I wanted to avoid anything that had to do with her for the first while. It was awful."

"Tate, I'm sorry."

"No, it's okay. Don't be. It's actually really nice to see this. To read the things people said about her, what an important part of the community she was. How loved." He pauses, lost in his thoughts. "And you know what? She really was that amazing. She was the best." He takes a deep breath and lets it out with a little shudder that makes me want to reach for him.

"I'm sure she was," I say. "Of course she was. She made you." The last words I say are a whisper. I'm not sure he's heard them as he sinks down into my desk chair, his eyes on the article again.

"Time has . . . well, not exactly healed it," he says. "I

don't think a day goes by that my dad and I don't miss her, think about her. We still talk about her a lot, which is nice. At first, we didn't, but then you came along. You helped me, Emory. I knew even after you were gone that if we didn't talk about her, we might forget all the best things about her. So we did. We do. And somehow, holding on to all those good memories, keeping them alive, has made it easier to live with, I guess."

He puts the article down on the desk. I forget about waiting for the kettle to boil and come closer to him, as if pulled by a force I can't control.

It has always been this way with him.

When I'm near enough, he reaches for my hand and looks up at me. My heart fills at his touch. My insides feel like the water in the kettle, bubbling over. We stand that way for a while, not saying anything, just looking into each other's eyes.

"Emory," he finally says. "I'm so sorry. For everything."

"You don't have to apologize," I tell him.

"But I do. I let you walk out of my life. I let your dad offering to buy the ranch come between us because I was ashamed that I wasn't able to handle it on my own, with my dad. That you even felt the need to help me. But that wasn't your fault. And I punished you for it. I've regretted it every single day."

"I walked away. I did it to us, too. I left without saying goodbye. But, Tate, we were young. We keep saying this, but I don't think we really accept it."

"Why do you think that is?" His voice is low. He

doesn't wait for me to answer his question. Instead, he answers it himself. "Because the feelings never went away. At least not for me."

My full heart leaps at his words. My emotions boil over. "I think it's pretty obvious they never went away for me, either. I'm here, aren't I?" I can't help but laugh softly.

"I thought maybe you just got lost on your way to somewhere else."

"Maybe, but I got found."

His gaze is soft and searching. "The first night I saw you, in my kitchen, you said you only stayed at my cabin because you didn't think I'd be there. It sounded like you wanted to avoid me at all costs."

"I guess that was true," I say, thinking about my emotions that night. It feels like so long ago. "But only because I didn't want you to see the state I was in. I had imagined seeing you again, over the years—but in my fantasy I had always just come from the hair salon, and was wearing the perfect outfit, and I was in a really good place in my life." I laugh at how ridiculous I sound.

Now it's his turn to laugh. "I never expected to find you in my kitchen in the middle of the night. Half naked." He raises an eyebrow, and the look he gives me causes the boiling to turn into a low, sultry simmer. But then he looks thoughtful. "Although, the truth is, it wasn't a surprise to see you. I talked to Charlie that night, and he said you were there. I think maybe he wanted me to come home and see you? He's always had a soft spot for you." This makes me smile. "As soon as he said Emory Oakes was back in town . . . well, I think I lost my mind a bit. I had been planning to leave the trade show Wednesday morning, but I just got in my truck and drove home. I *had* to see you. I couldn't let the chance slip away. But then I set about messing it up at every opportunity."

"That's not true," I say.

"It's partially true."

"Maybe it's safe to say we both seemed pretty intent on messing things up between us."

He nods. "We did, didn't we? Which is why I want to tell you the truth now. Very clearly. No chance for misunderstanding."

My heart is pounding. I think I'm starting to get scared. I have wanted this for what feels like always. But Tate Wilder and my feelings for him have only ever brought pain.

He's watching my face, and he looks concerned.

"Emory, this is real. It's not going anywhere," he says, reading my thoughts the way only Tate can. "I care about you. I always have."

I step back slightly because there's something I need to know. "If that's true, why didn't you ever call me? You had my number when I left."

There's pain in his eyes now, and I almost reach out to him, pull him up and into my arms. But I need to hear this, all of it.

"It's kind of embarrassing," he says. "Just after you left, I dropped my phone in the arena, and Walt stepped on it. Cracked it into a dozen pieces. Your number, which I hadn't memorized, was in there.

Your address, too. I wasn't ready to talk to you when that happened anyway, but by the time I was, I didn't know how to reach you."

"You could have come to the city."

He hesitates, bites his lip. "I did. About six months later, I looked up your address in the phone book, and I drove all the way to Toronto. I sat outside your house and felt really weird about that. Like if you saw me, you might think I was a stalker or something."

My heart feels like it's swelling in my chest.

"I called your landline, the one from the phone book, and I think your mom answered. I asked if you were there, and she said you were at the library." He smiles a little at this, but sadly. "I lost my nerve. I didn't leave a message. I just got in my truck and drove back here."

Now I step close to him again. I put my hand on his chest, and I can feel his heart racing as he continues to sit in my desk chair, looking up at me. "There's more," he says softly. "I used to go to the Royal Agricultural Winter Fair every year. I'd take as many horses, as many students as I could—so I could be there every day, just in case you happened to be there. Which you never were. I looked for you everywhere. I was convinced I'd see you in one of those fancy rich people horse show boxes you told me about." He smiles up at me for a moment as I shake my head, filled with regret.

"My parents kept wanting to get a box at the horse show, the way we used to when I was younger, but I always told them no. Being around horses, after you, was too painful. It reminded me of us. But to think that I could have seen you . . ." I trail off. Because there's still more I need to know, so I can be sure, once and for all, that the safest place for me is in his arms. "Last night, though . . . When you got so upset with me."

He sighs. "I don't want to make excuses for myself, because I wasn't fair to you last night. I know that. It's just . . . losing my mom when I did, the way I did, was hard."

"Of course it was," I say. "Tate. I can't imagine—"

He shakes his head. "Just let me finish, or I might lose my nerve now. When I saw you fall off Star, I was so afraid you were going to get hurt like my mom did. I know that's not reasonable, that you were right when you told me, years ago, that just because something bad happened one time doesn't mean it will again. But your fall triggered something in me last night that I think had already been opened up the first time you almost got hurt on Star, a few days ago." He's looking away from me.

"Tate," I say. "Look at me. Please."

He does. And I see so much pain in his eyes I can hardly stand it. I reach down to stroke his cheek.

"I've never cared about anyone this way, Emory. No one except my family." He reaches up for my hand against his face. Stills it, holds it there. "And I never want to let you go."

I don't know if he can hear my heart from where he sits, but it's officially galloping away from me now. There's so much I want to say to him, but I can't find any more words. Possibly because being so close to him, after so long imagining this, dreaming about it, is completely distracting. It's starting to consume me, like I'm a piece of paper and he's a lit match.

Then, suddenly, he's letting go of me. I feel bereft for a moment without his touch, until he stands and our bodies become aligned. Mere inches of space separate us. All my senses are on high alert. I can smell him. Woodsmoke and saddle soap, pine needles and leather. The air between us is electric.

"I missed you so much," he whispers. He touches a wisp of my hair. "I missed your hair. This color. Like the glossiest chestnut." Now he looks down at me. "And your green eyes, and your smile. Like the sun. You're everything I always imagined you would be, and more."

"How often did you imagine me?" I find myself whispering. Our lips are so close now. I reach up and bury my fingers in his hair, pull him one inch closer. He lowers his hands to my hips.

"All the time," he whispers back. "I dreamed about you, too."

I want to press myself against his body, but I also want to take it slow.

"This feels like a dream right now," he says.

"Do what you would do if it were," I say.

He tilts my face toward his and kisses my mouth. And if listening to him talk sets my insides to boil, if looking into his eyes fills me with unimaginable longing, if touching him sends sparks through my body, then kissing him undoes me entirely. Both my hands are on his face now. His stubble is tantalizingly rough beneath my fingers. But his lips are the softest thing on earth.

We're slow at first, and then our hunger for each other takes over.

"Come on," I say, pulling him toward the stairs to my apartment, feeling suddenly urgent. "Come upstairs with me."

We only make it as far as my tiny kitchen. I tug off his flannel, then his T-shirt. He pulls my sweater over my head as he pushes me against the counter.

"Emory," he whispers as he leans back to take me in. "You're so beautiful."

I grab the waistband of his jeans and pull him close. I don't want there to be any space between us, not anymore.

"Tate." I say his name, over and over, like a wish I'm making. Because he's all I want.

He kisses my neck, my shoulder, my collarbone. He gently pulls down my bra straps and kisses the tops of my breasts, then moves his lips lower as I moan.

"You're perfect," he says—and he does make me feel that way, like the most perfect version of myself. Every inch of my skin is tingling. I'm so filled with desire for him it feels like I can hear water rushing in my ears.

But then I hear something else.

A sound downstairs in the office. I didn't lock the front door, I realize.

"Hello?" It's a familiar voice.

The very last voice I want to hear right now. "Emory? Are you there?"

It's my mother.

Twenty-Seven

So many things are happening at once. My mother is still calling my name from down the stairs. I can hear her and her voice coming closer. *Shit.*

My phone, on the kitchen counter, is lighting up. I can see Lani's name, and the words I AM SO SORRY!! in all caps.

Tate is staring at me with alarm, and although we keep telling each other we are adults now, I feel very much like a teenager. I hustle him into my bedroom, tossing his flannel and T-shirt at him as he goes, then slam the door.

I pull my sweater back on and fix my hair, then call out, "Mom? I'm up here. Hang on, I'll be right down."

She looks so out of place standing in the middle of the *Evergreen Enquirer* office, taking it all in, a surprised look on her face. Then she sees me, and her face falls.

"Oh, Emory. You look terrible."

I almost laugh. It's so typically Cassandra Oakes to say that to me, when just moments before, the man I still love after all these years was telling me how beautiful, how perfect he thinks I am.

"Lani told me where you were. Don't be mad. I dragged it out of her. I'm sorry, Emory, I know you don't want to see me—but it's almost Christmas and I'm all alone."

"Oh, Mom. It's not that I don't want to see you. I got scared, of so many things, so I left. I don't think that was fair to you and Dad, but it felt like what I had to do."

She shakes her head. "Of course you did. I can't imagine how you must have felt. I could barely process it myself, and I did nothing to help you do that, the way a good mother should."

"Mom, I've been doing that a lot lately, placing all the blame on myself. But it's not right, and it's not healthy. So don't do that to yourself, either. I'm almost thirty years old. You don't need to mother me."

"What if I still want to?" she asks me—and it's so out of character for her, I find myself at a loss.

I swallow, clear my throat. "Dad called me," I say. "We talked. He sounds like he's feeling really awful about things."

"He's so sorry. You have to believe that. He is."

"I do, Mom."

She sits down in my desk chair and I try not to think about how, just moments ago, I was standing in front of that very chair, running my hands through Tate Wilder's hair, kissing him. And he's still upstairs. I need and want to talk to my mother—and I'm trying hard to focus despite being overly aware of every creak from overhead. Then my mom starts to panic. I can see it happen, because it's happened to her before. She, who has always worked so hard to keep up a perfect façade, has faltered a few times. And it's happening now. She's struggling to breathe, gasping for air. I go to her, tell her to take deep breaths.

"Oh, Emory, it's so awful," she says when she can speak again. "Every single person I invited to our holiday party declined. Every single one."

I wince. "Is that what you're most upset about? The holiday party?" I know she's in distress, and I don't want to call her out—but I can't help myself.

She closes her eyes for a moment, runs her hand over her face, smearing her makeup, which is not something she has ever done. She always looks perfect, but right now, she's a wreck. Still, I think she's about to deny it all, the way she did the last time we spoke.

"I know," she whispers. "It's awful. We've ruined lives."

The "we" is new. I didn't think my mom had it in her to admit that she, too, may be culpable. It makes me feel a wave of tenderness toward her I haven't felt in a long time.

"You know your father," she continues. "You know what it has always been like for him. Always striving for more, because that's how he was raised. The stakes always getting higher, the goalposts always moving." She pauses. "I think I got caught up in it all, too. I used to be idealistic, Emory. You may not believe it, but I was. I thought I could make a difference in the world—but in the circles we ran in, it just became about status and wealth. I don't know the exact moment I changed. But I did."

I shake my head. "It's not too late to go back."

"Go back to what?" she asks me, and this feels so strange—my mother speaking to me as if she is the child. "I don't know who I am, don't understand who I was." She rubs her eyes again. "You probably think what I'm most upset about is the party."

I smile ruefully. "I sort of did think that . . ."

"I am upset that the party isn't happening. It made me realize it's all over. Everything's ruined. We are not who we once were."

I say gently, "Were you happy in a life that was built on a house of cards?"

"To be very honest with you, Emory," she says, "I was. I was quite content to ignore my better instincts, to pretend everything was fine. Even though I knew, the way you probably knew, that it wasn't. I just assumed nothing would ever change. I didn't have to question what was going on in your father's business life. It wasn't my domain. My domain was what I saw as our *life* life—our social life. And to me, yes, it felt good. It felt like everything I ever wanted. Or, at least, everything I was ever supposed to want." She sighs, looks down at the desk, then back up at me. "I'm sorry," she says simply. "We've let you down. *I've* let you down. I understand that now. We're lucky to have a daughter like you. God knows how you managed to be so good when we were often so shallow, so selfish. But you did—and I know we made you feel like you didn't fit into our lives. I can see that now."

If the beautiful words Tate said to me earlier were what I always hoped to hear, these words from my mother are the ones I never dared to dream of.

"I never wanted you to feel bad, Mom," I say. "I just wanted . . ." But I trail off.

It's too much to tell her what I wanted. It would hurt her. I wanted to be a member of a different family because I never felt I belonged with them. And now here I am, in a place I belong, and I'm not sure what her presence is going to do to the fragile future I might be building for myself.

"This is hard," I say. "I love you, and I love Dad—you're my parents. But I don't know how I can help you right now."

"I did come here for a reason."

She reaches for her purse, opens it, and pulls out what I see is a cashier's check.

"I don't want money," I say. "Please."

I have no idea what she was about to say, but the fact that she's trying to offer me money is disappointing.

"No," she says, standing up. "It's not what you think. This isn't for you. I know you'll be fine. Look at you. A few days in this town and you have a job, a place to stay. You've never needed us, not really. Emory, what your father and I have realized is that money cannot buy everything. Certainly not happiness. But you are our daughter. There is no price that can be put on having you in our lives."

"And yet, you're holding a check."

"Which is for Gill. The restaurateur. Where it all

started. This check is for the money he invested plus interest. Your father knows he can't make it right with everyone—but we can at least make it right with him."

"Where did you get the money?"

"Your trust fund. And the rest of it, Emory, it's yours—"

"I don't want it."

She frowns. She's never understood this about me. "But why?"

Now my mind is racing. "Wait. Is this because Dad needs to do some good deeds so people will say nice things about him in court?"

Her frown deepens, and I feel a bit guilty for assuming there are bad intentions here. Then she sighs and says, "I can see why you might think that." She shakes her head. "But it's not true. Not at all. We've lost everything, Emory. We don't want to lose you, too. That's what this is about. That's *all* this is about."

I think about how scared I was earlier, with Tate. But also, about what I told him years ago: that just because something happens once, doesn't mean it will happen again. How he told me tonight he still believes that to be true.

And I choose to believe her. I choose to give her another chance.

"Let's go to Gill's," I say. "I'll show you where it is. There's just . . . something I need to get upstairs."

Only, when I open the bedroom door, the window is open, and Tate is gone.

Twenty-Eight

I t feels surreal, to be walking with my mother down Main Street in Evergreen—like this past week never happened. Like I imagined all of it, and I'm just Emory Oakes again, the person I was before I drove here in confusion and fear.

But I'm about to change one thing, I tell myself. There is one small way I will make things right here in Evergreen, on behalf of my family.

It's just that all I can think about is Tate.

I wonder how much he heard and what he thinks. If my mother's appearance has made him realize that he cannot have me in his life. Because back then, my parents did a really good job of ruining things between us with a check my dad tried to hand to Tate and his father, a pompous offer to buy the place out from under them. And although we keep trying to act like adults, somehow, we keep getting thrust back into the past, feeling like teenagers again.

But I push those thoughts aside now. My mother and I have something to deal with. We walk past Carrie's.

She's outside, wearing a Santa hat and giving out free hot chocolates—which I hope, for everyone's sake, are plain hot chocolate and not spicy or, worse, *meaty*.

"What a delightful town," my mother says. "Truly, Emory. I can see what you love about it. I never really looked around when I was here. It's so quaint. It's like . . . the perfect set for a holiday movie."

"I know exactly what you mean," I say. "Sometimes, it doesn't even feel real." This makes my heart start to ache a little, but I push it aside.

As we pass Young's Chinese, Mr. and Mrs. Young wave to me out the window. Inside, the lights are flickering on and off. Mya must be working on another electrical project.

"You seem right at home here," my mother says— but for some reason, this gives me another pang. I want to feel at home here, I realize. But will I ever, truly?

Now we're in front of Gill's. The window frame is outlined by twinkling green and red lights, and there's a big wreath on the door. The fishing-lure door chimes ring out as we enter. Gill is serving a customer, so we wait in line until he's finished. I feel nervous. I think about what Charlie told me, and Tate, too, about how upset he is, how wounded his pride is. What if he says no to us? Or tells us to leave? I know we can't really make any of what my father and his cousin did right, but I want to try.

Gill gives the customer their bag of takeout, and the woman smiles at us as she leaves. My mother smiles back and says, "Happy holidays!"

I've never seen her like this—so authentic and warm. As if Evergreen is having a positive effect on her.

Now we're at the front of the line and my heart is pounding hard. I swallow a few times, but my throat is dry.

"How may I help you?" Gill asks with a welcoming smile.

"I . . . I'm Emory Oakes," I say.

"Well, I know that," Gill says. "You're working with Bruce. Saw it in the Evergreen Business Owners' group chat."

I'm surprised. "Then you know who I am?"

"Of course I do. Everyone does."

"But you were so nice to me."

He looks surprised. "Of course I was. What did *you* do wrong?"

"Excuse me." Now my mother steps in. "I'm Cassandra Oakes. I'm her mother. And I'm here to apologize to you for what my husband took from you. I truly am sorry."

Gill pauses. "You didn't do anything wrong, either, ma'am," he says. "And I appreciate the sentiment, but it's all over now."

"No, it's not," my mother says. She's holding out the check. Gill hardly looks at it.

"No," he says firmly. "I do not want charity."

"It's not charity," my mother says. "It's the exact amount that you invested in the company. Plus a decade of interest. It's for you. Please, take it." She puts it down on the counter.

Gill looks down at the check for a long moment. Then he looks back up at us.

"I can't take that," he says.

"But it's your money!" my mother exclaims.

He shakes his head. "Are you able to pay back all the people who lost money in your husband's Ponzi scheme?"

"Well, no. The money simply isn't there. That's the nature of a Ponzi scheme, sadly."

"I can't," he says. "I appreciate it, I do. But it's just not right."

"But why not?" My mother's tone is pleading now.

"Because I can't be the only one to get my money back. I'm sure there are people far worse off than me. Why am I the one who deserves it?"

I don't know what to say to this and I can tell my mother doesn't, either. She opens her mouth, then closes it.

Finally, she says, "Well, we simply can't make it right with everyone. It's not possible. But we could try, we could pay back a few more people . . ."

He shakes his head again, picks up the check, and hands it to her. "I do appreciate the sentiment, really. But I've been thinking a lot since the news broke last week. Yes, my nest egg is gone, the money I inherited from my father. I've done just fine all these years without it. It was my retirement fund, but my wife died a few years ago and to tell you the truth, retirement doesn't seem so appealing. I don't know what I'd do with myself if I didn't have this place. I'll be just fine. I'll keep running this place and doing what makes me happy until I do finally decide it's time to retire. Then I'll sell the business and that will be my nest egg. I'm okay. Really I am."

I can tell my mother still doesn't know what to say—that maybe she has never experienced something like this before, someone being so selfless. The truth is, neither have I. I feel overwhelmed by his kindness.

And then he says, "Now, why don't you sit down and let me bring you some lunch? I imagine you've come a long way, Mrs. Oakes, and that you're hungry."

For the second time that day, I see my mother's eyes shining with tears. She looks down at the check for a long time, then tucks it back into her purse.

"I am hungry," she says. "Lunch would be really nice."

We sit by the window, looking out at Evergreen's snowy Main Street. Gill brings us his pan-fried trout and parsnip frites, and my mother declares it some of the best food she has ever eaten.

"I wonder if he does catering." But then she seems to remember herself, and who she is now.

"Just enjoy the moment, Mom," I offer, and she smiles and takes another bite.

We eat in silence. It's companionable. Speakers above our heads play "Silver Bells," then Anne Murray's version of "Winter Wonderland."

"I love this song," my mother murmurs. Another surprise. After a while, my mother puts down her fork and looks across the table at me. "Don't you think there's something you need to go deal with yourself?"

I frown. "What do you mean, exactly? Work? I'm pretty much done for the day."

"I saw that boy climbing out your window. Or man, I should say. You two aren't kids anymore, are you?"

I start to blush immediately. "You saw him."

"I didn't want to embarrass you. So, you two are still carrying on?"

"Mom, are you judging? Because I know you didn't approve of him back then."

Her face falls. "I know. God, I've been awful. But, Emory, you're *here*. That means something, right? I can see that you love this town. And even after just a few hours, I get it. I see why you love it here. But it's not just that. It's also *him*. And I very clearly interrupted something. Do you still care about him the way you did?"

In the past, I would have hidden my true feelings from her. But in the past, she never would have asked.

"I do," I say. "And yeah, we were sort of in the middle of a . . . conversation." My face feels like it's on actual fire.

"One I imagine you want to finish," she says. "Here, let me settle up with Gill. He has to at least let me pay for lunch. I'll meet you back at your apartment later?"

I stand. "Sounds good, Mom. Thanks." She reaches out and squeezes my hand, and the maternal gesture feels strange but also like the beginning of something between us. As if it might somehow be possible for us to make up for lost time.

"I love you, sweetheart," she says.

"I love you, too, Mom," I say.

Then I go outside and call Frank the taxi driver to take me out to Wilder's.

Twenty-Nine

The drive to Wilder Ranch seems to take forever. I'm torn between being excited to see Tate again after what happened between us in the apartment, and terrified. Should I really be coming out here? What if he doesn't want to see me right now? A few times, I almost tell Frank to turn around and take me back to town.

But what do I have to lose? And if my mother showing up at my apartment with a check is enough to send him running away from me again, this time forever, then I need to know that sooner rather than later.

The taxi turns down the road beside the lake that leads past the inn and toward the ranch. It's mid-afternoon now, and the sunlight is streaming through the snow-covered trees in that pretty way it does, waves of light rippling through the hardwoods.

We're at Wilder's. I get out of the car and see Charlie bringing horses into the paddock closest to the driveway.

"Hello there, Emory," he says with a smile as he closes the gate and walks toward me. "But I imagine it's not me you're here to see."

All I can do is nod. "Is Tate around?"

"He's in the south barn," Charlie says. "You'll find him there. See you around, kiddo."

And then he's gone and I'm heading toward the south barn, not quite sure what I'm going to say when I see Tate.

I push open the door just as Tate comes out of a stall. He stops walking.

"Hey," he says, fidgeting with the leg wraps he's holding. "Didn't expect to see you."

My heart swoops downward. "Why not?" I ask him.

"Your mom being here and all . . . I just figured you wouldn't be able to get away."

"Yeah, well, she mentioned seeing you jump out the window and suggested we might have some unfinished business to attend to." I raise an eyebrow as he grimaces.

"She saw that, did she? I was hoping I could escape unnoticed."

"And why did you feel the need to escape?"

He puts the bandages down and walks toward me, but I try to steel myself against him. I need to know where we stand.

"Jax banged his leg on a fence post out in the paddock yesterday and the vet was coming to take a look at him this afternoon. I knew I had to be here. And I didn't really think it would be the best idea to saunter casually by your mother and out the door, doing up my pants with no explanation."

I can't help but laugh. "You know, you could have done up your pants before you came down the stairs. And besides, I don't think we'd gotten that far. I hadn't undone your pants."

Now my cheeks are feeling hot—and if I'm being honest, so am I. I can barely understand what I'm saying. I can't look at him, so I look into Jax's stall instead.

"He's okay?" I ask.

"Vet gave him the all clear but he'll wear protective bandages when he's turned out for a while just to be on the safe side."

Tate steps closer. Woodsmoke, pine needles, leather, saddle soap, *Tate*.

I'm a goner.

"Emory?" he says. "Are *you* okay?"

I force myself to look at him.

"I don't know," I admit.

"What did your mom want? Actually, hang on." He puts the bandages down and locks Jax's stall. "Coffee and a chat at my place?"

He makes it sound so casual. As if we could ever have a coffee and a chat, as if it could be that simple between us. But I say yes and follow him out of the barn into the afternoon. It has started to snow again, thick white flakes that I can feel landing in my hair like confetti.

He turns back toward me. "I have something I want to show you, anyway," he says. "So it's good you came by."

He sounds so *easy* about everything—and meanwhile, I'm a simmering mess inside. Do I have no effect on him? I know it wasn't all one-sided earlier, it
couldn't have been. But maybe I'm wrong. I walk
along beside him until we get to his place, my thoughts
spinning.

He opens the door to his cabin and we walk inside.
It smells so good, it's almost overwhelming.

We have memories in here now, just like everywhere.

"Have a seat. I'll be right back."

I sit down on one of the stools at his pale granite
breakfast bar. I try not to think about myself standing
in the middle of this kitchen half naked, just days before, in a Fit-mas Tree T-shirt. I feel so nervous, it's like
I'm waiting for a job interview. And when he comes
out of his room holding a folder, it feels even more like
an interview.

He puts it down on the breakfast bar between us,
and now he seems nervous, too. But he doesn't address
the folder.

"So, your mom? Tell me what happened."

I start to explain, as much as I can. "I do think she
feels terrible and maybe my dad does, too." Then I tell
him about the check, and our visit to Gill's. "But he
wouldn't take it. He was just . . . so noble about it."

Tate smiles, a little sadly. "That's Gill for you,
proud and noble to a fault. Maybe a little stubborn,
too. He's been so helpful to us, as you know. He's such
a great guy."

"He is," I say, thinking about how he offered my mom lunch after what my parents had done.

Now, with Tate, the silence after my words stretches into awkward territory—yet I have no idea how to fill it. I look down at the folder. "What was it you wanted to show me?"

He pulls the folder toward himself, looks down at it, takes a deep breath.

Then he opens it.

It's a composition book, with the name *Emory Oakes* written on the front in familiar handwriting.

My breath catches in my throat. My old diary.

"I threw that away before I left here when I was eighteen," I manage.

"Yeah," he says. "And then, I was out for a walk on the road a few days after you left. Some animals had gotten into the garbage from your rental place," he says with a wry smile. "It was just there in the snow. I couldn't believe it. It felt like . . ." He looks down at the diary, then up at me again. "Like it meant something, but I never could figure out what. Not until now."

"This is so embarrassing," I say. "I wrote so much in there about . . ." *Us. You.*

"Don't be embarrassed," he says. "Please."

"Did you read it?" I ask him.

"I wanted to, but that wouldn't have been right." He pauses. "I gave it to Charlie, told him to lock it away. That I would return it to you one day if I ever got the courage. Then I brought it with me when I came to Toronto. And chickened out, as I told you. It turns out you were the brave one. You're the one who came back."

I pull the notebook toward me. I know every word by heart, but still, I open it to the final page. And with a sinking sensation in my heart, I start to read.

❋ ❋ ❋ ❋ ❋

Dear Diary,

I made a huge mistake.

I found my dad this morning, after our Christmas brunch, after we'd opened our presents and everyone was relaxing, and I asked for his help. I told him that I had become friends with Tate and his dad, Charlie.

"Your mother mentioned," my dad said, frowning, disapproval in his voice, but I chose to ignore it.

I explained to my dad as much as I knew about Tate and Charlie's financial issues.

"Dad, I never really ask you for anything, but do you think you could help them out in some way? Maybe offer to be a financial backer or something?"

I realize now how naïve I was being. It's never simple with my father. He's all business, all the time—always trying to get ahead, I guess. He asked if he could come with me over to the ranch, to speak with Charlie about an idea he had.

"I've been wanting to get into horse breeding for a while," he said. "And your mother did tell me what a quaint facility it is. I could definitely do something with it, make some positive changes."

This was when I began to realize this could be a mistake. But it was too late, I had already asked for his help. I couldn't say no. We headed over together. Tate looked confused when he saw me with my dad. I know he had expected me to come over by myself, so we could have some time alone on Christmas. He had told me he had a gift for me—but I didn't have anything for him! I think that's why I brought my dad into things. I felt sure I could solve any problems Wilder Ranch was having and make Tate happy. And Charlie, too. The perfect Christmas gift.

I was so, so wrong.

My dad walked up to Charlie and offered to buy the place.

It was awful. It was so embarrassing. But it was worse than that. It was shameful. How could my dad see a place like Wilder's as just something to buy, something to change completely and utterly? He started talking about how fun it would be to get involved with breeding Thoroughbreds for racing—when Tate and I have talked about how much he disapproves of racing, which is hard on horses and results in mistreatment, then the horses just being cast aside if they underperform. Sold off as horsemeat, if you can believe it. But my dad wouldn't know about any of that, nor would he care.

Tate looked at me like I was a complete stranger, and to be honest, so did Charlie. He just said, "No, thank you, Wilder's is not for sale" before heading off to do some chores.

"I tried, Emory," my dad said to me in front of Tate. "But it seems like these guys don't want what I'm offering. Maybe they just want to play small."

I had planned to stay, but Tate, his expression as cold as the ice on the lake, told me he had something important to do with his dad.

"You should go, too," he said. "I'll call you later."

I wanted to explain myself, but I couldn't find the words. What had I just done?

I told myself I'd give him some space, and I'd give myself some time to figure out a way to make it right, that when he called later, I'd come straight over and we'd talk.

He didn't call. So, I walked over there. It was late at that point, and I didn't want to knock on the front door of his house and wake up Charlie, so I threw handfuls of snow at his window, then tiny pebbles. His light was on, but he didn't come.

As I walked away, I had the most horrible feeling that I would never be coming back here. That Tate was finished with me forever.

Thirty

I blink back tears and close the diary. I never wrote in it again. I left it here in Evergreen, threw it in a trash bag. I told myself I needed to forget about Tate and that discarding the diary in which I had so painstakingly kept an account of our time together would be the first step. I didn't want to remember any of it.

But now I think about what happened next, all the things I didn't write down. I sat in the back seat of the Jaguar, my eyes closed, pretending to be asleep, refusing to look at the town I had so loved as we left it behind for what I was sure would be forever. Remembering all this is the most horrible feeling—one I've only ever experienced once before, ten years ago, right here in this place.

"Is this why you asked me here? To read this, and to remember why we should never be together?"

He gives me a long look, and then without a word, he stands and leaves the room.

I sit in stunned silence. When he returns, he's carrying a shoebox. He puts it down in front of me.

"Open it," he says.

I do, to reveal a stack of papers I realize are letters.

I lift the first one and start to read.

Dear Emory,

I miss you so much. I can't believe things ended between us the way they did. I'm upset, still. I wish you hadn't brought your dad into it. But I should have talked to you about it instead of just shutting you out like that. I was so hurt, but mostly, I think I was afraid. I have been afraid since the second I met you, and it felt like this perfect dream girl had just . . . dropped out of the sky onto my beach or something. I was afraid it couldn't be real. Instead of fighting for us, I made my worst fears come true. Because now it's not. It feels like you were never even here.

You came to my house, you threw pebbles at my window, and I ignored you. I don't think I'll ever be able to forgive myself for that. And now I have no way to reach you. I tried. I even went to Toronto. But I left without seeing you. And it's possible— more like probable—that you never want to see me again. That you've forgotten me already.

Because maybe my fears are true. I don't fit into your world. Maybe the sooner I accept that, the sooner my heart will heal.

Only, right now, it feels like it never will. I can't imagine ever getting over you. I have this thought sometimes that we'll find our way back to each other one day, if it's really meant to be. I guess I have no other choice but to wait and see.

For now, all I can say is . . .

Love,
Tate

I read through letter after letter. They become slightly less heartbroken, and almost conversational, after a while. He starts to share news with me, tells me about his experiences at the Royal Agricultural Winter Fair. That he looked for me. He tells me about the horses, and especially Star. *We've started training Star and she's spirited, but taking to it . . . This year will be Star's first time being ridden in the Starlight Ride; I'm the one who's going to ride her, but I wish you could, too . . .*

I look up at him. "Why didn't you ever mail these?"

"It's not exactly something I'm proud of," he says. "I should have had the courage to, but I felt like it would be better to see you first, to try to explain things to you in person, rather than just mailing all these. I mean, how would you have reacted?"

"I would have driven straight here. All these years, all I wanted was to know that you were thinking about me, too." Then I sigh, and I put down the letter I'm holding. "Because I was. I thought about you. I waited for it to stop, and it didn't."

We stare at each other in silence, what could have been hanging between us.

"Can you forgive me?" he asks. "For letting it go this long?"

"It was my fault, too. What was I thinking, bringing my dad over? I should have known he would act that way."

"I blamed you for his behavior. I was so unfair. I'm sorry, Emory."

"We had no idea what we were doing, did we?" I

shake my head. "And I could have called you. I could have written. It didn't need to be all on you."

More silence. I can feel the air between us filling with all our regrets. But then, he ventures, "Maybe this is the way it needed to be. Maybe the timing would have been wrong if we had done it any other way."

I nod. "I like that. It makes it feel less like being apart was wasted time . . ."

"And more like, we just had to wait for the right moment." Now he smiles, and I do, too.

"A moment that arrived with me standing in your kitchen in the middle of the night, thinking you were a burglar."

He laughs. It's the softest, sweetest sound. "There you were. You know, if I could have made a Christmas wish, it probably would have been something along the lines of, 'Emory Oakes, standing half naked in my kitchen.'" Now he grins. "You looked so cute in that damn T-shirt. What did it say?"

I groan. "'Do you have the balls to try the Fit-mas Tree?'" I admit, laughing.

"What the hell does that even mean, Emory?"

"Oh, trust me, you don't want to know."

Now I'm reaching for his shirt, and it's like I've turned on a switch. We pull at each other's clothes, desperately, hungrily. He presses me against the breakfast bar, undressing me further and kissing me all at the same time. I pull off his shirt and his firm, smooth chest is tantalizing as my hands explore down to the low waistband of his jeans.

"Let's go to my room," he breathes.

I make a noise of assent and he pulls me up, lifts me off the ground. I wrap my legs around his waist as he carries me to his bedroom. In the doorway, he holds me against his body with one hand, bumps his door shut with his hip, carries me toward the bed and lays me down.

He kisses me all the way down my body as I recline. His lips are on mine, then my collarbone, my breasts, my thighs, my knees, my calves, my toes. I truly think I might pass out from the pleasure of his mouth all over my body. This is everything I ever dreamed of with him—and more, so much more. He kisses my stomach, whispers into my navel how beautiful I am, how perfect. I lose my hands in his hair, and my mind in the sound of his breath, the touch of his fingers, his tongue.

Soon, I can't take it anymore. "I want you," I breathe. "I need you." I pull him up, reach for his belt buckle. "Also, how am I totally naked and you've still got your pants on? We need to fix that, right now." I unbutton his pants and pull them off, pull him on top of me, slide his boxers down and away.

"Wait," he whispers, rolling away from me, reaching into his nightstand for a condom, which I help him put on as he lies on his side, so dizzy by now with my desire I have no idea how I manage it, but I do.

His lips are on mine again, he's back on top of me, his chest against mine, our hips aligned. "Please," I whisper—and with a shuddering sigh that I echo, he slides himself inside me. "Pleasure" is not the right word to describe how this feels. It is dizzying bliss; it is coming home. "Tate," I whisper, and he says my name, too, in whispers, in moans. I run my hands down his muscled back, grip his backside so I can greedily pull more of him inside me. How is this possible, that anything could feel this good, this right? I wrap my legs around his thighs as I look into his amber-brown eyes. My desire feels bottomless, but he meets it, meets *me*, thrusting as hard and as fast as I need him to, while still kissing me tenderly and making me feel perfectly safe, entirely loved.

"Oh God," he groans. He kisses my mouth, then lowers his head, runs his tongue over one of my nipples. And it's all over for me. I couldn't wait if I wanted to. And I don't have to; he's right there with me, our sighs of gratification mingling into one, the orgasm lasting so long my entire body is shaking and spent when it's over.

After a few minutes, he leans up on one elbow and looks down at me, smiling.

"You look rather pleased with yourself," I say.

His grin widens. "Well, I mean, I just got *laid* . . ."

I swat at him, and he rolls over onto his back. We stay like that, side by side, still breathing heavily, looking up at his ceiling.

"Emory?" I turn to him. His expression is now serious. "That was amazing. Everything I ever dreamed. It still doesn't feel real." He kisses me softly. I lean up on my elbow to look down at him.

"But it is real," I say. "You and me."

He nods. "The best thing I've ever known."

I lower my head so it's resting on his chest, where I

can feel his heart, still racing from everything we just did together.

"I have to ask you this," he says. "Will you stay here for Christmas? Will you come with us on the Starlight Ride? I know you have obligations in the city—but I just got you back, and I want you to stay a little while."

I think about Lani, how I told her I'd be at her place in time for Christmas. But I know she'll understand. Despite my protests, she's been rooting for Tate and me this whole time.

"Yes, I'll stay," I say, and Tate pulls me closer, holds me tighter, like he never wants to let me go. I feel the same. I could stay here like this forever.

As I continue to listen to his heart, it slows. He relaxes. This new cadence of his heart calms me, too. I close my eyes and breathe along with him, slowly and surely, until we're both asleep, dreaming of nothing at all because our biggest dream has just come true.

Thirty-One

The night of the Starlight Ride is true to its name. No snow, just the clear and starry sky above. The way is lit by the lanterns on the horses and in the hands of the townspeople walking along with us—as well as someone who isn't from town, but who I can tell feels at home here, too.

My mother walks beside me as I ride a sweet older gelding named Beau. She has a lantern in her hand. She looks up at me from time to time and smiles. This is new; so new, it's taking some getting used to. She's stayed a few days in Evergreen, and I've found myself happy to have her around. I feel sure I've never spent time with my mother like this before, doing what I like to do in a place I love rather than something she or my father have orchestrated. There was a time I felt sure I needed to be free of my family, that my happiest life could never include them. Now, as my mother walks with me on this beautiful, special night, Christmas Eve, I think maybe my life could take a different path. The one I always wanted.

"Emory! Hello!"

Bruce has caught up with us. He walks with his arm tucked into that of a tall man with red hair and a matching beard.

"This is my husband, Michael," he says. "And this," he says to his husband proudly, "is my brilliant Emory. I've so loved having her around. I'll be completely lost without her."

"Bruce," I say, and a pain tugs at my heart. "I think I'm going to be lost without you, too."

"But we still have tonight," Bruce says with a smile. "And what a magical night I'm sure it will be."

Tate, up ahead, riding Inez, looks back at me and smiles. I smile at him, feel that pull I always do when he's near.

"I feel sure it will be, too," I say.

I reach down to pat Beau's shoulder. I feel sad I'm not on Star, but I know Star is happy tonight, out in a paddock with a few of her other horse friends who also don't like being ridden on the trail. Maybe Star will come around one day, but for now, it's not something I can change. I'm determined to enjoy the moment, knowing I'll be able to ride her again. And that with patience, things are likely to get better.

"Looking good there, Ms. Oakes." A warm growl of a voice coming up beside me makes me smile even wider than I already was.

"Why, thank you, Charlie."

He's riding Hank. He looks down at my mother. "She's a talented rider, your daughter."

I laugh. "I don't know about that," I say. "I only

rode four times while I was here and got thrown off two of those times. Not the best average."

"Ah, but you know that wasn't your fault. You were riding a horse who hadn't taken to anyone in ages. You have a real way with horses." He pauses. "A shame, though, that you probably don't get to do much riding in the city." He gives me a meaningful look but leaves it at that, then rides on ahead.

We all move slowly toward the woods, a mix of riders and walkers, all with lanterns. There are also lanterns hanging from trees to light our way. Tate and I walked through the woods together this afternoon and set up for the Starlight Ride. We pulled the lanterns on a sled and stopped often to kiss, to talk. He told me how glad he is I am staying for Christmas.

Beyond that, I don't know. He didn't ask for more, and my answer seems just out of reach.

Bruce and Michael are just ahead now—and I hear Bruce begin to sing. His voice is a stunning baritone. I had no idea he was so talented. The opening lines of "Joy to the World" ring out, as pure as fresh snow.

Michael joins in with a low bass. Soon, more people are singing, both those on horses and those walking. Even my mother joins in, and so do I. At the end, Bruce sings one last verse alone. It's a verse of the carol I've never heard, with a line so beautiful I want to write it down later. Perhaps in my diary, which still has a few blank pages left to fill. *And hearts unfold like flowers before Thee . . . opening to the sun above.*

After the song, there is silence, just the sound of boots and hooves crunching through snow. Then, a child's voice begins to sing next: "Jingle Bells," and I recognize that little voice as Sam's. She's at the front of the pack, riding a peppy little pony named Mags. Reesa is walking beside her holding a lantern. I hear her voice, too, a pretty alto—and then the whole group is singing along. *Laughing all the way . . .*

I don't think I've ever been so happy—but maybe I have. Maybe I was this happy ten years ago, and I'm finally finding a way to let it all in again.

We're deep in the forest now, and our voices are ringing through the trees just like the sleigh bells we're singing about.

"Emory." Tate is beside me on Inez. For the briefest of moments, he reaches out to touch my hand. He looks at me and smiles. I smile back. "Come on," he says. "Come to the front." Beau and I follow him. Together, we lead the group on a gentle loop through the starlit woods, and then back to the barn.

. . . .

It's eight o'clock by the time the bonfire is over, and we get the last horse put away, the ranch closed down for the night. Charlie invites my mother to dinner—his traditional, *very* homemade fondue, he says with a wink. And while the past version of my mother probably would have gotten a haughty look on her face and said *no, thank you,* as if eating store-bought fondue was a new low she did not care to excavate, she instead thanks him genuinely for the invitation, but says she had better get home so she can visit my father on

Christmas morning. I feel a pang when she says this. I ask her if she'd like me to come back with her.

"That's going to be hard," I say. "Going to see Dad in jail on Christmas morning. It's so bleak, Mom."

But she just smiles sadly. "It is. And there is no way I would take you away from this beautiful place you're in, from how happy you are, to do that with me. I can handle it. I promise."

"Will you call me after? Will you ask Dad to call?"

"Of course. Now, would you like to walk me to my car?" my mom asks.

I take one of the lanterns from the Starlight Ride to lead our way and we walk along the snowy path past the stables and out to her car.

"This place is just so peaceful," my mother says, pausing and standing still. She looks up at the starry sky, then back at me. "Thank you, Emory."

"For what, Mom?"

"For making me feel so welcome here."

"Of course. I'm glad you came to Evergreen." And I find that I mean it.

"I'm really sorry, you know. I'm just realizing now that we could have been doing things like this together for your whole life—and you're twenty-eight years old." She sniffles, reaches into her purse for a tissue.

"Oh, Mom. It's not too late, you know. These past few days, and tonight, they proved that."

She dabs at her eyes, then puts the tissue back in her purse. "I believe you, Emory."

I hesitate, but I know I need to say this. "When I'm back in the city, I'll come visit Dad with you."

Her face lights up. "Oh, he would love that."

"I know it isn't going to be easy and that we have a long journey ahead of us, but we're still family," I say.

"Maybe someday, we'll have gotten to a place where you feel proud to call us that," she says.

"I'll talk to you tomorrow," I say softly.

She nods. "Yes. And I'll miss you. But I have to get back to the city and your father, and I know how happy you'll be here—which makes *me* really happy."

"Everything's going to be okay," I tell her—although I'm not certain of that. I know this is going to be a strange, hard year for my family. "I'll be there for you through all of it," I amend. "You won't be alone."

My mom pulls me in for a hug. I hear her sniffle a little more, but when she pulls away, her eyes are dry. "All right, I really should get on the road."

"Text me when you get home," I say. I stand and wave until her car's red taillights disappear from sight. Then I turn and walk back toward Tate's cabin.

He's standing at the door, waiting for me. "Did that go all right?" he asks, pulling me into his arms.

"It did," I say. "It was a nice goodbye."

He looks down at me with his beautiful amber eyes. "She must be so proud of you."

I can't help but smile. "That's sweet, but I'm twenty-eight years old and I don't even really have a job. Not a ton to be proud of."

"That's not what I meant. She's proud of *you*. Who you are." But now he looks thoughtful. "You could, you know. Have a job. Bruce would have you on permanently in a second. And you know he'd also let you keep the apartment."

"It's a nice thought," I say. "Except Bruce doesn't have enough money to pay me."

He pulls away, then tilts his head up toward the sky.

"What are you doing?" I ask him, feeling bereft when he's not near me. He reaches for me and pulls me close again, and I feel relieved.

"Making a wish," he says, nodding up at the stars. "Wishing . . ." Now he ducks his head, his lips brushing against mine. "Wishing you'd stay. That we'll find a way."

Inside, through the open door, I can hear Charlie in the kitchen, humming along to Loretta Lynn's *Country Christmas* album.

I look up, too, at the starry blanket above—and then back into the eyes of the man I love and cannot imagine my life without, ever again.

When we kiss, I know his wish will come true. I'll figure it out. Because I'm home.

* * * * *

One Year Later . . .

Dear Diary,

This is the last page left in this notebook, so I'd better make it good. It has been quite a year.

I stayed, dear Diary. I stayed!

I found out about a community newspaper grant and helped Bruce apply for it. He got it, meaning he's able to pay me. So, I took a permanent job at <u>The Evergreen Enquirer</u>. I moved into the apartment—although I spend most of my time at Tate's cabin.

The summer here was as magical as the winter. Long trail rides, with me working on Star, who it turns out maybe just prefers trail rides when it's warm, rather than cold. Long walks with Tate, swims in the lake, hours on the dock once all the barn work was done. Plans for the future. He's training more and more horses, making a name for himself in the equine world. He was at the Royal Winter Fair this fall and could hardly keep up with all the people who wanted to speak with him, tried to hire him to work with their horses. I keep telling him he should change the name of Wilder's to "Heartland" and he just laughs—but I know it makes him happy. He's doing what he's meant to be doing.

And so am I. It's not a big-city newspaper, but working here, in this community, is what I'm meant to be doing, too. We started a website, got the newspaper online, and hired a high school student to do our social media, which has had some great results. This summer was busier than the town has been in years. And it turns out that even if I don't like Carrie's wacky cookies and donuts, other people do. They've become a viral internet sensation, and she comes up with a new flavor every week. There are lines out front almost every day in summer. But since I'm now a local, and in the know, I always get there early so I can get the good cookies.

Although I'm writing exclusively for the Enquirer now, I realized I had a lot of contacts at city newspapers and magazines, so I put together a media and influencers event earlier this year, inviting as many journalists as I could to come to Evergreen for a day and check out the atmosphere, sample the food at local establishments. Mya and her parents' secret menu is now a not-so-secret sensation, and foodies travel from all over to sample it— then post about it. Gill's Fish n Chips n Bait n Tackle is doing so well. One of Canada's top food writers took one bite of his fish a few months ago and declared it the best on the planet. He's been writing about him all over the place, and now Gill sells out of fish every day, even in the offseason. Especially the Haliburton Gold. I know I can never truly make up for what my family did to Gill—but this does help, and Gill is so happy.

Reesa's inn has gotten some great press, too. A journalist from Food & Drink magazine tried her scones, then ended up basing an entire feature on the inn and its recipes. It's been on several "Best Road Trip Destinations from Toronto" lists, and they're so busy now, Reesa can't keep up. They've had to hire someone to help.

I'm keeping myself busy, too. In addition to my work at the paper, I used my trust fund to start the Starlight Foundation, which provides scholarships for underserved youth in the region so they can do the activities they love but their families can't afford: horseback riding, hockey, dance. It doesn't make everything that happened with my family go away, but it feels so good to give back. My mom is helping me with the foundation, too. She's in her happy place, planning galas. We had a fundraiser at the beginning of the month that was better than any holiday party she has ever thrown. Some of her old friends even came.

My dad's trial is in the new year, and I know that's going to be hard. He wrote an op-ed in <u>The Globe and Mail</u> apologizing for his actions, but public sentiment seems to be that he's just trying to curry favor. I know him, so I know he really is sorry. But he's going to have to face the consequences of his actions. I keep telling my mom she's not alone, and telling him that, too. My relationship with my parents continues to grow and change. I sometimes can't believe any of us are the same people. Maybe we're not.

And then, there's Tate. What can I say about Tate?

We're so in love. Every moment with him feels the way it used to, except so much better.

But I'm burying the lead here, dear Diary, something Bruce always tells me not to do.

Last night, after the Starlight Ride, when we went inside for Charlie's fondue, the lights were all out. And when they turned on, the room was full of everyone I love: Tate, of course, and Charlie. My mom, with my dad somehow on speakerphone. A beautiful surprise: Lani and the twins. New friends, too: Mya and her parents. Reesa and Sam. Bruce and Michael. Gill.

And then, in front of all those people, in that room already so full of love, Tate looked at me with his amber-brown eyes reflecting everything I feel for him so perfectly back at me. He got down on one knee and asked me to marry him, offering an amethyst ring that belonged to his mother, and that he had engraved with three words.

"Hey, City Girl."

I said yes, of course.

Acknowledgments

I'm grateful to: my incomparable agent and friend, Samantha Haywood, and her team at Transatlantic Agency; the dazzling Dana Spector at CAA; talented dream editors Tara Singh Carlson at Putnam and Deborah Sun de la Cruz at Penguin Random House Canada; Molly Donovan, for so tirelessly (and kindly!) taking care of the details; Natasha Tsakiris and Katie McKee, publicists extraordinaire; Talia Abramson in Canada and Tal Goretsky in the US, for two gorgeous covers; Catherine Knowles, Molly Pieper, Bonnie Maitland, Katie McKee, Alanna McMullen, Jazmin Miller, Alice Dalrymple, Madeline Hopkins, Beth Cockeram, Sabrina Papas, and Marion Garner.

Dear friends: Sophie Chouinard, Sherri Vanderveen, Asha Frost, Nan Row, Nance Williams Jonkman, Beatrix Nagy, Lori Dyan. Writing-life sanity savers: Kerry Clare, Chantel Guertin, Kate Hilton, Liz Renzetti, Bianca Marais, Laurie Petrou, Uzma Jalaluddin.

Beloved family: Bruce, Shane, Griffin, and Drew Stapley; James Clubine; Joe and Joyce Ponikowski; and, as always—with an ache in my heart and a joyful understanding of unconditional love—Valerie Clubine.

My children: Joseph and Maia—with that same unconditional love I learned from my mother.

And finally, my husband, Joe, who has now added "chops down own Christmas tree" to his list of sexy attributes.

Julia McKay is the pen name of Marissa Stapley, the *New York Times* bestselling author of the Reese's Book Club pick and future Apple TV+ series *Lucky*, as well as many other international bestsellers. She has coauthored several holiday rom-coms, including bestseller *The Holiday Swap*, writing as Maggie Knox. She lives in Toronto with her family.

CONNECT ONLINE
marissastapley.com
📷 MarissaStapley